Q: What do you get when you cross Avon Ladies with Charlie's Angels?

A: A world-class intelligence organization run by women who really know their foundation. You get CARRIE MAE.

In *Bulletproof Mascara* Nikki landed unexpectedly in a world of international intrigue and learned to navigate the treacherous waters of her first professional job where it was learn fast or literally die trying. In *Compact with the Devil* the internal politics of Carrie Mae nearly got Nikki killed as she raced to protect the devilishly handsome pop star Kit Masters. Nikki's first two adventures were complicated by her attempts to hide Carrie Mae's real purpose from her family and her boyfriend/CIA agent, Z'ev Coralles. Juggling her work, her love life, and her family might be difficult, but in *High-Caliber Concealer*, Nikki never thought that a vacation at home on her grandmother's farm could lead to anything disasterous. But when Nikki Lanier's nemesis Val Robinson returned from the dead with a request to rescue Nikki's long-absent father, Nikki dropped everything to go do it. Now, Nikki realizes that if wants to her life back, she's going to have not only save her father, but convince her boyfriend that Carrie Mae isn't a terrorist organization, and stop an international arms dealer. Can she do it, or is it a *Glossed Cause*?

Blue Zephyr Press
2661 N. Pearl, #360
Tacoma WA 98407

This book is a work of fiction. Names, characters, and incidents are products of the author's imagination or are used fictiously. Any resemblance to actual events or persons living or dead is entirely coincidental.

Cover art by **LILTdesign.com**.

ISBN-10: 0692924949
ISBN-13: 978-0692924945

GLOSSED
CAUSE

a novel

BETHANY MAINES

SOUTH AFRICA I
APPROACH VECTOR

Death hadn't changed Valerie Robinson a bit. Tall and lean, with a model's angular face and severe black bob she looked just as Nikki remembered. Unfortunately, she also acted just as Nikki remembered. If anything she was more sarcastic, explicit, and blunt than before she faked her own death. Nikki blamed this on Val's switch from cigarettes to nicotine gum. When they had both worked for Carrie Mae, the international cosmetics corporation / espionage agency, Val had been Nikki's first partner and role model. Val had seemed to be everything that Nikki wanted to be; right up until Val betrayed the company and tried to kill her. And now, three years after being presumed dead, Val was back and instead of taking her into custody, Nikki Lanier had decided to trust her.

Nikki looked out of the plane window at the distant ground. From the air, what had been a post-sunset world was now a twilight sphere of advancing shadows as the sun retreated beyond the curve to the earth. Below, the farm fields of South Africa unrolled like a patchwork quilt sewn by a half-rate seamstress. Somehow she hadn't pictured Africa having this much green.

"This is a terrible plan," she said, unintentionally speaking her thoughts.

"I know," said Val, leaning over to look out the window with her.

"You say that now!" Nikki's head snapped around to look at Val.

Val popped a piece of nicotine gum in her mouth and grinned. "I said it when you came up with it."

"I can't believe I let you talk me into this," said Nikki.

"Hey, I just asked you to help rescue your father. I didn't say you had to jump out of plane without a parachute," said Val. "That was your idea."

"Coming up on the drop point," yelled the co-pilot coming into the cabin, and yanking open the exterior door. Nikki shuffled to the door, her wingsuit dragging behind her. The co-pilot checked his watch and held up three fingers, counting down. Val pulled her goggles down on her face.

"Yeah, but—" Whatever Nikki had been about to say was deliberately cut off as Val pushed past her and dove out of the plane.

Nikki rolled her eyes and checked her watch, marking the time. "Drama queen," she muttered. She pulled down her goggles and glanced at the co-pilot who gave her a thumbs-up. Still shaking her head, Nikki stepped from the plane.

For a moment, there was the delicious sensation of pure speed, unhampered by anything so mundane as a vehicle. Freedom, for Nikki, was going fast. If she went fast enough she could leave everything behind. Unfortunately, Val, the person that worried her the most, was in front of her.

After Val's presumed death in Thailand, Nikki had been haunted by the idea of Val—by the idea that maybe she could have saved Val from her own bad choices. Her friends had wanted her to forget, but leaving Val behind had proved to be far more complicated than she had thought it would be. All too soon, her watch flashed and with reluctance Nikki widened her arms and spread her legs so that the fabric webbing between them could catch the air like sails. Val was below her, already angling her body for the descent. Nikki squinted in the dim light trying to match her approach.

Nikki didn't trust Val. She still wasn't certain that Val wasn't leading her on a wild goose chase. The fear that they would arrive at their destination only to find that her father had never been kidnapped, never was in any danger, and all of this was just one more elaborate hoax from Val to exact her revenge on Nikki loomed in the back of her thoughts like a lingering ghost. But the idea that her long absent father was in mortal danger was a hard thing to shake. And the letter she had received had definitely been in his handwriting. How he had become entangled with Val still wasn't clear, but Nikki felt like she had to take the risk. She had to keep going. If she could save her dad, she would.

Nikki was buffeted by a gust of wind and found herself slipping off target. Battling back, Nikki corrected course, and blinked back tears from the cold air that blew in around the edge of her goggles. It was true; there were easier ways to get into the farm where her father was being held. But all of them would leave a footprint of some kind. Abandoned vehicles, changes of clothes, traces of hacking. Nikki wanted to drop in, collect Philippe Lanier from whatever hellhole he had been confined and disappear into the night. After that—well, Nikki couldn't think about after that.

Because after that meant thinking about what to do about Val and her... aliveness. Not to mention what to do about her job, the one she had unexpectedly quit, or her boyfriend, CIA Agent Z'ev Coralles, who she had left sitting in her grandmother's living room with no explanation. The *after that* list on this mission was extensive and scary. Nikki avoided the thought and concentrated on not falling out of the sky like a rock.

The lights of the farmhouse, if you could call a sixteen bedroom mansion with on-call chef and a rooftop pool, a farmhouse, were ahead of them, forming a distinctive pattern in the darkness. The two story house, possibly in a nod to the Dutch owners, or possibly because even architects sometimes take drugs, was built in two long strips like a *V*. At the point of the *V* was a windmill. Their goal was the right wing of the house, which had a long narrow pool on the roof.

Nikki had chosen this approach for the simple fact that it was the only entrance to the house that wasn't under video surveillance. The owner of the farm, a thirty-year-old, dark-haired Dutchman named Maaravi Meise, had more security on his flower farm than a drug cartel. Nikki assumed this was because, even though there were flowers in the fields, Meise was not actually in the flower business. At best, he was *also* in the flower business. Nikki chose not to investigate—she didn't actually care. She just wanted to get her dad and get the hell out of the country.

However, her chosen entry method—wingsuits—were meant to be deployed in conjunction with parachutes, but parachutes were unwieldy and too easy to spot from the ground. Instead, Nikki had chosen to use an alternative method to soften their landing—the pool. Nikki watched as Val angled her body up, slowing her descent even further. Too much angle and she'd become vertical and gravity would take over. Not enough angle and she'd hit the rooftop at fifty miles an hour then bounce off the water with leg breaking intensity like a skipped stone.

Nikki swung onto her approach vector. From the air things were always so much clearer. The roof was lined with lights focused on the grounds below and ambient light and altitude illuminated the roof clearly. But once she touched down, she knew there would be a period of darkness as her eyes adjusted to being behind the lights. That was the moment of danger. She and Val had debated bringing night-vision goggles. Nikki had been reluctant to pack a giant, clunky, standard issue army pair, which was all they could afford on the black-market, and Val seemed to think night-vision was for sissies. Either way it had seemed sort of silly when it was only going to be for this one moment. But now, as the moment approached, Nikki wondered if maybe they had made the wrong decision. But then, all of her decisions since leaving her teammates, family, and boyfriend seemed worthy of being questioned.

Val disappeared into the darkness beyond the row of roof lights. Nikki checked her watch. If she had timed the jump properly she should be thirty seconds behind Val. Time enough for Val to make the landing and get clear. Nikki angled, spreading her arms and legs, slowing down as much as possible. The roof still seemed to be approaching far too quickly.

Slow. Slow. Slow. Nikki lifted her chin, and clenched her tongue carefully inside her teeth, hoping for a graceful bellyflop that would glide her into the shallow end of the pool. There was a heart stopping moment of impact and the rush of water. She was going to make it. Son of—it's a pool noodle! Ducky! Ducky! It's a ducky. Nikki took the long piece of wet foam and bobbing rubber duck to the face, before feeling them bump over her hair and down her back.

She felt her momentum lessen and she reached for the zippers on her suit. Arriving safely only to drown in the pool would be the definition of a failed plan. She floundered briefly and then found her feet. There was a dim light near the stairs. She sloshed over to them and hauled herself out—stripping out of her suit as she went. Her eyes, not yet adjusted, saw only indistinct blobs of white deck furniture. No alarms seemed to have been triggered. No running feet. Also, no Val.

"Val?" she whispered. There was an annoyed grunt from ahead of her. "Val?"

"Over here," said Val, her voice filled with resignation. "I'm stuck."

"Stuck how?" Nikki inched forward, hampered by the dragging fabric of her suit.

"I'm not entirely sure," said Val. "I think it's a hammock."

Nikki began to bundle the suit down to a manageable size to be stowed in the flattened backpack that she was wearing underneath. She crept a little farther forward and finally saw Val.

"Oh dear," said Nikki.

"That bad?" asked Val.

"Well, it's not good. What happened?"

"I landed on a damn pool floaty. And for a minute there I was body boarding. But then I got kicked over the edge of the pool and straight into this thing. I think it's a hammock. Couldn't see it. Caught me like a spider web."

Val was indeed bundled inside the hammock very much like a wayward fly.

"Just use a knife," Val said, thrashing slightly against the ropes.

"Hold still," commanded Nikki. She finished stowing her suit and took a closer look at the hammock. Her eyes were finally beginning to adjust to the lighting. Squatting down she saw the edge of the hammock. She remembered camping once with her childhood friends Donny and Jackson. They had snuck up on her as she lay in a hammock, grabbed the ends and spun her. The centrifugal force had rolled the hammock shut and she had been trapped, much to Donny and Jackson's amusement. The same thing appeared to have inadvertently happened to Val and now Nikki applied Jackson's technique to release her. Grabbing the edge of the hammock she yanked straight up, unrolling the hammock and Val spun out and onto the ground with a hard smack.

"A little warning might have been nice," said Val sounding annoyed as she picked herself up.

"But not as much fun. Hurry up. Let's get the hell off this roof before someone spots us."

Val grunted in response, already packing her flight suit down into her back-pack. Nikki crept to the door and tried to listen for voices or footsteps, but above her the creaking arms of the windmill seemed unbelievably loud. No wonder no one had come up to the roof after their landing; probably no one heard them over the windmill.

"Who the hell puts a windmill on their house?" complained Val.

"The floor plans indicated he was using it to generate electricity," said Nikki.

"Well whoo-de-freakin-hoo; he's an environmentalist. Let's all give a cheer. Meanwhile, whoever stays at his house has to listen to that all night long? No thanks."

"I don't think that—oh never mind. I'm not arguing the finer points of environmentalism with you. Let's just go, shall we?"

"You used to be more fun."

"You mean I used to fall for all your crap."

"That too."

They both drew their guns and Nikki cracked the door, looking through the sliver of an opening into the hall. She didn't see anyone. Pulling open the door farther, she stepped into the hall.

"Hm," said Val, coming in and closing the door behind her. "Very modern. Not what you'd expect from a man with a windmill on his house."

"It is sort of…" Nikki looked around trying to pinpoint why she didn't like it. "It's like if a hipster were a house—one of those dorky ones with 1920s moustaches who wears scarves even in ninety-degree weather."

Val nodded. "He probably has a ceramic deer head on the wall somewhere because…irony. Anyway, my contact said Philippe was being held on the second floor, south wing, third door on the left from the stairs. This way."

"OK, but if I see a deer head—"

"Oh, we're smashing it," said Val. She held up two fingers, and gestured from her eyes to Nikki's. "I'm there with you, kid."

Val led the way quickly, her steps firm, but quiet in the gray carpeting. They didn't see anyone and arrived at the indicated door without incident.

"This doesn't feel right," whispered Nikki. "There aren't any guards?"

"Maybe they don't think they need any with the door locked and all the security on the ground floor?" Val looked around nervously.

"How do we know this isn't a trap?"

Val rolled her eyes. "We don't. Pick the lock and let's just get this done." Nikki knelt down and examined the lock and then stood back up again. "What?" demanded Val. "Don't tell me you forgot the lock picks."

"No," said Nikki, twisting the knob, and swinging the door open easily. "I didn't."

Val's expression seemed genuinely confused. Then, she shrugged impatiently, and slithered into the room, gun at the ready. Nikki followed, her 1911 pistol leading the way.

The suite, like the hall, was modern. All crisp white sheets, pale gray furniture and sleek touches of sparkle from glass or marble. Over the top of this interior decorator's photo shoot was a layer of real life.

"Well, Philippe is definitely here," said Val picking up a pair of boxers that had been left on the back of the couch.

Nikki pushed her way through the detritus of clothes, empty chip bags, wine bottles and receipts to the desk. The designer tchotchkes had been shoved ruthlessly on the floor and a new computer with two massive screens had been set up. Photoshop was running and the image of a document was on the screen. Nikki twisted her head, trying to read the enlarged, curved text that made up part of a seal—South Africa, she guessed.

"What is going on Val? Why wasn't the door locked? What the hell is Dad doing here?"

"Like I know?" hissed Val. "He should be here!"

There was a small clunk and both Val and Nikki whirled, pointing their guns at a closed door. It opened and a man in a bathrobe and slippers shuffled out, toweling his hair.

Philippe Lanier removed the towel from his face and looked

at the pair of women with evident surprise. His hair, now laced with gray wasn't as vibrant as Nikki remembered, but it still stood up in a curly red shock from the top of his head. His gray eyes had more lines, but they still seemed to radiate enthusiasm and life.

"Nikki? Val? Wow! How did you get here? This is so great! I'm so happy to see you!" He held out his arms for hugs.

"We don't have a lot of time, *Papa*," said Nikki, grabbing a pair of pants from the nearest clothing pile and throwing them to Philippe. "We're here to rescue you."

Philippe caught the pants easily, but didn't move to put them on. "But girls…" he was still smiling, beaming really, so happy to see them. "I don't want to be rescued."

SOUTH AFRICA II

LIBERATION FRONT

"I'm sorry, what?"

Nikki shut her mouth and looked at Val, who seemed to have gone straight through surprise and arrived at pissed way ahead of Nikki.

"I went through a lot of trouble to rescue you. I flew to the US. No, I went to the sticks to get Nikki. She was in some damn garbage dump in Washington State—"

"Hey!" Nikki interjected, resenting the characterization of her grandmother's farm as a dump. Val ignored her.

"And I went and got her so I could rescue your ass! Now get your clothes on!" Val tucked her gun away and began selecting random clothes off the floor.

"And I really, really appreciate it, *chère*," said Philippe. "But my ass doesn't need saving." There was a push-of-war between Philippe and Val over the clothes. Philippe eventually won and Val threw the clothes back on the floor in fury.

"Dad, what is going on? Val said you'd been kidnapped."

"I was kidnapped," agreed Philippe nodding enthusiastically. "Scared the crap out of me."

"So what happened?" asked Nikki. "It took us a week to plan this little shin-dig and I assume it took Val a couple of days to find me. How in the world did you get Stockholm Syndrome in less than two weeks?"

"I don't have Stockholm Syndrome," said Philippe. "That's

a ridiculous idea. Do you really think I could be brain-washed so easily? *Je suis offensé!*"

"Philippe!" growled Val.

"*Bebe*, don't be upset, but I have this great idea for making some money."

"No, no, no, do not *bebe* me. I am not listening to this. We are taking you out of here, now!" Val looked absolutely furious, and Philippe petted her arm soothingly.

"Val, I swear it's a great idea. Maaravi, that's the guy who had me kidnapped. Do you know Maaravi?"

"Maaravi Meise. He's the owner of this farm. We're aware of him," said Nikki. She knew her father wasn't going to budge until he'd said his *great idea*. Also, she wanted to prevent him from calling Val any more pet names. It was burning a hole in her brain. The letter she had received from Philippe before leaving the States had said that he was in a new relationship, and in some tiny part of her brain she knew that meant that Val and Philippe might be *special* friends. She'd been attempting to deal with that concept by ignoring it. But hearing the linguistic tics of a genuine relationship between her father and her arch-nemesis was more than a daughter cared to listen to.

"Yeah, he's a great kid. I really appreciate his family loyalty. And I mean, he grows great flowers." He pointed to a vase full of gorgeous roses on the coffee table.

"He actually grows flowers?" Val looked as surprised as Nikki felt. "We assumed that was a cover."

"Oh no, this is a fully functioning flower farm. They export them to Europe. How else do you think you get roses in the middle of winter?"

"I never really thought about it," said Nikki.

"That's probably because he doesn't buy you flowers," said Val.

"I swear to God I will punch you in the face if you so much as say his name."

"Ooh! Nikki has a boyfriend? *Dis m'en plus.*" Philippe dropped down into an armchair and grabbed up the candy dish full of M & M's.

"Oh jeez! Dad! Pants!" Nikki threw up her hand and averted her eyes as Philippe's robe gaped a little too much at the bottom.

"Oh, sorry. Went a little hospital gown on you there." Philippe stood back and grabbed the pants that Nikki had originally thrown at him. Turning his back, he pulled them on. "Anyway, my point is," he said, turning back around, "did you research Maaravi at all?"

"No," said Val. "We did not. We were trying to rescue you before something horrible happened. Apparently, we wasted our time." Val folded her arms across her chest; her lips pinched tight in disapproval.

"No, no, this great. Because see, Maaravi is the son of an old friend—well, friend might be stretching the point. I stopped talking to him after that incident with his wife, but," Philippe shook both his head and his hands at them, as if trying to erase his previous sentence like the drawing on an etch-a-sketch. "That's really irrelevant. Maaravi is the son of Arjan Meise."

"That wack-job bastard in the Netherlands?" Val asked, looking suspicious.

"That's him!" Philippe seemed pleased that Val knew where he was going with his story.

"We don't want anything to do with him. I've done business in the Netherlands; that guy is bad news."

"Oh, yeah, totally," agreed Philippe. "But Maaravi is a nice kid. Anyway, apparently the cops are finally putting the screws to old Arjan, and now in order to come up with some quick cash for his dad, Maaravi is taking a chance on the family business."

"What is the family business?" asked Nikki.

"Arjan is an arms dealer. Buys, sells, trades. First come, first serve, as long as you're the highest bidder. He's not a nice person. But, I mean, you can't help who your family is, and Maaravi wants to help his dad."

"I'm sympathetic," said Nikki. Philippe glared, but disregarded the comment as he sat back down to the dish of M & M's.

"Anyway, so Maaravi's trying get a big score and get his dad some money. And he's got guns, but he needs to get the guns to Europe, so he can sell them and give the money to Arjan."

"OK, I understand why Maaravi would want to do this, but why did he kidnap you?"

"Philippe's a great smuggler," said Val, managing to sound both annoyed and proud. "He got me out of China." She perched on the arm of the couch and pulled the gum out of her mouth, placing it on the head of a crystal owl that held a place next to the vase of roses.

"That's how we met." Philippe and Val beamed at each other.

"Barf. Moving on. So Maaravi wants you to help smuggle weapons into Europe so he can sell them and give his father the money. And what are you getting out of this? Flat fee? Percentage?"

"Percentage."

"You do realize he's probably just going to kill you once you're done."

"Well, Arjan certainly will anyway. But that's not my great idea. That's just what Maaravi wants to do."

"Oh, my God. You're killing me. What's the great idea?"

"Well, I want to take all the money and turn Arjan over to the cops. I wish I didn't have to grass on Maaravi at the same time, because I really do like him, but I think that's how it'll have to be."

"Arjan is still going to kill you," said Val. "That's never going to work."

"Well, it wasn't going to work before, but now that my two best girls are here I'm sure we can figure out something."

"That's a terrible plan," said Val.

"I didn't say it was a plan," protested Philippe. "I said it was an idea."

"That's even worse than Nikki's plans."

"My plan was fine," said Nikki. "You're just mad because you got stuck in a hammock."

"You got stuck in a hammock? That seems difficult to do. I mean, it's basically just a piece of cloth, yes? I guess some of them are more like fishing nets. Was that it? Did you get netted? Seriously, how do you get stuck in a hammock?"

"It was dark," Val said in a tone that could have cubed water. "The point remains that this is a terrible idea."

"I have other points in my favor," said Philippe. "I really do, but I can't talk about them right now because Maaravi's going to come upstairs in a little bit to look at my progress on the documents I'm working on."

"What? Dad! Then we have to go now!"

"Well, you two do, *oui*. But look, Maaravi and I are flying out day after tomorrow. I think you should go too. Meet me in Amsterdam. It will be great. We can talk more there."

"Amsterdam?" repeated Val, as if to make sure she had heard him correctly. "You want us to meet you in Amsterdam?"

"Yes!" said Philippe, nodding emphatically. "Amsterdam. It's all working out perfectly."

"Dad, this is ridiculous. We're not going—"She stopped speaking as the sound of voices from the hall filtered through the door.

"Time to go, *chère*," said Philippe grabbing Nikki by the elbow and pushing her toward the far wall. He threw open a cupboard door and revealed a dumbwaiter inside. He hugged her and then pushed her at the dumbwaiter. "Really happy to see you! Love you! *Au revoir*!"

"Oh good grief," said Val. "You might as well."

Reluctantly, Nikki crammed herself into the tiny compartment and Philippe hit the button that lowered the dumbwaiter. She climbed out in a gray-tiled service area and the dumbwaiter was immediately whisked back up. There were multiple dumbwaiter openings on one wall and a set of double doors on either end of the room. Through one, kitchen noises could be heard. A large rolling bin was filled with dirty linens and pegs on the opposite wall were lined with coats for the kitchen staff. Nikki crept to the door and looked into the kitchen.

The staff was doing what kitchen staff do when none of the bosses are looking. They were standing around, drinking beer and criticizing the one who was actually cooking. Nikki went to the other door and looked out. It led down a long hallway to an exterior door. Nikki guessed it to be the service entrance, which had been their original planned exit. There was a whoosh as Val arrived in the dumbwaiter.

"Son of bitch! You have no idea how lame that was!" Val spilled out of the compartment in a tangle of limbs.

"Shhh. Keep your voice down. And I just came down in the same dumbwaiter. What do you mean I have no idea?"

"I'm older and taller. It's more difficult for me."

"You are so full of crap."

Val inspected her jacket for dumbwaiter crumbs. "I choose to think I'm under appreciated."

"Whatever. Anyway, the service entrance is this way. I guess we leave according to the original plan?"

Val threw up her hands in an exasperated shrug. "Yes? Otherwise I think we have to go back upstairs, knock him out and drag him with us? And I think that would just really piss him off. Plus, I hate lugging bodies around."

"It is kind of lame," agreed Nikki. "They get so floppy."

"I always manage to bounce the head off a wall or something," said Val looking embarrassed.

"I suppose it's really awful of me," said Nikki, "But those are the times when I think a man on the team would be really handy."

"Oh my God, yes. They have all that upper body strength, might as well be doing something useful with it."

Nikki looked at Val. There was an awkward moment of silence as they realized they were agreeing about something and that something was body removal.

"So, we should probably just go then," said Val.

"Right behind you," agreed Nikki.

The journey to their hotel in the laundry van was not very pleasant and smelled of rancid olives. The driver, who wouldn't budge until they'd paid the rest of his bribe, said someone had spilled olive oil all over a tablecloth and Val complained about the stench under her breath. Nikki put her head back against the wall of the van, letting her ponytail cushion her head and tried to think about what to do next, but couldn't seem to focus.

She had been standing in her grandmother's living room.

Z'ev had been looking at her with an expression that said he was re-evaluating their entire relationship and the very idea that he would stop loving her had overwhelmed her with a panicky fear that was worse than anything she had ever felt on a mission. Her grandmother had shoved a letter in her hand from Philippe and Val had said he was in danger. And Nikki had just... left. Not because she trusted Val so much, or because she really believed Philippe was in so much danger, but because she was too scared to stay. And now? Now she was stuck in South Africa with the woman who had betrayed everything Nikki believed in and they hadn't even rescued Philippe. Nikki had destroyed her life and she had literally nothing to show for it. Even if she left right now, what were the odds that Carrie Mae would take her back? Would her teammates—Jenny, Ellen, and Jane—forgive her for running out on them? Z'ev would probably have told his superiors in the CIA about Carrie Mae by now. She was probably black-listed as much as Val.

The van eventually stopped and Val got out, angrily leading the way back up through the hotel to their room.

On the other hand, the girls knew that Nikki and Val were going after Philippe. With that much information, and a week to work with, Carrie Mae should have been able to find them. Nikki glanced around nervously as Val unlocked the door. They ought to have Carrie Mae agents raining down on them by now. Nikki felt a sliver of hope. Was that because her teammates hadn't turned her in? Or was it because they were too busy dealing with the CIA?

"I'm not flying to Amsterdam," said Val, slamming the door of their hotel room. "I mean, I really..." she hesitated just slightly, "like your father, but I'm not going to Amsterdam."

Nikki took off her back-pack and dropped it on the bed. All

of their luggage had been packed and the room cleared out. They had only been planning on stopping long enough to pick up their luggage and leave the country with Philippe in tow. Nikki pulled her suitcase over and put it on the bed next to her back-pack, and stood staring at the pair. How much time did she have? She couldn't actually abandon Philippe. She had to get him clear of this mess before she could worry about her own mess. But maybe there was a way she could turn this to her advantage. Would Z'ev at least not expose Carrie Mae if she could convince him that she and Carrie Mae were on his side? If she could, for instance, hand him an international arms dealer?

"It actually might be better," Nikki said.

"Better? Better how?" Val angrily yanked off her boot and threw it at the wall with a resounding smack. "Are you telling me you like his idea? You're both crazy!"

"No, I think it sounds like a terrible idea. I don't know anything about this Arjan Meise."

"Be glad you don't. From what I hear, he's a vindictive son of a bitch." The second boot was thrown with equal force.

"Well, sounds like someone my father shouldn't mess with then. But my point is, now that we know Dad is helping them willingly, and they only really need him to get weapons to Amsterdam, what if we just kidnapped him back? You know, if we can't talk him out of his crazy idea? Because if he gets their weapons to Amsterdam, which I'm not convinced he will, honestly—"

"He will," said Val, shaking her head. "He's really good at what he does.'"

"All right, well, assuming he does, once they get to Amsterdam, what do they need Dad for? They won't. And if he were to suddenly get kidnapped, do you really think they'd look that hard for him?"

Val looked thoughtful. "That idea is not entirely without merit. But I'd want to get there ahead of them."

"Yeah, you'd have to put your boots back on and we'd have to go catch our original flight."

Val looked at her boots. "No. No, no, no, no. I really can't go to Amsterdam."

"Why not?" asked Nikki impatiently.

"Because," Val said and stopped, her lips pinching together as if holding words back.

"Because?"

"There are people who want me dead in Amsterdam."

"There are people who want you dead everywhere," Nikki said with a shrug. "You're not a very well-liked person. You keep shooting people."

"Just the inconvenient ones," said Val picking up her boots.

"Well, fortunately for you, you are already dead. No one will be expecting you. And I don't think we'll be there that long. How long can it really take to fly in, get a lay of the land, kidnap Dad and fly out?"

Val grunted. "I don't know," she said, but she was already lacing up her boot.

"Do we have another choice?"

"We could leave him here to deal with his own problems," snapped Val.

"If you were going to do that, you wouldn't have gone all the way to the US to get me. Roll with the punches. Isn't that what you used to tell me to do? I mean, I didn't know they'd be your punches, but it's still sound advice."

"You're going to have to get over that at some point."

"And yet, I doubt that I will. Now put your other shoe on and let's go."

THE PAST I

WHAT'S LEFT

Kaniksu Falls, Washington

Nell threw the phone across the room, where it hit the wall with a jangling smack that left a dent in the plaster. The phone landed in a tangle on the floor, still making an odd ringing sound that faded off to the very edge of hearing.

Twelve-year-old Nikki walked down the stairs. It had been three days since her father had left for the hardware store. The first day there had been flurries of phone calls and Nell driving out to look for evidence of a car wreck. Her mother had returned and locked herself in her room. Nikki had heard her crying all that afternoon and into the night. The second day had been hushed conversations between her mother and her grandparents. Nikki kept working up the courage to ask where her father was, but every time she lost the nerve. She'd finally asked Grandpa if her father was alive.

"Yes, peanut. Try not to worry," he'd said, and then rushed off to the orchard.

Finally, now on the hot, airless third night, twenty minutes after Nikki had finally fallen asleep, the phone had rung.

"Mom?" she asked, blinking in the glare of the overhead light. Nell was sitting on the floor. "When is Papa coming home?"

"He's not," answered Nell, her voice grating across the air between them.

"Why not?" Nikki had asked, not understanding.

"Because he's a selfish jerk who doesn't know the meaning of the word responsibility."

"He's leaving us?" It was the only explanation Nikki had been able to come up with. She knew her parents sometimes fought. She could taste the bitter tang of dissatisfaction that flowed between them sometimes. But she'd clung to the idea that, while maybe Papa and Mom might separate, surely, surely Papa would never leave her. She was his *petite lapin*. She was his princess.

Nell stared at her for a long time. "Left," she corrected. "He's already gone." She climbed to her feet, stiffly, as if her muscles were sore. Nell brushed her hands over her dress, straightening and cleaning, then she patted her hair in the same way, and pushed back her shoulders, standing up as straight as possible. "But we're going to be OK. Sometimes life likes to knock you down a bit, but we just need to roll with the punches and we'll come up all right. You'll see." Nell attempted to smile reassuringly. "We don't need him. You can't really count on men anyway. And as long as we've got each other, then we don't need anyone."

AMSTERDAM I

YOU BETTER RECOGNIZE

Nikki shivered in the cold wind that swept along the loading zone outside the Amsterdam airport. It was a shock after the humid, oppressive heat of South Africa. Val flipped up the collar on her coat and waved her arm angrily at a cab.

"Seriously, I hate this city. Too much flipping beer. Never trust a town that doesn't serve decent cocktails."

"Well, if you hate it, then you know it well enough to find us a place to lay low," said Nikki pragmatically.

"Stop being reasonable at me," Val said. "You know I find it antagonistic."

"It's the only way to deal with unreasonable people," replied Nikki. "And since all my parent figures are crazier than you, I get a lot of practice."

"Don't be ridiculous. No one is crazier than me."

Nikki decided not to pursue that line of conversation; it would only end badly. "What's the next step, do you think? Do you have any contacts in Arjan's organization?"

"None that would actually talk to me," said Val waving again. "I think we should probably do a little basic surveillance, check out his house and office. Nothing fancy, just get the lay of the land. Philippe said the cops were closing in, so he could be anywhere.

A cab pulled up and Val leaned in to talk to the driver. A moment later she gestured for Nikki to get into the cab. "We'll go see a friend of mine. She'll know a place to stay."

Nikki tried to visualize a friend of Val's and found she was having trouble.

The cab delivered them to the old part of the city. Narrow roads, cobble stones, brick buildings heavy on the crenellations, and bicycles everywhere. And Val hopped out, paying quickly.

"This way," she said. "Let's move it along a bit."

"Afraid you'll get recognized?"

"A bit, but also, I hate this place. It always feels like I've driven onto the damn movie set of a European city. It feels like if I hang around too long there's going to be group singing."

A cluster of football fans poured out of a bar ahead of them, full of good will and beer, giving off whoops of celebration. It did feel like singing was probably imminent. Bad singing. Singing with more burps than words. But singing.

"I hate singing," said Val glaring suspiciously at the men, whose zest for life withered under her stare.

Val pushed into the bar. Amsterdam had several bars that claimed to be the oldest in the city, and this was clearly one of the contenders. The paneling was dark wood, not that you could see it through the array of knick-knacks dotting the wall. It was if someone's beer obsessed grandmother had been collecting tchotchkes for several hundred years. Nikki did not think they were going to fit in; if a record player had screeched into silence as they entered, Nikki would not have been surprised.

Val looked back at the tables of Dutchmen who were staring at them. She pumped a fist toward the ceiling and yelled "Goooooooo Ajax!"

"Goooooo Ajax!" The bar bellowed back and conversation levels returned to normal.

"Ajax the Greek hero from the Iliad?" asked Nikki as they

made their way to the bar.

"What? No! Where do you get this stuff? Ajax the number one football team in Amsterdam."

"So sue me for having an education."

"I don't mind the education," said Val, "But the Ajax football scarf is displayed over the bar and those were the colors on those jackasses who just left. You should pay attention."

"Whatever," said Nikki, annoyed.

The bartender was a large brawny woman with cascading ringlets of dirty blonde hair tied up in a bandana and a large tattoo of the Madonna down her left bicep. She hefted a tray of tankards from the table with ease, slid them into the dirty dishes bin, wiped her hands on the bar rag and then turned to face them, finally focusing on the new customers.

"*Wat kan ik—Bokkelul!* I heard you were dead."

"Rumors of my death have been greatly exaggerated. And I'd like to keep it that way Femke, if you take my meaning," Val said.

"*Ja.* No problem, but what are you doing here then? You know half the players in this town want you dead."

"I have a bit of a problem, and I need a place to stay for a few days. I figured you could set me up."

"Ja. I think. Give me a minute to make some calls."

Femke used the landline in the kitchen, and Nikki watched her, while Val watched the bar. Nikki appreciated that they didn't have talk about this division of labor; they just did it. Val had left a lot of things about Carrie Mae behind, but her training wasn't one of them. She'd been with Val for a week now and she was no closer to understanding why Val had done what she'd done in Thailand. Had she really betrayed Carrie Mae for a boyfriend? If nothing else, it seemed unlike Val to care about anybody that much. She wondered if Val would ever tell her the truth. She wondered if Val had ever told Philippe the truth.

Femke came back with an address scrawled on the back of an order slip.

"I had a little trouble finding something that wouldn't... where you wouldn't be noticed. This is the best I can do. It's not the Ritz, but it's private. And Val, I suggest you not come back here. There are too many *slechte mannen* who come here for a pint and to remember the old days."

"Thanks Femke," said Val, taking the piece of paper. "Don't worry; I won't be back. I don't like to remember the old days."

"The thing I want to know is," began Nikki, following Val out of the bar.

"Why does everyone here want to kill me?"

"Not really. I mean, I just figured you smoked a cigarette at someone and then shot them."

"There was a little more to it than that, but..." Val moved her hands up and down, as if weighing the past, "Yeah, more or less. What were you going to ask then?"

"*Bokkelul?* What does that mean?"

"I don't know, my Dutch isn't that good. Something about goats and penises?"

"Really? That's a swear word with promise."

"Possibly not goats? Possibly some other sheep-like animal. You'll have to find a Dutch person to—turn around, walk quickly, do it now."

Nikki followed the direction of Val's stare and saw a black Mercedes parking just down the street from the bar. A blonde man with a Viking-esque beard was exiting. He glanced their direction just as Val turned and began to speed walk away. He frowned, puzzled, like he was trying to place them.

"*Hey wacht,*" he called after them.

"Keep walking," said Val.

"Seriously? We've only been the country like twenty minutes."

"Irene Adler!" shouted the man, she could hear his footsteps on the sidewalk, quicken to a jog.

"Irene Adler? Really?"

"What? You're not the only one who can read. I told you it was a bad idea for me to go to Amsterdam. This is not my fault."

"Whose fault is it then?"

Val lengthened her stride reaching the intersection. A smattering of bicyclists were stopped waiting for the light to turn. Val shoved a bicyclist over, sending him sprawling onto the pavement.

"Personally, I blame Philippe." Val grabbed the man's bike and hopped on. "Better move it kid!"

Nikki glanced back, the Mercedes had u-turned and was heading her direction, the blonde man was already running. The bicyclist was up and yelling at Val and turning to clutch at Nikki's arm. Nikki swept off his grasp and began to run, her back-pack jouncing along on her back. This was not the ideal chase equipment. There had to be a better way.

Nikki took a hard left into an alley. The blonde ignored her, sprinting after Val, while Mercedes turned after her. Nikki eyed her chances of making it to the end of the alley without getting run over. The odds were not in her favor. She pushed her legs and looked around for an opportunity. Mrs. Boyer, her training officer, had been fond of saying that opportunities were everywhere, but people who panicked saw only closed doors. Which in this case was literal because the alley contained nothing but closed doors and dumpsters. There was shouting from the car and Nikki knew she was running out of time. Stripping off her backpack she tossed it up onto the closed lid of the nearest dumpster and scrambled after it. The Mercedes screeched to a halt and a man got out of the passenger side door. He had a gun in his waistband and he yelled something in Dutch, gesturing for her to get down. He sounded annoyed, but clearly didn't expect her to do anything other than follow his instructions.

His eyes widened in shock as Nikki launched herself off the dumpster and his right hand instinctively began to pull the gun out. He staggered backward under the impact of catching a Nikki to the chest. Nikki dropped low, kicking out as she spun, aiming for his legs. His feet shot up in the air and she heard his head smack off the car paneling before he landed, unconscious, with a meaty sound like someone had dropped a side of beef. Nikki had to scramble to seize the gun from his far hand. Grabbing it by the barrel she turned, just as the driver was rounding the front of the Mercedes, drawing his own pistol from a holster under his arm, and hurled the gun at his face. She dodged left and prepared to come back for further assault only to realize there wasn't any need. The gun had hit the driver square between the eyes, knocking him unconscious.

Nikki dusted off her hands and surveyed her handiwork. She collected the guns, a 1911 and a Beretta M9, and then after a moments thought, collected the car keys. She pulled her bag off the dumpster and dropped it in the trunk.

Val was relatively easy to find, she just had to follow the swath of angry pedestrians, bicyclists and motorists. Her pursuer had acquired his own vehicle, which might have gone badly for Val except that he had stolen possibly the most under-powered moped on the planet.

Nikki followed them down a street forced to move at the pace of traffic while Val wove her way through the cars with an impressive nimbleness. However, it seemed inevitable that the moped would catch her eventually.

Val suddenly broke free of traffic, swinging onto a side street, her bike tipped at a dangerous level. The moped driver roared in fury and drove up onto the sidewalk, taking the corner close to the building, hoping to cut the distance between himself and Val.

Nikki honked her horn and bullied her way across traffic, finally rounding the corner, only to find the moped laid out on its side in traffic. Val was standing over the sprawled blonde.

"Get in the car!" Nikki yelled, honking the horn.

"He's going to talk!"

"Everyone on the street is going to talk!" Nikki yelled back. "Forget him and get in the car!"

Val grimaced unhappily, then shrugged and did as she was told. Nikki could hear the distinct uneven sound of European police sirens as she put the pedal down.

"Nice bike work, by the way. I thought for sure he was going to catch you."

"No way. I used to be a bike messenger when I was a kid. Before Carrie Mae. There was no way he was going to catch me."

"How'd you take him down? I didn't get to see the end."

Val laughed. "Oldest bike messenger trick in the book. I just hit him with the bike. What'd you do—steal their car?"

"It seemed like the thing to do at the time," said Nikki easing to a stop at a light. "I mean, considering that they were driving around with US army issue side-arms that don't look like surplus, I don't really think they'll be reporting their car stolen anytime soon."

Val picked up the guns from the floor of the passenger seat where Nikki had dropped them. "You think those guys were ex-military?"

"They didn't fight like it. I think it's more likely that those guns weren't obtained legally, if you know what I'm saying."

"Sounds right. You want the 1911?"

"Yes, please."

"Cool." Val tucked the Beretta into her bag. "God, I could really use a cigarette."

AMSTERDAM II
VISITING HOURS

"You have got to be shitting me," said Val as they stared up at the disaster that was their safe house. It looked abandoned and possibly condemned.

"She said it wasn't the Ritz," said Nikki.

"Not the Ritz? This isn't even a Motel 6. I've seen heroin dens that look nicer. I've seen war zones that look nicer," said Val. "I've seen hotel rooms after spring break that looked nicer."

"Maybe it's nicer on the inside?"

"Well, yes, that part of the inside I can see through the hole in the wall does look nicer," agreed Val.

Suddenly Nikki laughed. "Just go inside," she said, still chuckling. "Get set-up. See if you can find us a dry place to sleep. I'm going to go check out Arjan's house."

"OK, but keep an eye out for Anders Hoek—the dickwad who was chasing me. He's going to be pissed once he scrapes himself off the sidewalk."

"We've probably got a few days before we have to worry. The police probably caught him. What did you do to him anyway?"

Val shrugged. "I shot his brother. I don't know why he's so mad. I didn't kill him or anything. I just shot him a little bit." She held up two fingers to indicate how much she'd shot him.

"He probably thinks getting shot is on the pregnancy scale—you either are or you aren't. A little bit doesn't factor into it."

"Pansy ass, if you ask me. Anyway, you're right. We might as well camp out here. Philippe is going to owe me a week at the Blue Lagoon after I get his ass out of this mess."

"Ooh! I've never been. But the pictures look amazing. Is it as nice as it looks?"

"Better. Get what's his face to take you when we're done here. The geothermal pool is to die for." She opened the door and slid out. "I'll do some poking around online once I get set-up. See if I can find out anything about Arjan and his situation with the cops. Call if anything interesting happens."

Val slammed the car door either not seeing or totally ignoring Nikki's frozen expression.

Using her phone, Nikki navigated to the right neighborhood and parked the Mercedes, still trying to decide if Val was totally oblivious to the fact that she had ruined Nikki's relationship, or if she had just forgotten because she didn't care. Z'ev would not be taking her on any impromptu spa vacations in Iceland. She and Z'ev would not be doing anything together in the future and the loss of future possibilities was like a knife in her gut.

Nikki changed into a hoodie and running shoes from her bag. The weather was cooperating with her desire for anonymity by spitting out a few cold sprinkles of rain. Zipping up her sweatshirt, she jogged slowly along the road toward Arjan's address, taking in the street. A canal occupied the left side, while the right was a mish-mash of grand old row houses jammed tight to their neighbors, each one's architecture fighting for prominence. Nikki frowned. She hated row houses. With narrow back gardens that were highly visible to neighbors and long streets with no good viewing angles, they were very difficult to run surveillance on.. The best solution was usually to gain entry to adjacent house where a clever spy could listen through the walls. The second best solution was to gain entry to a house across the street where you could cover the front door. The absolute worst solution was to attempt to park a van full of surveillance equipment on the street. And then order take-out.

Nikki watched as the Chinese food delivery person, a kid in his early twenties, backed his scooter up to the white van parked two doors down from Arjan's house and knocked on the back panel doors. The door opened and the Chinese food was exchanged for cash. Nikki tried not to stare in disbelief as she jogged by. Not that she thought they would notice. They had to be police. No one else would be that stupid. Nikki picked up the pace and went a few more blocks before looping back to try the alley that ran behind the houses. The house next to Arjan's had an empty parking garage and a tiny dog yapping behind a French door leading into the kitchen. It took Nikki mere moments to pick the lock and let herself in.

The tiny Pomeranian exploded in a furry of barking, attempting to protect his home from this unknown invader. Nikki ignored the dog and stood on the mat listening. The kitchen was Nordic modern minimalist meets handicraftsperson, or in other words, it looked as if an upscale IKEA had barfed on it. From the pale wood to the copper pots hanging over the stove, everything looked spotless and ready for a photoshoot. She listened for a sound in the house, but nothing moved.

The Pomeranian bounced higher, enraged at her disregard. Finally, she picked him up and held him at arms length. He snarled ferociously until she reached for the bag of kibble treats on the counter. She grabbed a handful and began shoving them in his tiny maw with one hand and checked his collar with the other. His tags were hidden in a neoprene bag that was labeled "Quiet Spot".

Nikki rolled her eyes. Don't have a dog if you don't like the jingle of dog tags. But his collar was elaborately embroidered and what was presumably his name was stitched into it.

Funske.

"I don't think I get the Dutch sense of humor," she said. Funske wagged his tail and begged for another treat. "Well, my fun-sized Funske. Let's go see what the police are doing, yes?"

Funske did not appear to care where they went as long as they took treats with them. Nikki went to the front of the house. The anonymous white van was still there. At least it didn't have tons of radio antennae on top or a camera lens sticking out the window.

"Still pretty embarrassing," she told Funske, who clearly agreed with her. Jogging up to the second floor master bedroom, Nikki finally abandoned the dog and went out on the balcony. From the balcony, she could see that the Meise house next door had a security camera, located above the lintel and trained on the backyard.

"But nothing up above," she commented, shaking her head. "Someone should really talk to them about the possibility of an aerial assault." Working quickly, she boosted herself onto the balcony railing, where she paused long enough to get her balance and then launched herself at the underside of the third floor balcony next door. A few seconds of scrambling, a prayer of thanks for her personal trainer back in LA, and she was onto the Meise's property. She inspected the glass door. It was as antique as the rest of the building. The lock was so basic she could have jimmied it with a nail file.

Sliding inside the Meise house, Nikki paused to get her bearings. She was in a bedroom similar to the one next door, but the bed was bare, stripped of sheets and the furniture was wrapped in white, sheet-like Holland covers. Nikki paused to wonder if people from Holland actually used the term, or if they just called them furniture covers. Then she decided she needed to stop reading Jenny's Jane Austen collection.

She walked out of the bedroom and stood at the top of the stairs listening, but heard no movement. The house was cold and felt as if the thermostat hadn't been adjusted upward in weeks. Nikki walked slowly downstairs, passing by the second floor, and then arriving at ground level. Both floors had their furniture covered, the refrigerator was empty except for several bottles of water. The only room that showed signs of life was an office in the rear of the house. It had a small space heater plugged in, the furniture was uncovered, and the waste paper basket yielded a few crumpled pieces of paper and some junk mail. Nikki straightened the papers and found tightly-spaced text that had been heavily gone over with red pen. She snapped a picture with the thought that she could get Jane to translate it, only to realize as the camera made the familiar and totally fake shutter noise, that she didn't have Jane's help on this mission. Angrily, Nikki recrumpled the pages and placed them back in the trash.

The rest of the office was empty, as if someone had swept all the shelves bare. Only the desk phone and printer remained of the office equipment, and a quick check of the phone interior revealed a discreet phone tap. Nikki replaced it and looked around the office—it was probably bugged. Whoever was working here was not working in privacy.

Her phone buzzed, vibrating in her hand, which caused her to jump. Quickly, she left the office and retreated to the stairs.

"What?" she demanded, answering Val's call in a whisper.

"We've got a problem," said Val without preamble.

"In addition to the ones we already have?" Nikki marched back up the stairs.

"A modification on an existing problem, I guess. You know how Philippe said Maaravi was doing this whole thing to keep Arjan out of jail?"

"More or less," agreed Nikki.

"But that was Philippe's end solution, right? To get Arjan arrested?"

"Yeah."

"Well, I finally got set up at the house, and got the computers up and rolling. Thought I'd dig into Arjan's past a bit. Just to get a briefing together and see what we're up against."

"OK, where are you leading with this?"

"Front page of the paper is where I'm leading. Arjan was arrested by INTERPOL three weeks ago. As in, before Maaravi kidnapped Philippe. Somebody has been lying."

AMSTERDAM III

PHONING IT IN

Nikki found that she was holding her breath. She had been pinning her hopes on Arjan as a golden ticket back to her life. Turn him in and she'd be able to prove to Z'ev that they were on the same side. She'd be able to stop him from exposing Carrie Mae. She'd be able to go home again.

"In prison, Nikki. He's already in prison. What does that mean?"

Nikki let out a long gust of air. She could rally. There had to be an alternative solution. She couldn't let Val smell the wave of fear washing over her. Think Nicole, think. What *does* it mean?

"It explains why the police think it's OK to order Chinese, for one thing. But who's using the office?"

"I don't know what that means."

"I'm at the Meise Manse—"

"Really?"

"Meise Manor?"

"You're at Arjan's house."

"You should take more joy in language."

"You don't approve of the language I take joy in."

"*Merde* balls," said Nikki, which was a swear that Jane had invented, and Val snorted in laughter. "Anyway, as I was saying, I'm here and the house is closed up, but there's a police surveillance van parked outside. And I know this because as I jogged by, their lunch delivery pulled up."

"You're *merde* balling me."

"I am not."

"Well, if they've got Arjan in prison, then why are they watching the house?"

"I'm not sure, but the only room that appears to be still in use is the office. Someone is using it, and the police seem intent on listening in."

"Well, none of that explains why Philippe lied to us. He had to know we'd find out Arjan was in prison the minute we started poking around in Amsterdam. Why even say that?" Val's voice had a sharp, angry tone that Nikki sensed was hiding disappointment and a little bit of fear. Maybe Val was more hung up on Philippe than Nikki had originally thought?

"I don't know," said Nikki. "It's possible that Maaravi lied to him. It's possible that he simply *condensed* to make a better story. We won't know until we ask."

"I bet Maaravi did lie to him," said Val, the tension in her voice easing slightly. "But I don't understand why."

Nikki wanted to argue with Val's immediate acceptance that Philippe wasn't to blame, but realized that arguing against Philippe wasn't actually in her best interest.

"Me neither." Nikki went to the front of the house and parted the window sheers slightly to look out at the police van. "Uh-oh, the boys in the police van just got caught red-handed."

"What do you mean?"

"Some blonde chick pulled up and she caught one of the guys making a trash run with the Chinese food boxes. He's getting an earful. She is not happy. Oh, splat, there goes the left-over General Tso's onto the sidewalk." Val laughed.

"Bad timing on their part."

"Yeah, but it would be perfect timing for me to make my exit. Text me the address of where we're staying? I'm not sure I can find my way back."

"Yeah, no problem."

Nikki hung up and went back to the balcony, then she slipped over the railing and dangled for a long minute, working up enough momentum to launch herself onto the second story balcony of the neighbor's house. Funske was waiting for her in the bedroom. She fed him another kibble treat and he barked, excitedly this time. She carried him back downstairs and saw that the text from Val had come through.

"Time to go Funske," she said kissing his fuzzy head and placing him on the floor. He followed her to the kitchen, trotting after her on prancing little feet, his tail wagging. She wondered if the owners would notice the depletion in treats when they came home as she carefully re-locked the kitchen door and exited through garden. She jogged back up the alley and then to the corner. The blonde was still berating one of the van lurkers. Nikki snapped a picture while pretending to check the time. They were too busy arguing to notice. The blonde had a wide Scandinavian face with high-cheek bones and was wearing a Burberry trench and her hair down in long waves that, while most fashionable, were not particularly practical.

Someone's been watching too much CSI Miami.

Nikki jogged back to the rental car and got in the driver's seat, trying to assess the situation and formulate her next steps.

She had two problems. Philippe, as always, was her first problem. She had no intention of helping Philippe steal money from an arms dealer, but even if she had decided to help, it was becoming increasingly clear that his *great idea* was not as simple as he'd made it sound. Which left her with the same situation she'd had in South Africa—Philippe was choosing to place himself in danger on the theory that he could financially benefit, and the assumption that she and Val would help him. The second problem was the Carrie Mae / Z'ev situation and the mess she'd made of her life.

If Nikki were being honest with herself, which she occasionally was, without the Carrie Mae / Z'ev situation, she would most likely just re-kidnap Philippe and then leave. Let Val and Philippe do whatever it is that they did when Nikki wasn't around and she would just go back home and pretend the whole thing had never happened and that she didn't know Val was alive.

But there was the Carrie Mae / Z'ev situation. Val had done in two seconds what Nikki hadn't been able to work up the courage to do in two years. She'd told Z'ev the truth about Carrie Mae and what Nikki did for a living. And if only he hadn't worked for the CIA, Nikki might have been able to talk him into being OK with that. But he did work for the CIA, and Val's revelation had placed the entire organization in peril. Only, she didn't know how much because she had chickened out and left.

Nikki thumped the steering wheel in aggravation. She didn't have any way of knowing if there was a way to fix it because she didn't know how big of a smoking crater Val had left in her life. Nikki started the car and glanced into the review mirror checking the road, and then checking her hair. She was startled to see an expression of angry dissatisfaction that made her look remarkably similar to her mother. She was used to seeing glimpses of her father in her reflection. She wasn't prepared to think that she was anything like her mother.

Nikki pulled out into traffic, chewing her lip, still troubled by her problems, but more troubled by her own reflection. Two blocks later she pulled over and picked up her phone, dialing a number that was all too familiar.

"Hello," said her mother, sounding cautious.

"I am nothing like you," said Nikki.

"Nicole Lanier, what the hell is the matter with you?"

"I am not over-reactive and clingy and social climbing. I trust people."

"You do not! You don't trust anyone! I am your mother, and did you ever once tell me the truth about your job or your boyfriend? No!"

"You lied about Dad growing pot and going to prison! You lied my entire life!"

"I wanted to keep you safe!"

"Well, ditto!" Nikki bellowed into the phone and there was silence.

"I don't social climb," said Nell. "I'm socially ambitious. And sue me if I wanted more for you than to live on a farm your entire life."

"There's nothing wrong with living on a farm." Nikki rolled her eyes even though no one was in the car to see.

"You get to say that because I didn't make you grow up there."

"How do you think Grandma feels when you talk that way?"

"She thinks I'm ungrateful. But just because she and Dad loved farming doesn't mean I have to. And I will not be blackmailed into feeling something just because it might hurt someone else's feelings. I have a right to feel my own feelings."

Nikki paused and assessed Nell's last sentence.

"Mom, have you been reading feminist self-help books?"

"Don't be silly—you know I hate feminism. Feminists are

unshaven and angry and I think I have always made it clear that I am pro-man, aside from the fact that you can't really depend on them. But Jane left me this really good book that I think makes some excellent points about how women aren't always trusted to feel our own feelings, or that people don't believe us when we say what we feel."

Nikki slapped her free hand into her forehead. "Jane has a lot of good books," she managed to squeak out in a voice free of all laughter. Leave it to Jane to have the appropriate feminist literature on hand for any occasion.

"Well, she's a bit kooky, but you said she was a Mensa member and they're really smart, so I thought I'd give it a go. It turns out that it's a really good book."

"I'm glad you're enjoying it," said Nikki trying to figure out how to work into her real questions. "Mom," she hesitated, uncertain of what to ask first. Finally, she settled on the one that was the least useful, but potentially the most emotionally satisfying. "Seriously, why didn't you ever tell me that Dad went to prison and that's why we moved to Seattle?"

"It wasn't safe. And after he got out, well, I met some of the people he was associating with." She managed to imbue *associating* with a level of disgust that registered on the scale of nuclear contamination. "It was not safe for you to be around him. He is careless and irresponsible. And I had to keep you safe."

Nikki opened her mouth to rebut and then paused, feeling as if some emotional tumblers had clicked into place. All the times in her childhood when she had been warned to *be careful, stay safe*, and *be responsible* seemed to echo in her ears.

"I'm not my dad," said Nikki.

"I know that!" said Nell sharply.

"But I am like him in some ways," said Nikki.

"I know that too," said Nell sadly.

"I like adventures and travel and excitement. But, that doesn't mean that I'm going turn to smuggling and a life of crime. I'm not an irresponsible idiot."

"Oh really? Then what do you call running off with that horrible woman who shot you?"

"Val's not horrible," said Nikki. "She's just selfish."

"The girls told me. She shot you," said Nell flatly.

"And she beat me up pretty bad," said Nikki. "But I've learned a lot since Thailand. I really think I could take her. And anyway, what am I supposed to do—let Dad get killed?"

"Wouldn't hurt my feelings any," said Nell. "He still owes about fifteen years of back child support."

"Mom, you ran off with the proceeds of his drug smuggling business. I don't really think you have a leg to stand on."

"I don't wish to discuss my financial arrangements with your father," said Nell, falling back on formality. "We are discussing the fact that running off like that was extremely rude and shocking."

"Mom, did you spend my entire childhood thinking that Dad was going to show up and kidnap me?"

"I didn't think he'd kidnap you, not really. I just thought he'd show up and promise to show you the moon over the Alhambra, or some nonsense like that, and then the two of you would be off. It was his friends who worried me. I did worry about one of them kidnapping you."

"Is that why you had that freak out when I was in high-school and wanted to change my last name to Connelly?"

"He called and said everything was probably fine, but that the two of us should be careful for a couple of weeks and then he hung up. What was I supposed to do?"

Nikki sighed and tilted her head back, leaning against the headrest. So many things about her childhood suddenly made sense.

"Mom, I love you. And even if I were to go see the moon over the Alhambra, I would still come home for Christmas."

"You didn't come home last Christmas," said Nell with a sniff.

"That was a work emergency," said Nikki. "And I apologize. I'll make a bigger effort this year."

"Ok," Nell sounded watery and slightly defeated, which is how she always sounded when she'd won an argument.

"I'm sorry I was so rude and shocking," added Nikki for extra buttering.

"What do you want?" asked Nell, seeing through Nikki's apology like cellophane.

"I want to know what happened after I left."

"Oh! Well, let me tell you, your boyfriend was not happy! And the girls were not happy! There was so much freaking out! Z'ev wanted to call his work immediately, but then Jenny said she would hog-tie him and Ellen threatened to shoot him and Jane yelled, *Calmness is the cradle of power.* I don't know what that means, but it was at least so surprising that it stopped everyone from fighting. And then Z'ev stormed out of the house, but Jackson told us to all wait inside and he went out to talk to him. And I don't know what he said, but I could see from the kitchen window—"

"You spied on them?"

"Yeah, of course! We wanted to know what was going to happen. And there was a lot of arm waving and yelling from Z'ev. Jane could only make out a word or two with her lip-reading—that's a handy skill—because he was turned away a lot and they were down in the paddock. But the basic gist was that you were crazy and dishonest."

"What did Jackson do?" The idea of her ex-boyfriend being in charge of talking her current boyfriend out of being mad at her was not a pleasing one.

"The horse whisperer thing. You know where he stands real still and pretends he's a stump."

"He's good at that."

"Yeah, so anyway, after a while Jackson got him calmed down and they came back up to the house. And Z'ev said he was taking his things and he was flying back to L.A. And he would talk to them when they got back. And he looked very serious. Jackson said after he left that the girls had better keep an eye on him because he didn't know how long Z'ev would take to decide anything."

"What did the girls do?"

"They packed up, made some phone calls, and then Mom and I drove them to the airport later that afternoon. They all seemed really upset, particularly that Val was alive."

"She has that affect on people," said Nikki.

"Anyway, do you want the number that Jane left for you? She said you would call."

"Jane left a phone number for me?"

"Yeah, I've got it here somewhere." There was the sound of rummaging. "Do you have a pen?"

Nikki reached in her bag for the notebook and pen that she always carried. "Yeah, I do. Thanks Mom."

"Sure sweetie. But please remember next time you go running off with a crazed psychopath that I'm not your answering service. I do have better things to do with my day than deliver messages for your friends."

Nikki got the number, hung up and checked her watch. If she took too much longer Val was going to be suspicious. She put the car in gear and headed back to the house.

So Z'ev hadn't immediately ratted her out. Jackson had bought her some time. She felt a burst of affection toward her ex. He was definitely on the Christmas card list this year. Sure, the Arjan thing probably wasn't going to work out, but maybe she could still pull out of this nosedive. She could probably still save Philippe, even with Val unable to walk outside without getting recognized and shot at. And she could probably still get her life back without Arjan; she would just have to come up with something clever. She was good at clever—she could do this. She felt a tiny blossom of hope struggle up in her soul. The question now was, had the girls told Carrie Mae about Val? How much time did she have? Nikki dialed the number her mother had given her while at a stoplight and then put the phone on speaker, dropping it into her lap as she drove.

The call connected and began ringing. By the fourth ring Nikki thought it was going to go to voicemail. On the fifth ring she was debating whether or not to leave a message when Jane picked up.

"Oh my God," said Jane. "Stop calling me," and hung up.

AMSTERDAM IV
RECOVERING FROM THE PROBLEM

Nikki stood just inside the doorway and stared. How the house was still standing was beyond her. Peeled paint, missing floorboards, broken or boarded up windows—the place was unlivable.

"It's my life as a house," muttered Nikki.

Something squeaked its agreement from the dark.

"I'm upstairs," yelled Val.

"My life has vermin," said Nikki.

She trudged up the stairs. She didn't know what else to do. She felt utterly abandoned. Cast adrift in a cold sea from a shipwreck of her own making. All she had left was Val.

"The iceberg to my Titanic," she muttered.

"What are you grumbling about?" demanded Val from above her.

Nikki took another stepping wincing at the hideously loud creak. "This place is a disaster." She looked up at Val, who was leaning over the banister; she was chewing nicotine gum again.

"It's not so bad up here, and the good news is that we won't need to set any alarms or traps, the stair treads take care of it all. Come on up. I've got the upstairs drawing room warmed up. I even took off my jacket." She held out arms, noticeably bare, and waved them in a Vanna White pantomime.

"You're too happy," said Nikki sourly.

"I bought alcohol," said Val, and disappeared into a room

beyond the banister.

Nikki shrugged and continued her trudge up the vocal stairs. At the top of the stairs was a bedroom with what appeared to be a camping pad and sleeping bag stretched across an empty bed frame. Val's bag was already plopped proprietarily at the foot of the bed. A bathroom with what appeared to be functional plumbing was the next door along the hall and then another bedroom with the same camping set up as the first. Nikki put her bag down on the bed and took the left that lead into what appeared to be some sort of upstairs drawing room. The windows had been boarded over, which hid the garish strings of Christmas lights and camp lanterns from the outside world. An ancient, burn-marked table occupied the center of the room, Val's computer glowing from one end, and a space heater emitted a blast of heat from where it had been nestled in the niche of a filled-in fireplace. The computer had acquired new peripherals, including a printer.

Val was standing at the opposite end of table from her computer, cooking something over a single burner. Nikki had to admit that whatever it was, it smelled delicious.

"Where did we get all this stuff?" she asked surveying the room.

"Came with the house. It's part of Femke's service."

"Oh."

Nikki dropped down at the table. A pile of papers had been binder clipped together and placed neatly in front of the chair as though it were a place setting. It was a dossier on Arjan Meise. The top page was the print out of the newspaper article on his arrest. The photo showed him walking into court in shackles, accompanied by his lawyer—a petite man with a pointy white beard and glasses. Arjan had a craggy, arrogant face dominated by a pair of icy blue eyes and a shock of blonde hair gone to white, and his expression was one of angry disdain. Charges ranged from gun smuggling, to theft and money laundering. His assets had been frozen and property seized as evidence. Which explained the almost empty office and lack of heating at his house. It didn't explain who was using the office though.

The article described the courtroom scene as a three-ring circus with Arjan mocking the lawyers and judges, while his lawyer, a thin man with a neatly trimmed beard, elegant curved moustache, and wireframe glasses, tried ineffectually to make him sit down and be quiet. Nikki flipped through the rest of the packet. Maaravi Meise was barely mentioned. He seemed to have played almost no role in his father's life or business before now.

Nikki looked up and realized that there was a wine glass already poured and a cheese plate already cut.

"The house came with cheese?"

"No, there's a shop down the road. I popped out after we talked. Realized I was starving."

"And you thought you'd drink away the pain of how screwed we are?" asked Nikki, taking a large swallow of the wine. It was faintly spicy and smelled like summer, which Nikki resented. She felt as though she had left summer behind in Washington, with Z'ev and everything else she cared about.

"We're not that screwed," said Val, continuing to stir.

"How are we not screwed? Dad has some wack-a-doodle plan about stealing money from an arms dealer that hinges on the idea that the arms dealer will get carted off to prison, except that the arms dealer is already in prison." Val nodded her agreement. "You have some Viking looking *bokkelul* following you, who, if he didn't want you dead this morning, will surely want you dead after he wakes up in a prison hospital with bike tread imprinted on his forehead."

"Heh. Yeah." Val nodded some more as she sprinkled a little salt into the pan.

"And I came all the way across the damn world, after you blew my cover to the CIA, to rescue my father and now I have no father, no job, no team, and no damn boyfriend! How are we not screwed?"

"I didn't say we weren't screwed. I said we weren't *that* screwed."

"That's like the Captain of the Titanic saying that the boat is only sinking a little."

"I disagree. *That* screwed is being the orchestra on the Titanic. We're the women and children in first class. We're going to get put on a lifeboat or something. Besides, I really feel like you're over reacting to this boyfriend situation. I mean, come on, he had to know. How could he not know? If he didn't know, it was because he was maintaining plausible deniability."

"He suspected I was... something. But he didn't know about all of Carrie Mae until you opened your big mouth."

Val shrugged. "It's better anyway."

Nikki fought the urge to throw the wine glass at Val's head. "How is it better?" she asked through clenched teeth.

"It's better to have everything out in the open."

"Honesty is the best policy? So you've told my father all about Thailand, have you?"

Val stopped stirring for a brief second. "No, I have not. I have given him a brief overview and implied that our split was not amicable and that it was mostly my fault, but no, I haven't given him any of the particulars. And I would appreciate it if you wouldn't either."

"Well, I would have appreciated it if you hadn't blabbed to the CIA about Carrie Mae, but that didn't seem to stop you! How do you not get how much danger you've put us all in?"

"Meh," said Val. "That guy's crazy about you. He's never going to tell the CIA about us."

Nikki thumped the glass down on the table and stood up.

"You don't know him. You don't know me. And even if you were my best friend, it wasn't your call."

"No, it was your call, but you weren't making it, were you? Admit it, I helped you out." Val carried on stirring as if nothing was the matter. Nikki wanted to punch her. She wanted to shoot her. She wanted to do something violent and permanent. None of which was going to be productive to her situation.

Nikki snatched up a chunk of brie and threw it at Val where it splatted against her collar bone and stuck to her shirt.

"Hey!" Val stopped stirring, her expression locked in disbelief.

"Stop talking to me," said Nikki picking up her wine glass. "Just stop talking to me." She took her wine into her room and sat on the bed frame. After a while she put her head between her knees and concentrated on breathing deep.

She sat back up and took a large swallow of wine and unrolled the camp pad and sleeping bag and laid down, staring at the ceiling. The room had twelve foot ceilings with a wide molding and a window over the door. She heard Val go down the hall to her room and back again. Probably to change her shirt.

"Dinner's ready!" Val yelled.

With a sigh, Nikki took her wine back to the drawing room. Val had magically created a gourmet, homemade mac n' cheese.

"That was a perfectly good piece of brie," said Val sternly as she sat down.

"It was either that or shoot you." She didn't even try to hide the bitterness in her voice.

"I forgot that about you. You're a doer."

"I don't know what that means."

"So many people need permission to do… anything. You don't ask; you just do."

"Some people call that being hot-headed."

Val shrugged. "That was always the challenge with you: channel the impetuous impulses to appropriate behaviors."

"The challenge? Val! Stop talking like you ever intended to train me. You planned to kill me the whole time!"

"Not the whole time," protested Val. "I really thought you had potential. I kind of hoped we could both get out of there with what we wanted. And in retrospect, I realize that it was a bad idea to go along with Jirair's plan, but… *c'est la vie.*"

Nikki fell to the side of her dinner bowl and clunked her head on the table repeatedly. "You do this on purpose to persecute me," said Nikki, still resting on the table.

"No, really, I don't. That's where you get screwed up. None of this is personal. It was never personal."

Nikki sat up and looked at Val who was calmly eating her mac n' cheese in delicate forkfuls as if savoring every bite. "Is anything ever personal to you?"

"My cooking," said Val. "I don't generally cook for anyone."

Nikki hefted a forkful of noodles set in a creamy white sauce. It smelled delicious. She bit into it. It was as good as it smelled. It was as far better than any blue box Kraft dinner she had ever eaten.

"It's good."

"Thanks." Val graciously inclined her head as if Nikki had uttered more than a sentence that could be mastered by a two-year-old.

They ate in silence and eventually Nikki refilled her glass and sat back in her chair. The problems besetting them swirled around her head in a jumble. *Divide and conquer.*

"What are we going to do about your fan club? We're going to have a hard time doing anything if you're enemies keep popping up everywhere."

"That's a toughie. Although, personally I blame you for that."

"Excuse me? How are your enemies my fault? I thought you said you shot his brother?"

"I did shoot his brother, but if you hadn't destroyed all my shit he wouldn't dare make a move against me."

"What?"

"After I died, you sold or confiscated all my shit. I have been in this business a long time and I had collected lots of good," Val hesitated, looking for the right word, "leverage."

"Black mail material?" Nikki was skeptical.

"Useful information that kept people like Anders Hoek on my side. But no, Carrie Mae knows best. Let's just destroy everything."

Nikki pursed her lips.

"What? What is that face?" Nikki avoided eye contact. "Are you saying that you didn't destroy everything?"

"I'm saying nothing," said Nikki.

"Ha! You didn't, did you? What'd you do with it? What would you have done with it?" Val narrowed her eyes, trying to divine from Nikki's past actions from her current face. "It got put in storage, didn't it? Well, then it must have been evaluated when you closed my case file. So all of the dirt I have is on the main frame somewhere?"

"Yeah," said Nikki. "Not exactly."

"What does that mean?"

"Well, Rachel's girls went through everything from your house in California. But you still had that storage unit in Cologne from when you were with the German branch. Astriz still hates you, by the way."

Val grinned. "She should. So the German branch has my shit?"

"Not exactly."

"Who has all my gear? I had some good stuff in there."

"Well, the thing is. It's not so easy to set up a crime lab without getting noticed. It's not like the US where we can just wave our hand and declare it to be a product testing facility. And in the seventies when Carrie Mae expanded into Europe they didn't have the resources to set up their own anyway, so... they developed a work around." Nikki cleared her throat and adjusted the salt shaker.

"This is why I hate Carrie Mae," said Val flatly. "We're so third rate. What did we do?"

"We recruited crime lab employees and now we essentially... share space with INTERPOL. Which generally works out great. But sometimes it's difficult to get our stuff processed because we have to account for the INTERPOL case load. So your stuff is actually still in the evidence lock-up."

"I'm on the waiting list. I was the number one threat to Carrie Mae, but hey, as soon as she's dead, slap her on the God damn waiting list."

"Stop being over-dramatic," Nikki said, drily.

"Ooh! That's what we should do!" said Val. "We should break into that evidence locker and get my case book."

"Absolutely not. What are you, crazy? If Carrie Mae hasn't disavowed me already, that would do it."

"Oh come on," said Val. "You said it yourself, we're screwed. We need to start eliminating some of our problems."

"You could keep a lower profile," suggested Nikki.

"I can't believe you just suggested that. It's like you don't know me at all. I'm telling you, if we had my old case book I'd be able to stop Hoek from coming after me and I might even have some dirt on Arjan Meise in there. We should do this."

"We should *not* do this. We should kidnap my father and get the hell out of town before this becomes a disaster of epic proportions."

"He is not going to be happy with that as a solution." Val shook her head and reached for the wine bottle.

"Arjan is in jail. You're being hunted. And I have no resources to help us without my job. We're out of options. You know my father isn't going to do the responsible thing, so we're going to have to. You know I'm right."

"I know we need to talk to Philippe. He has to know more that half-assed idea he was spewing in South Africa."

"OK, so we should go meet them at the airport and kidnap him back."

"We can't kidnap him; he'll be pissed!"

"So we won't kidnap him. We'll just... forcefully rescue him. And if he can come up with a good reason not to vacate the country, then we'll stick around."

Val looked unconvinced.

"Val, INTERPOL is all over this guy. How are we supposed

to do anything?"

"I guess," said Val. "I just don't think Philippe's going to be happy."

"At the moment," said Nikki polishing off her wine, "his happiness is the least of my concerns."

THE PAST

THERE AND THEN

Lethbridge, Canada

"Time is important. Like money, it should not be wasted; it should be spent judiciously on things that matter."

"Riding my bike down to the store matters," said thirteen-year-old Nikki.

"But not as much as your Latin lessons," said Grand-Mère and Nikki's face squished in on itself, her expression clearly denoting how she felt about Latin lessons.

"Sometimes we have to do things that don't always make us happy. But," added her grandmother sternly, pointing to the tea-cups and saucers for Nikki to collect, "It's not always about what makes us happy. It is about responsibility." Grand-Mère walked stiffly across the golden finished oak floor, the tip of her cane making a click with each step. Nikki wrinkled her nose at her Grandmother's choice of words; they were all too familiar.

"Don't slop the tea into the saucers!"

Nikki came back to attention quickly, covering her lapse into the past with a smile and correcting the dangerous tilt of the tea-cups. She followed after Grand-Mère, paying careful attention to the tea level.

"That is why I make sure you come to see me every summer," continued Grand-Mère, "If my son is delinquent in his responsibilities then it seems I must pick up the slack, as usual. It is clear that it was a mistake to let him indulge in his artistic fancies.

Let that be a lesson to you. Do not make the mistake of thinking that the liberal arts are a suitable career choice."

Grand-Mère settled her bulk into her favorite high backed Victorian armchair. Nikki followed and set one teacup on the small, ornate table next to her, trying not to spill. Taking her own cup to the smaller stiff backed chair next to the window, Nikki settled into the chair trying to remember all of Grand-Mère's rules of etiquette.

As Nikki sat down, the edge of her skirt climbed above her knee. The skirt was a faded pink and left over from last summer. Nell had packed it, knowing that Grand-Mère would expect Nikki to wear skirts, but not bothering to buy a new one, since Nikki refused to wear them anywhere else. The skirt was now two inches too short and revealed Nikki's gangly legs, and scab-covered knees at inopportune moments. Grand-Mère stared at the scab on her left knee with a ferocious intensity. Nikki tugged her skirt down, but Grand-Mère kept staring. Nikki lowered her gaze to her grand-mother's swollen ankles that were so fat that even in support hose were purple with uncirculated blood. There was a long moment and then Grand-Mère withdrew her gaze.

"Now, turning our attention to your Latin. Yesterday we were discussing verbs and adding verb modifiers in translation. Since *is*, *does* or *does not*, and *es* are all from implication rather than stated in a text, our translation must depend on context. Let us turn to page sixty-four and examine some more of the complex translations. You'll see that we have Roman, Greek, and Christian samples, please point out the places where verb modifiers are necessary."

Nikki dutifully picked up her Latin textbook, but her mind was drifting. It dodged around the maid in the hallway, clambered through the tall stained glass window in the library, tumbled down over the meticulously trimmed lawn, across the road, through the gates and eventually made a break for the border to Washington where she just knew that Donny Fernandez and his sisters were having fun without her. Even Jackson, whose parents had moved to the west side last fall was going to be there for the fourth. She was missing everything really good. Her other grandma would be putting up peach preserves. And Grandpa would take the leftovers and make ice cream. And there would be pie, all kinds of pie. Peach of course, but also rhubarb and apple and chocolate peanut butter. Nell had said that she was going to move them to Seattle and that she'd look for a house there while Nikki was in Canada, but Nikki didn't believe that Nell would willingly leave behind Grandma's pie.

Grand-Mère did not believe in pie. Grand-Mère said pie led to diabetes. Nikki didn't know what diabetes was, but she thought it must be some sort of sin, like gluttony or sloth. *Thou shalt not commit diabetes.*

In Grand-Mère's world there was the sin of diabetes, the sin of freckles, and the sin of irresponsibility. She was already lost to the freckles, no matter how much sunscreen she wore, and the pie was a definite no-no, but irresponsibility loomed over her head, just out of sight, hiding in the foliage, always waiting to pounce.

Her father was irresponsible for leaving. Everyone said so, but Grand-Mère always seemed to imply that it might be contagious. *Better watch out or you'll catch the irresponsibility.* She usually managed to imply that he'd caught it from Nell and that Nikki needed to be inoculated against any further exposure. Nell always implied that it was hereditary and that Nikki might inherit it like she had his hair and eye color. Nikki wished faintly that she could just catch it and get over it like chicken pox, so that they could all stop poking at her.

She felt like her world was a tornado and she was stuck help-less in the middle as everything went spinning away from her.

"*Hic et nunc*," said Grand-Mère.

"Here and now," translated Nikki automatically, watching the gardener trim the hedges and wondering if Donny's mother would make tomatillo salsa for the Fourth of July picnic.

"Which is what you are not," snapped Grand-Mère, thump-ing her cane on the floor for added emphasis. "Pay attention. I am giving you tools to succeed in life. If you can understand why people use the words they do, you can understand why they do the things they do."

"Yes, Grand-Mère," replied Nikki dutifully, holding her text-book more firmly.

"Words are everything." Grand-Mère thumped her cane again, but softer.

"Yes, Grand-Mère," repeated Nikki.

"For instance, if I say *go get an apple from the cook*, why do you think I would say it?"

"Because…" began Nikki, uncertain how to proceed.

"I can only assume that your lack of articulation is due to hunger. Go get an apple from the cook."

"Yes, Grand-Mère," said Nikki, grinning. Closing her book, she slipped out of her chair and hurried to the door.

"And come directly back when you're done!" Grand-Mère called after her.

"Yes, Grand-Mère!" Nikki yelled over her shoulder, as she ran.

AMSTERDAM V
LIFE IS GREAT

In the space of a heartbeat Nikki went from sleep to a hair prickling wakefulness. Moving slowly she wrapped her fingers around the 1911 and breathed out slowly, listening for what had caused her to jump from a jumbled dream to heart pounding alertness. She cracked an eyelid, and surveyed her room; nothing seemed to have moved. She hurriedly pulled on her underwear, bra and a sweatshirt and stood up. Then she heard the soft creak of the stair board.

Climbing onto the ancient roll top desk she risked a look through the transom window above the door and into the hall. Val's door was wide open and through it Nikki could see that her window was also open and that Val had one leg over the sill. Glancing up, Val saw Nikki, and gestured out the window and then held up two fingers and pointed at her watch. Nikki sighed and nodded. Val tossed her bag out the window and then followed it. It was every woman for herself.

Nikki looked around her room. The first thing she really needed to do was put on pants. Just as she was reaching this decision a man appeared at the top of the stairs, Baretta M12 held casually in one hand a cigarette in the other. He glanced along the hallway, looking in the open doorways, before homing in on the only one that was closed—hers. She waited until he had one hand on the doorknob and then boosted herself up and through the transom window. He let out a bleat of surprise as she landed on him. The impact widened his too loose grip on the gun, sending it skittering down the hallway. Nikki grabbed him around the neck and pulled him into a hip throw. He staggered upright, using the railing for support and blinked at her in surprise. Before she could launch herself in an attack, a hand reached up and pulled him over the banister, throwing him down the stairs. Nikki waited, guard up, ready for a fight.

Z'ev Coralles walked up the stairs, dusting off his hands.

The first time she had met the six-foot-something, half-black, half-Jewish, hair always buzz cut, eyes always the color of melted chocolate, voice like Jack Daniels whiskey, Z'ev Coralles, Nikki was literally left breathless. This morning he had managed to repeat the effect.

"You couldn't find someplace less decrepit to stay? I think I just breathed in lead based paint chips."

"Z'ev?" Nikki gaped, unsure of what to say or do.

"We have to go now," he said glancing at his watch impatiently.

"No," said Nikki.

"No?"

"Well, for one thing, I'm going to put on pants. I'm not running naked through another European city."

Z'ev opened his mouth, shut it and then tried again. "Which European city did you run through last time?"

Nikki shook her head. This was not how a reunion with Z'ev was supposed to go. And if she wanted a reunion with Z'ev to go at all, she had better not mention Paris and Kit Masters. "Technically, it was just the hotel," said Nikki going back into her room. "And technically, I wasn't naked; I had a coat on. But let's just say it's an experience I'm not anxious to repeat."

She began to shovel her belongings into her duffel bag,

starting with the file on Arjan Meise, before Z'ev came into the room.

"We don't really have time to pack," said Z'ev, over the sound of running feet pounding up the stairs.

"What? You want me to go around pantsless?" Nikki threw more crap in the bag. "Look," she said, risking a look out into the hallway, "I get that you're a little upset." She pulled her head back around the corner and tried to keep her voice down. Several men were running down the hallway. "But—"

"Upset?" Z'ev cut her off, his voice rising in volume. "No Nikki, I am not upset. Upset is when I find that you've eaten the last of peanut butter and then put the jar back empty."

"There is peanut butter on the sides; you can still scrape the jar," said Nikki, sounding lame even to herself, as she pulled on her jeans.

"Upset is when you go to the bathroom during dinner, don't come back for a half hour and when you do you have a black eye."

"I only had a black eye the one time." Nikki petered out, knowing that the black eye hadn't been the point. She focused on tying her shoes.

"I am not upset," he repeated. A gunmen burst through the door. Z'ev grabbed him by the shirt, yanking the man off his feet and head-butted him. The man sagged back unconscious and Z'ev dropped him, stepping over his body to grab the second man. Nikki winced as Z'ev punched him twice and shoved him away. "I'm not upset," he said again, watching the man slide down the wall. Anders Hoek arrived, a gear mark on his left cheek, and swung a knife. Nikki watched as Z'ev stripped him of the knife, lodged it in his foot, kneed him in the groin, and then punched him repeatedly until he fell over. She winced a little at the sound of crunching nose cartilage. "I'm pissed," said Z'ev, breathing heavily. "I'm angry. I'm hurt. And I feel like a fool."

"No," protested Nikki.

"You were supposed to be on my side," he said, still looking at the unconscious bodies of the gunmen. "Instead, you made me look like an idiot. Jenny, Ellen, and Jane must have thought the situation was real funny."

"No," said Nikki. "They thought I was being unfair to you and they thought I should have broken up with you after Paris."

"Then why didn't you?" he demanded bitterly.

Nikki took a ragged breath, blinking back tears. "I'm not that tough."

He stared at her and she saw him soften—saw the slight unbending in the spine. Some part of him believed her. Then he shook his head. "You do this on purpose, don't you?"

"Do what?" Nikki asked.

"Do you even have any idea what kind of situation you've put me in at work?"

"Yes, I do! That's why I didn't want to tell you! And here, here," she walked over and grabbed the head of the last victim of Z'ev's rage, lifting it off the floor. "This one is Anders Hoek. He's mad at Val for... doing Val things. But he's got to be on someone's most wanted list. Won't that be good for work?"

"I know who he is," said Z'ev. "I'm here with INTERPOL."

"Oh." Nikki let Hoek's head drop with a thunk.

"I'm supposed to bring you in for questioning about the Arjan Meise case. I'm assisting the INTERPOL task force that arrested him."

Somewhere in the back of Nikki's mind, the part that never really stopped working, a little signal flare went up.

"Why?"

"Because I was assigned to assist by my boss. Because I have a real job with a real intelligence agency."

"Yeah, one with a sterling reputation for honesty and correct decision making. I meant, why am I wanted for the Arjan Meise case. I've never even met Arjan Meise."

"The B.O.L.O. didn't name you specifically. Just a crazy redhead and a brunette. Forgive me for assuming that was you and Val. You'll have to come in, if you want to find out what they want."

"I'm sorry, I can't," said Nikki, standing up.

"This isn't a choice Nikki," said Z'ev. "You have to come in."

"No, my Dad is still in danger. Besides, I don't actually have any information about Arjan. I won't be of any use."

"We might be able to help with your Dad's situation. After all, we're the good guys and it is our job. As opposed to someone who just decided to *help* with international terrorism."

Nikki wanted to argue with the last barb, but realized that it wouldn't lead the conversation to a useful destination.

"Well, the problem is that I'm pretty sure that the people who took my Dad want him to do something illegal because he's good at illegal things and if I answer questions about that than I'm pretty sure that you *good guys* will arrest my Dad."

"I don't have a problem with that. And frankly, if you want me to believe that our relationship was anything but one long con game then you'll come with me right now."

Nikki folded her arms across her chest, guilt suddenly dropping away in favor of righteous anger. "So I have to prove I love you, by turning in my Dad? What kind of dick move is that?"

"I don't think it's a dick move," said Z'ev. "I'd say it's fair play. You've spent the last three years manipulating me. Now it's my turn."

Nikki was unprepared for the sudden return of guilt or the lump of tears in her throat that threatened to overwhelm her.

"Is that what you really think? That it was all a lie and that I manipulated you?"

"You're not trying to manipulate me right now?"

Nikki looked away. If that was really what he thought, she didn't stand a chance.

"No, I'm not. I swear I have never tried to manipulate you. I only ever tried to," she struggled for the right words, "work around you. I never wanted to get in your way. I just wanted to do my job and have everybody I loved be happy." She couldn't look at him anymore, so she dabbed her eyes with the cuff of her sweatshirt. She heard him step over the pile of offenders and she could feel the heat from his body as he moved closer.

"You really don't know you do it, do you?" he asked.

"Do what?" she asked impatiently, blinking up at him through tears.

"Oh God," he said, half-laughing, then kissed her. It was an angry kiss, half-rough, half-tender, half-something wild, but Nikki didn't care, as long as he kept kissing her.

Downstairs the front door banged open. "*Politie. Niemand zet!*"

"That will be my colleagues from the INTERPOL task force," said Z'ev. "You'd better go."

"What?"

"But I expect constant contact and updates. If I don't hear from you every three hours, I'm giving your name to the task force. Do you understand?"

Nikki gulped in air. "Right. Right." She ducked into her room and grabbed her duffel, then ran down the hall to use the same exit as Val. "Wait, wait," she turned back, panicked, "How do I get in touch with you?"

Z'ev held up his phone, and managed to shake it with an entirely sarcastic air. "My number hasn't changed. You just forgot how to dial."

Nikki would have liked to argue, but she could hear more police arriving. She settled for an angry glare and slid over the windowsill, dangling by her fingertips for a long moment before dropping onto the grass below.

AMSTERDAM VI
TIPPING POINT

Nikki checked her watch again and cautiously sipped her espresso. She was uncertain if she wanted to tell Val about Z'ev, but that was an irrelevant decision if Val never showed up. Nikki checked the street and then the interior of the café reflected in the window; nothing was moving. She hadn't been followed and no one in the café appeared to be watching her. Nikki drummed her fingers and mentally retraced their steps. Replaying Z'ev's words in her mind.

The B.O.L.O. didn't name you specifically. Just a crazy red-head and a brunette.

She was absolutely certain that she hadn't been spotted at Anders house, but it was possible that she had missed a surveillance device. So it was theoretically possible that INTERPOL had gotten her description there. But Val hadn't been there. How had they gotten a brunette?

I'm supposed to bring you in for questioning about the Arjan Meise case.

The incident with bearded Anders Hoek had surely attracted a lot of attention—it's not every day you see a bicycle fight—but that shouldn't have been connected to Arjan Meise. Unless, there was more to the story with Hoek than Val had said?

Nikki found herself tearing up little bits of paper napkin, and rolling them into tiny spheres as she rolled around thoughts of the last week with Val in her mind. She and Val had been discreet.

Despite chiding Val about keeping a lower profile, they honestly hadn't been that many places in public, together or separate. The only way to have kept a lower profile would have been not to go anywhere at all. The hotel in South Africa, the Meise Farm, onto a plane, Amsterdam, the bar, slight detour to deal with Hoek and back to the house. That was it.

Nikki began to build a pyramid of paper napkin balls. In the reflection in the window, she saw a figure approaching her table.

"Architecture school missed out on your genius," said Val.

"They're not the only ones," said Nikki. "We've got a problem."

"More than the ones we already had?"

"INTERPOL has a B.O.L.O. out on two women matching our descriptions in connection with the Arjan Meise case."

"What? How?" Val dropped down into the second chair. "And how do you know?"

"INTERPOL showed up after you left. I did a little recon. I'm still not sure how Hoek found us. I checked the car for GPS."

"Femke, I think," said Val, taking a sip from Nikki's coffee cup. "She's got a new girl handling dispatches. She said she'd deal with it. But what about INTERPOL?"

"I've got an informant on the inside, but how they got our description, or how they connected us to Meise... I've been sitting here trying to figure out," said Nikki, "and I'm coming up with bupkiss."

Val took a deep breath and let it out. She shook her head. "I'm starting to think you were right. We need to just get out of here. There are just too many unknown factors."

Nikki wrinkled her nose.

"What? Now you want to stay?"

"I don't like mysteries," said Nikki, unwilling to discuss her meeting with Z'ev. "But, yeah, let's get Dad and go."

"I've got the flight time and a car out back."

"Where'd you get a car?" asked Nikki, digging money out of her wallet, as Val chugged the coffee.

"Stole it." Val finished off Nikki's croissant in a bite

"Of course you did. Finished with my lunch?"

"Mmm," said Val, her mouth still full. "Tanks."

The drive to the airport was carefully law abiding and within designated speed limits.

"What's the plan?" Nikki asked as they approached the passenger loading zone.

"I don't know. Why get fancy? Let's just park the car on the strip. We'll wait for them as they come out of baggage claim. I'll stick a gun in Maaravi's back and say we're taking Philippe and you cover whatever bodyguards he's got with him and then we walk Philippe to the car, get in and drive away."

"Works for me," Nikki said, digging through the contents of the stolen car's glove compartment. She found a ridiculous Gilligan-esque plastic rain hat, and put it on, tucking up her hair. She wondered if she should dye it. It was a very recognizable color and that B.O.L.O. was going to make life difficult if she couldn't get Z'ev to quash it.

There were a few refinements to the plan, of course. Nikki ended up waiting for the party in baggage claim, so she could alert Val. Philippe spotted her right off and winked in an overtly conspiratorial manner. Nikki tried not to roll her eyes. *Why are parents so embarrassing?*

"They're headed your way," muttered Nikki, into her phone, following the group from a safe distance.

Maaravi Meise was a dark-haired man in his thirties. Neatly trimmed beard. Blue eyes like his father, but with a more thoughtful air, and fisherman's sweater to accommodate the cooler weather of the Netherlands. His bodyguard was a Neanderthal in a black leather jacket with a protruding forehead and the profile of a Dick Tracy villain.

"Starting my approach now," said Val. Nikki could see her through the sliding glass doors about fifty feet down, wearing a purple scarf and wheeling a small piece of luggage that she had undoubtedly purloined from somewhere. As she walked she undid the scarf and Nikki knew it would be used to hide her pistol. Nikki closed in, getting ready for her own encounter with the bodyguard.

A car pulled up at the curb and a woman got out. Maaravi waved.

Val stretched out her legs, and Nikki saw Philippe spot her. Philippe adjusted his angle slightly, putting himself between the bodyguard and Val.

Nikki began to jog. Maaravi and the woman were embracing. Nikki slammed into Val knocking her over.

"I'm so sorry," gushed Nikki. "I'm so careless. Are you alright?"

The bodyguard's eyes drifted over to them. Val looked furiously from Nikki to Maaravi and Philippe.

"No, I'm not alright!" she said sharply. "I think you've torn my new scarf."

"I'm so sorry. Come inside. I'll buy you a new one. My apologies."

Nikki continued the stream of apologies until the sliding door had shut between them and Maaravi. Philippe watched them go with a puzzled expression.

"What the hell was that all about?" demanded Val.

"See that woman in the lip-lock with Maaravi?"

Val took a subtle look over Nikki's head. "Flashy blonde. Yeah, so?"

"That's the police woman from Arjan's house who chewed out the guys on the surveillance team."

Val grinned. "And just like that, we are back in the game."

AMSTERDAM VII
NO DOUBT

"You're following too far back," Val said.

"My distance is fine."

"You're going to lose them."

"I'm not going to lose them," said Nikki, through gritted teeth. "She's police and the bodyguard might have more brains than he appears to. If I follow any closer we're going to get spotted."

"Twenty bucks says you lose them."

"Twenty bucks says I punch you in the face."

"I'll take that action," said Val.

"You can't bet on getting yourself punched in the face!"

"Sure I can. I'm really annoying. I know, because you keep telling me."

Nikki spared a glance away from the silver Mercedes Range Rover in front of them, to look at Val, who grinned. Nikki tried not to laugh, and was about to respond when Val pointed ahead.

"They're turning!"

"I can see that! Put your arm down."

Nikki turned left, following the Range Rover at cautious pace.

"Is it just me or do those things look ridiculous anywhere other than Africa? I mean, a Mercedes faux Jeep, in the city? Yuppie, please."

"Maybe there's more countryside around than we know about?" suggested Nikki, half-heartedly.

"It's like having a $1700 rain poncho," said Val. "If you can afford it, you're not going to use it. You're going to pay someone else to use their twelve-dollar poncho and go get wet."

"I see your point. I didn't know there were $1700 rain ponchos, but sure, theoretically I'm with you. Although, I also didn't realize you were so offended by the dilettante spending of the rich."

"Meh. I've been spending too much time with your father. Income inequality. The pleasures of the idle rich are killing the planet. Blah, blah, blah." The car ahead changed lanes and Nikki concentrated on her job. "It's actually really annoying."

"The constant sermonizing, while attempting to get more money through illegal means?" asked Nikki, not sure which part of her really annoying father Val was referring to.

"No, the fact that once he points it out, you can't stop seeing it."

"Oh, that. Yeah, Jane is constantly pointing out instances of white privilege and after a while you want to strangle her and then you realize that she's gotten inside your head and you can see it everywhere."

"Wouldn't work with me. I enjoy mine," said Val. "It's very convenient."

"I don't think you're supposed to say that," said Nikki.

"Why not? I'm benefiting from an unfair system that gives me far more leeway and assistance simply by being white. It's like the pleasant tailwind of life. Yay me!"

"But I'm pretty sure that Jane would say you're supposed to feel guilty about it. Or work to stop it. Or you know, at least not celebrate it."

"I don't feel guilt. Guilt means that you made an incorrect

decision in the past."

"Oh, and you never made an incorrect decision?"

"Certainly. I've made lots. But I have always made decisions with the best information available or with the full knowledge that what I was doing was stupid or wrong. Having consciously made the decision, why would I then feel guilty about it? Doing anything else would mean that I didn't embrace my true self or my own emotions. And feeling guilty about something that's entirely outside of my control is even stupider."

Nikki pursed her lips, trying to channel her inner Jane. "I'm pretty sure that Jane would say that you should then be working to change the unfair system."

"But I don't actually care that much," said Val. "That's why I always donated to the Carrie Mae Foundation's actual charity wing. It was so they could hire other people to care for me."

"I'm pretty sure morality can't really operate like a carbon off-set plan."

"It's a system that works for me. I think they're parking. What is that—a hotel? Drive by and then circle the block."

"What block? The damn thing is right on a canal!"

"Well, just drive past and then double back."

Nikki did as she was told. The hotel was an enormous castle looking structure of red brick, banded in white stone with a copper roofed tower on one corner. It was built on a promontory of land that jutted out into a canal giving the whole thing a fairy tale appearance of presiding over a medieval moat. She slowed down as they passed. The party was definitely disembarking. Nikki stopped at a stoplight and Val opened the car door.

"Find parking and meet me at the hotel," she said slamming the door behind her.

"Feels no guilt," said Nikki bitterly. "I really ought to punch her in the face."

She parked the car around the corner, bullying her way into a space and then dialed Z'ev as she walked back to the hotel.

"It's been over three hours," he said without preamble.

"So sue me, but I didn't think letting Val know you were in town was a good idea. Meanwhile, hold on, I'm texting you a picture." Nikki took the phone away from her face and flipped to photo files to find the picture of the blonde police woman she'd taken the day before.

"I need you to run the photo I just sent through the police database. I think she's with the police and I need to know who she is and what she's up to."

"I'm not helping you spy on the police!"

"It's not spying if the police aren't on the side of the police. Also, what did you find out about Anders Hoek?"

"He's still being processed. And you're going to have to make better sense than that if you want me to help," he snapped.

"All right. You want me to make sense? How about making sense of something for me? The B.O.L.O. you said matched the description of Val and me— who put it out? Where did they get our description? And why is it in connection to Arjan Meise? Because up until yesterday, I'd never heard of Arjan Meise."

There was silence on the other end of the line.

"It originated from the INTERPOL task force on the Meise case," he said at last. "My turn. What do you know about Arjan Meise?"

"I know that he's an arms dealer and smuggler, that he's currently under arrest, and that all of his bank accounts have been frozen. And I know the police are watching his house even though it looks like no one is living there."

"And?" Z'ev prodded.

"And nothing. That is literally all the information I have on Arjan Meise. My turn. Have you looked at that picture I sent you?"

"Hold on." Z'ev whistled softly through his teeth as he put the phone on speaker. She could picture him, sorting through the phone's commands, his large hands delicately maneuvering across the screen. She found herself simultaneously missing the tiny routine gestures even as she ground her teeth at his continued bullish attitude.

"What kind of crap is this, Nikki?" he said, his voice echoing slightly as if he were in a stairwell.

"That's the police woman I want you to run through the database and identify."

"I don't have to run her through the database," said Z'ev. "That's Petra Gilles. She's INTERPOL. She's the head of this task force."

"Uh…"

"Nikki, seriously, where did you get this picture? She's one of the rising stars in the department—a total straight arrow."

Nikki dodged a bicyclist and stood on the front steps of the hotel. Across the lobby from her Val was entering an elevator. She gestured impatiently and then held up four fingers as the doors began closing. Why did she always feel like Val was one step ahead of her?

"Nikki!"

"Z'ev, I'm going to have to call you back," said Nikki. "Um. I would recommend not trusting her."

"No. She's great. It's you I don't trust."

"Yeah, I know," said Nikki. "I'm going to have to work on

that. OK, I really gotta go."

"Nikki!"

Nikki hung up the phone without saying goodbye.

THE PAST II

MAZATLAN

Seattle, Washington

The mall was crowded with shoppers. The sky was still overcast and the periodic downpours were accompanied by a biting wind, but the idea of spring had permeated the shopping consciousness. Shorts and itty-bitty tops were suddenly in high demand.

"So you're really going on the Mexico trip?" asked Caitlin Barcourt.

"Yeah, my mom said I could if I paid for it," said seventeen-year-old Nikki, holding up a pair of earrings to her earlobe and turning slightly in the mirror to visualize how it would look against her neck. "I figure I can use the money I was saving."

"I thought you were going to buy a car?"

"Everyone I date has a car; so what's the point? Besides, when will I get to go to Mexico again?"

"You don't think you'll go after college?"

Nikki shrugged. The idea of *after college* seemed as inconceivable as the Jurassic era. Both were theoretically possible, but neither seemed particularly convincing when viewed from the immediate now.

"You should come with us," volunteered Nikki.

"With my Spanish grade?" Caitlin tried on a bracelet and then put it back down again. "Mrs. Trawly hasn't exactly invited me."

"Oh, come on. They just want to pretend like it's exclusive, but really just about anyone who raises the money can go."

"Probably true," agreed Caitlin as they drifted away from the jewelry section. "Want to go down to Beauty Place and mix our own perfume?"

"Sure," agreed Nikki. "You really should think about going. It would be so much fun!"

"Do you really want me there?" she asked, frowning.

"Of course," said Nikki, uncertain of what Caitlin meant.

"I mean, sure it would be fun, but I just never really thought of us as you know, the backpacking buddy types."

"Well, it's not really backpacking. The class is staying in a hotel."

"Well, you know what I mean."

The mall was busy, but Nikki dodged the shoppers without noticing, concentrating on what Caitlin was saying.

"No, I don't think I do."

"Well, we're not best friends or anything. I mean we're friends and all, and lord knows I've tried to get to know you, but I'm not sure I can."

"Are you calling me shallow? You dumped Brett in the middle of Junior Prom because you didn't like his aftershave."

"It wasn't just that," said Caitlin airily.

"He was crying in the bathroom and you left with John Weinmen."

"I'd moved on. I don't know why he couldn't. Look, I'm not saying we're not friends. I'm just saying you're kind of hard to get to know and ever since you broke up with Billy Hollis, you don't even hang out with us anymore."

"I hang out," said Nikki plaintively.

"Sure, practices, games and stuff. I'm just saying that you

don't really… Well, you're not really like everyone else, are you?"

"Yes, I am," muttered Nikki, wishing she didn't want to cry.

"I'm not trying to be mean, I swear."

"Then what are you trying to do?" demanded Nikki.

"I'm just saying, that cheerleading is more than just an after-school activity. You're going to have to try harder. I mean, next year is senior year! I'd just hate for you not to make the team on your senior year. Can you imagine?"

Nikki, swallowed an angry retort. There was no point in arguing; there was never any point. It would just create a big scene and then Caitlin would tell everyone at school and then Nikki wouldn't be invited to anything anymore. Caitlin was right; she was going to have to try harder. Eventually Caitlin had mixed enough orchid, Patchouli and Sandalwood to satisfy her nose or an unbathed hippie and Caitlin drove her home.

"See you tomorrow," said Caitlin cheerfully, as Nikki slammed the car door. Marching up to her house, Nikki felt a tide of unexpressed anger churning in her gut, but her swift strides slowed as she approached the porch and saw a big box squatting in front of the door.

"Mom," Nikki called, unlocking the door, but the house was dark and quiet. Nikki checked her watch. Nell was late, but it was tax season at the office, so it Nikki didn't really expect her home for another half hour.

Pulling the box into the front hall, Nikki noticed it was mushed in at the corners and tied with string; it looked as though it had come a long way. Nikki looked at the return address. The address had been stamped and marked over, but after some deciphering Nikki read the words "Hong Kong." She puzzled over who could be sending her mother something from Hong Kong and then she read the labels again. It wasn't for Nell. It was for her.

Nikki looked over her shoulder nervously. It was from her father. It had to be. He was the only person she knew who went anywhere. She carried the box upstairs to her room, afraid that Nell would come home and catch her with it.

Nikki ran downstairs for the kitchen scissors and then, ignoring all strictures about running with scissors, ran back up the stairs to her room. Once in her bedroom, she began to hack at the string and tape that held the box closed. Breathing hard, she wrenched the box open.

Standing in her room, Nikki pulled out the bag in puzzlement. It was a big pack, with padded shoulder and waist straps, perfect for traveling. She hadn't spoken to her Dad in months. There was no way he could have known about the Mexico trip.

She tried on the pack and then took it off and examined it more closely, pulling open the pockets and finding out what all the zippers did. In the front pocket she found a 3 x 5 card with the name, address, and return policies of the shop where the bag had been purchased. Curious, Nikki had flipped the card over. There on the back was her father's firm handwriting.

Nikki,

We all experience life as individuals, but what I have learned from traveling is that individual is not the same as alone. Find the unique things in life, treasure the unique things about yourself and you will never be alone.

Love Always,

Papa.

Underneath the note her father had written a quote in block letters.

Own only what you can carry with you; know

LANGUAGE, KNOW COUNTRIES, KNOW PEOPLE. LET YOUR MEMORY BE YOUR TRAVEL BAG. - ALEXANDER SOLZHENITSYN

Nikki felt a lump form in her throat and tears spring to her eyes. Her parents had been divorced for five years, and she could count the times she had seen him since then on one hand. But it seemed like just when she had begun to believe all the crap her mom said about him, he did something like this.

Sniffing fiercely, Nikki flattened the box and carried it downstairs to shove into her neighbor's garbage can. When her mother came home, Nikki would claim the backpack was from Grand-Mère.

KNOCK THREE TIMES

Nikki arrived on the fourth floor and looked around. Val was nowhere to be seen. She stood in the hallway and scratched her head. She imagined at times like this that Z'ev had some secret CIA trick for divining the correct path and, if pressed, she would have admitted that being unable to solve such a simple puzzle made her feel like a failure as a secret agent. Her entire job was predicated on knowing what to do when other people didn't. Moments of indecision were what haunted her.

"Hey!" Val poked her head out of a room further down the hall. "Are you coming or what?"

"Yeah, I was trying… never mind. What'd you do, rent a room?" Nikki jogged down the hall and entered the door Val was holding open.

"Are you kidding? This place is like $600 a night. I just stole a master key from one of the maids."

"Well, smart, I guess. But what are we doing here? Where's Maaravi and Dad and the woman?"

"They're upstairs," said Val.

Nikki looked around the hotel suite. It was a jewel box in blue and white, coordinating with the China pattern displayed in the reproduction Dutch Master painting hanging on the wall. She stared at the lovingly depicted water jug and fruit. "Nice place." She bounced on the bed, mounded with white linen, and a matching blue duvet.

"Yeah, it's nice," said Val, opening the door to the balcony and staring upward. "The bathroom is all Italian marble. It's got class. Who were you talking to on the phone?"

"What?"

"Downstairs. You were talking to someone on the phone."

"I was calling my INTERPOL contact. I wanted to find out about the woman."

"Good. What'd you find out?" Val took the desk chair outside wheeled it outside onto the balcony, then stood on it. Appearing to stare intently at the underside of the balcony directly above. "Well?" she demanded, climbing down.

"Sorry, I was waiting until you weren't standing on a wobbly surface four floors above the ground. Her name is Petra Gilles. She's in charge of the INTERPOL task force that arrested Arjan Meise."

"Oooh! A double cross!" Val sat down on the chair and began to push herself back and forth across the balcony. "But who is double crossing who? Is she using Maaravi to help her case against Arjan?"

"Or is he using her to help free his father?"

"It could—" Val held up a hand, and cocked her ear toward the ceiling. Nikki heard the door to the balcony above them open.

"This place is great," said Philippe. "I'm going to order room service. Do you want room service?"

Nikki couldn't hear the response of the other person in the room.

"Yes, but I know they're a mayonnaise town. I don't know if you're all right with that." Philippe tapped quickly on the wrought iron railing of the balcony, with what sounded like the idle drumming of adult ADD.

Val reached and tapped a quick reply on the railing nearest to her.

"You're going out for smokes? No problem. I'm not going anywhere."

Nikki listened intently as she heard footsteps crossing the ceiling above her. A few moments later, Philippe's head dangled over the edge of the balcony.

"*Mon chère*! And my own Nicole!"

"Hey babe," said Val.

"Don't call him babe. It grosses me out." Nikki came out to the balcony to stare at her father's upside down face.

"You're just going to have to deal with it," said Philippe. "Your mom and I have been divorced for a long time. You're going to have to deal with the fact that we have other relationships. Someday your mom will probably want to date too, you know."

"Oh my God. *Papa*, she's been dating for years."

"What? Really?"

"Yes, really. My objection is not based on you being related. It's you dating Val."

"I know you two didn't part on the best of terms, but could you please try to bury the hatchet for my sake? Val is a really great woman."

"Thanks baby," said Val seriously, but Nikki recognized the twinkle in her eye.

"I'm not having this conversation with you while you're upside down!"

"Fair point. Also, we don't have a lot of time. That Igor of a bodyguard only went downstairs to buy cigarettes.

"Mmmm, cigarettes," said Val longingly.

"Stay strong, *chère*, you're doing really well. What's going on?"

"Maaravi's girlfriend," said Nikki ignoring the further use of the objectionable pet names, "what do you know about her?"

"I think she's been feeding him inside information about the police. She said we couldn't go to his house because INTERPOL was watching it."

"That's because she is INTERPOL," said Val. "She's in charge of the task force that locked up Arjan. As in, Arjan is already in jail. As in, not available for us to put him in jail. As in, you perhaps weren't entirely truthful with us in South Africa?"

Val's tone was calm, but her arms were crossed in a defensive posture. Philippe blinked rapidly as if assessing new information.

"He's already in jail? Are you sure?"

"Yes," said Nikki. "It was all over the papers here. INTERPOL arrested him and froze his accounts. The trial date hasn't been set yet, but it's looking like it's going to be a thing."

Understanding seemed to bloom across Philippe's face. "That makes so much more sense! I knew Maaravi wasn't telling me the whole story. I couldn't figure why he wasn't just using his dad's network for a lot of this shit. I mean, why did he even need me in the first place? And he kept saying that INTERPOL was onto them and they had to be careful. But if the accounts are frozen, he can't use his dad's network! He'd have to pay them! And of course, INTERPOL probably is watching them. This really makes it all clear. No wonder Arjan needs cash." Philippe moved his hand as if to stroke his chin, started to wobble and then grabbed the balcony railing again. "And, also somewhat more complicated for my plans. And what did you say about Maaravi's girlfriend?"

"She's INTERPOL and she's the one who arrested Arjan," repeated Val.

"But is Maaravi using her or the other way around? *Intéressant.*

I will have to consider. Meanwhile, I think you two must have gotten caught on security footage somehow when you came to see me. Maaravi has been asking about my daughter. And considering that I have only mentioned you in passing, he seems rather more interested than he should. And he's also put that bodyguard on me. The man has been sticking to me like a leech."

"Impossible," said Val. "We were careful."

"What Val said."

"On the other hand, it would explain the B.O.L.O.," said Val. "You know, if Maaravi told his girlfriend."

"She put a B.O.L.O. out on you? That's dirty pool," said Philippe. "My sympathy for her is waning fast."

"I think your sympathies are irrelevant. The point is the leader of an INTERPOL task force is sleeping with the son of a man she just arrested. We've got to be able to use that. What is Maaravi's plan anyway?"

"Maaravi plans to ship the guns in with his next batch of flowers. I've forged inspection documents and it should all go off without a hitch. The trouble is actually getting them off the plane and back out of customs, but I think I've solved that too. I came up with a great idea—"

"Time, Philippe," said Val tapping her watch.

"Right. Never mind that. The problem Maaravi's facing is that he doesn't have a buyer. And his father won't tell him where his black book is."

"Well, with INTERPOL tapping his everything I'm not surprised. I wouldn't be telling anyone anything over the phone either if I was Arjan."

"Well, now that I know he's in prison it makes a lot of sense. Previously, I just thought he was being a dick to his kid." Philippe momentarily picked himself up and looked back into his room. "Anyway, that's why we had to come here to Amsterdam. Maaravi hasn't ever actually done this before. He wants to talk to his father and get his list of customers. That way he can find a buyer and get the sale over with quickly. Get the finances back in the black."

"Well, if that's the case," said Val, "he doesn't really need Arjan at all. He just needs the customer list."

"I believe Maaravi concurs," said Philippe. "And I think he believed that Arjan's black book is at the house. He seemed put out when his girlfriend said we couldn't go there."

"He's not going to find anything at the house," said Nikki. "His girlfriend swept it clean."

"Maybe that's his play," said Val. "Maybe he's planning on using her to get the book back?"

"That at least sounds likely," said Philippe.

"They could actually just be in love," offered Nikki, and was rewarded with disbelieving stares from both Val and Philippe.

"And pigs could fly over the moon, *mon petite lapin*," said Philippe. "But it's not likely any time soon. Anyway, all of that kind of complicates my plans. FYI, I did offer to help him. After all I know a few people who could really use those guns. But so far he hasn't taken me up on the offer. But I think— gotta go. Love you!"

Philippe hauled himself back over the banister rail and they could hear the suite door opening above them.

Nikki looked at Val, who shrugged, and gestured to the door. Nikki nodded.

"Well, what now?" asked Nikki when they were out in the hall.

"I think you should dye your hair," said Val. "That B.O.L.O. is going to be a bitch and your hair is pretty recognizable."

"I've never dyed my hair," said Nikki, hesitantly. "I mean, I've thought about it. But... I've never actually done it. I don't know if I want to Jason Bourne it up though."

"Oh God no! We'll get you an appointment at a salon like a normal human being. It's only a B.O.L.O. it's not like we're on the lam or anything."

"Actually, I think that's what it does mean. Police are supposed to Be On the Look Out for us, and we are running away from them."

"Yeah, but that's just the cops. It's not like our faces are on the news or anything. No one else is going to be looking for us. Certainly not hair dressers. There used to be a good place near here," mused Val as they exited the lobby on to the street. "Maybe I could get a massage. Yeah, let's do that." Val nodded decisively and immediately began striding off in a direction, then stopped. "Where'd you park the car?"

"This way," said Nikki, pointing the opposite direction.

"Right."

AMSTERDAM IX
GET A HAIRCUT

Nikki stared into the mirror and let out a deep breath. Her red hair, naturally full of curls, had been freed of its pony tail and now hung loose around her shoulders—past her shoulders, she realized. It had been awhile since she'd made a trip to the hair-stylist. Val had already disappeared into the back to get a massage and a facial. Nikki was waiting for Mr. Tang—the special, special stylist that Val had recommended.

Her phone, clutched nervously in one hand beneath the draping robe, rang, startling her. She held it up, expecting to see Val's number with a last minute tip. Instead it was a number she didn't recognize with a California area code. She hesitated and the phone rang again, earning her dirty looks from the other women in the salon. She hit the answer button and put the phone to her ear.

"Hello?" she said cautiously.

"Oh, good, you picked up," said Jane. Nikki felt a wave of relief wash over her and she sank down into her chair, her muscles releasing tension she didn't know she had.

"Jane! You called back!"

"Yeah, sorry about yesterday. I was standing right next to Darla and I had to pick up, but I had to spin some lie about how you were a guy who wasn't taking the hint. So I couldn't let you talk, and then I had to go see Mr. Merrivel to get one of his burners in case I was being followed, or in case Darla decided to tap the one you called on."

Nikki let the information flow over her, reorganizing it and chasing down implications. If Jane had been lying to Darla, the interim head of the West Coast Division while Mrs. Merrivel was on medical leave to help her husband recuperate from open-heart surgery, then it was possible that Darla did not know about Val or Nikki's abrupt departure. If Jane had borrowed a burner from Mr. Merrivel, then it was probable that the Merrivels did. Jane came to a stop, and Nikki shook her head.

"Never mind that Jane. I really need your help. I have a very serious question to ask you."

"Anything," said Jane.

"I have to dye my hair. What color should I dye it?"

"Oh God, you're not letting Val butcher your hair in some crappy gas station bathroom are you? We can do better than *The Fugitive*."

"No, I'm at a salon. An expensive salon. And the stylist is going to be here momentarily and I don't know what to tell him."

"That's tough," said Jane. "Because if you go blonde then it will look like you're copying Jenny when you come back." Jane's voice started to peter out at the end as if she realized half way through the sentence that she implying that Nikki would be coming back.

"That's what I was thinking," said Nikki, jumping into the awkward silence that followed.

"Can't go black," said Jane.

"Right, because I'd look like I was trying to *Single White Female* Val or something. And you've already got the Goth angle covered on our team."

"Which leaves brunette," said Jane.

"And I'm resistant to that idea, because when I was growing up the only thing that saved me as I was being called Pippi Longstalking and Wendy—"

"Wendy?"

"Like the fast food restaurant."

"Ah."

"Was that at least I wasn't boring brown like everyone else. And now that I've finally embraced my hair, it feels like going brown would be going backwards."

"I see your point and I have the solution. Balayage."

"I don't know what that means."

"It's that fun color fade hair. I've pinned a ton to my hair board on Pinterest."

"Is that going to look OK on curly hair?"

"It will probably flatten out your curls a bit," said Jane knowingly. "Ok, I'm texting you a pin. I think it will look perfect for you."

Nikki held the phone away from her face to look at the incoming message. "Oh! Um. Hm." She put the phone back to her ear. "That's more daring than I was thinking."

"But super awesome, right? Besides, you already are riding the disaster wave. You can't quibble that hair dye is scary."

"It is scary."

"Tough cookies."

Nikki sighed. "OK, I know we need to actually talk, but it'll have to be in an hour or so because my stylist is approaching."

"Call this number," said Jane. "I'm playing indoor putt-putt golf in a bowling alley, wasting time and drinking Blue Hawaiian's."

"You're where?" Nikki couldn't imagine Jane going to play putt-putt golf on purpose.

"I'm waiting for Jenny," said Jane, and Nikki could practically hear the shrug.

"Oh, that makes better sense. Meanwhile, if I sent you some pictures of some text, do you think you could figure out a way to get them translated?"

"Probably. It's got to be better than putt-putt golf."

"You should either drink more or not play when it comes to putt-putt."

"Wise words. Talk to you soon!"

Jane hung up and Nikki felt a warm glow. Things seemed possible. Solutions seemed imminent. She wasn't alone out here. She quickly texted the photos she'd snapped at the Meise house to Jane.

Mr. Tang arrived. His English wasn't great, but his hair was gorgeous. When Nikki showed him Jane's picture he snatched the phone out of her hand, zooming in and out, and then pausing to feel her hair, scrunching it between his fingers, lifting it at the roots and then watching it fall back.

"Yes," he said, handing the phone back to her. "Also, cut. Because..." His hand gestures made it clear that Nikki's current look was unacceptable. Nikki nodded her agreement and he set to work. An hour later, as she was being wrapped in tinfoil, there was a ping on her phone—it was an invitation from Jane to join Snapchat.

Nikki dutifully followed the link and built a profile with the name Rita Hayworth. Jane was logged in as Morticia Addams. She ignored the snap function and headed straight to chat. Snapchat's claim to fame in the social media world was that after a few seconds any image, or "snap," sent would delete itself off both the sender and receiver's device. It had a similar rule for the *chats*; the instant messaging function would automatically delete anything typed once they left the chat. It wasn't fool proof, but it was a pretty good defense against surveillance.

I SENT THE TEXT TO A FRIEND TO TRANSLATE. SHE SEEMED TO THINK IT WOULD BE DONE BY TOMORROW, UNLESS IT WAS SUPER COMPLICATED.

Thanks, typed Nikki, dodging the stylist as he worked his way around her head. I TALKED TO MY MOM. WHAT HAPPENED AFTER EVERYONE GOT BACK TO LA?

WE WENT TO MRS. MERRIVEL. MR. MERRIVEL TALKED TO Z'EV. MR. M SEEMED TO THINK THAT Z'EV WAS STILL REALLY ANGRY WITH YOU, BUT THAT IT HELPED THAT MR. M WAS EX-CIA.

Nikki breathed out a small sigh of relief. It hadn't occurred to her that Mr. M's past as a CIA agent might work in her favor with Z'ev.

WHAT DID MRS. M SAY? YOU DIDN'T TELL DARLA, RIGHT?

The girls had left LA on Darla's orders, after a little adventure of Ellen's had landed them on the wrong side of Carrie Mae politics. Darla was all right, but she wasn't one of the girls and currently she was already digging them out of one mess with The Council. Adding this to her plate would be a bit much.

NO, WE DIDN'T TELL DARLA. MRS. M SAID NOT TO.

Nikki waited for Jane to continue. But nothing was immediately forthcoming. She flipped over to snaps and captured a selfie of her hair, sending it to Jane.

YOU LOOK LIKE YOU'RE TRYING TO PREVENT ALIEN COMMUNICATION.

IT DOESN'T WORK. VAL STILL TALKS TO ME.

SNORT.

There was dead air again. Nikki waited this time. Whatever

Jane was typing was apparently either lengthy or difficult. The stylist picked up speed as she put the phone down. Nikki was beginning to get nervous when the phone finally plinged.

OK, SO I'M JUST GOING TO SAY THIS BECAUSE I CAN'T THINK OF A GOOD WAY TO SAY IT. AFTER Z'EV CAME BACK FROM WASHINGTON, WE PUT HIM UNDER SURVEILLANCE. BUT HE WAS CALLED OUT ON ASSIGNMENT IN EUROPE, AND WE COULDN'T UTILIZE CARRIE MAE RESOURCES TO KEEP TABS ON HIM. THEN YOU CALLED YESTERDAY, AND WHEN I WENT OUT TO THE MERRIVEL'S TO GET A NEW PHONE, MRS. M SAID THAT WHEN YOU MADE CONTACT AGAIN TO TELL YOU TO THAT IT WAS TIME FOR THE LOOKING GLASS PROTOCOLS.

Nikki's hand hovered over the keyboard. She tried to think of something to write other than *Oh, shit*.

WHAT DOES THAT MEAN?

Nikki sighed at Jane's question.

NIKKI?

MRS. M AND I HAVE EXPLORED VARIOUS HYPOTHETICAL SCENARIOS AND WHAT TO DO IN CASE CERTAIN SOMEWHAT UNLIKELY EVENTS OCCURRED.

LIKE WHAT?

RANDOM STUFF. WHAT IF CALIFORNIA GOT HIT WITH ANOTHER MASSIVE EARTHQUAKE? WHAT IF MRS. M GOT KILLED? WHAT IF MY BOYFRIEND EVER FINDS OUT ABOUT CARRIE MAE?

WAIT A MINUTE... YOU MEAN YOU ACTUALLY HAVE A PLAN FOR THIS? AND YOU DIDN'T TELL ANY OF US?

The words practically vibrated on the screen with outrage.

WELL, AFTER THE INCIDENT IN SOUTH AMERICA, AND AFTER PARIS, MRS. M DEMANDED THAT WE COME TO AN AGREEMENT ABOUT WHAT TO DO ABOUT Z'EV IN A WORST CASE SCENARIO. UNFORTUNATELY, I AGREED THAT IF Z'EV DIDN'T TAKE FINDING OUT

ABOUT MY JOB WELL, THAT CERTAIN MEASURES COULD BE TAKEN.

WHAT DO YOU MEAN MEASURES?

YOU KNOW, LIKE ELLEN TYPE MEASURES. PERMANENT MEASURES.

YOU AGREED TO LET MRS. M KILL Z'EV? WHAT THE HELL WERE YOU THINKING?

I WAS THINKING THAT HE WOULDN'T FIND OUT. AND I MADE HER AGREE TO A TIMELINE. I HAVE A WEEK.

THAT'S NOT RIGHT.

SEE IT FROM HER POINT OF VIEW. THE COVERT WING HELPS THOUSANDS OF INDIVIDUAL WOMEN A YEAR. THE NON-PROFIT WING REACHES OVER A MILLION. MILLIONS MORE RELY ON THE BUSINESS ARM FOR INCOME. IF Z'EV TELLS THE CIA ABOUT US, IT'S NOT JUST A PROBLEM FOR US AND OUR JOBS; IT'S A PROBLEM FOR ALL OF THE WOMEN WHO DEPEND ON US.

I DON'T UNDERSTAND HOW YOU CAN EVEN THINK THESE THOUGHTS. HOW CAN YOU EVEN CONSIDER THE POSSIBILITY OF KILLING Z'EV? DO YOU THINK ABOUT HAVING TO KILL ONE OF US TOO?

Nikki sighed and rubbed her eyebrow between the tinfoil dreadlocks that now encircled her head. She obviously couldn't reply honestly to the last question.

LOOK, THE LOOKING GLASS PROTOCOLS ARE SUPPOSED TO BE FOR WHEN SOMETHING THAT YOU NEVER THINK IS GOING TO HAPPEN, HAPPENS. I DIDN'T ACTUALLY THINK I WAS GOING TO HAVE TO FIGURE OUT HOW TO SAVE Z'EV FROM CARRIE MAE. I JUST FIGURED I'D BREAK UP WITH HIM BEFORE THINGS GOT THIS FAR.

WELL, HOW EXACTLY ARE YOU GOING TO SAVE Z'EV? YOU DON'T EVEN KNOW WHERE HE IS!

I DON'T HAVE TO GO FIND Z'EV. HE'S ALREADY FOUND ME.

What, really? How?

Coincidence, I think. I've blundered into the case he's working. I'll just have to get my Dad out of the country, figure out what to do about Val, and save Z'ev.

Oh. Well, no problem. I don't know why I was concerned. That's only three things. You can totally do that in a week.

I know sarcasm when I read it, Jane.

How are you not freaking out?

I'm getting my hair done. You can't freak out when you're getting your hair done. It's a well known fact.

You're in denial.

Also a well known fact.

What should I tell Mrs. M?

Tell her that I've made contact with Z'ev, and I'm in communication with Val. Tell her that I'm handling the situation, and that I understand the timeline.

I don't know what she's going to say to that.

Just tell her.

OK.

Nikki put the phone down and closed her eyes for a moment. How had she gotten herself in this mess? The phone pinged again.

Are there any Looking Glass Protocols about me?

Nikki typed three letters and then backspaced. Of course not. Is Jenny there yet?

Yes, but she's on the phone. The Council is breathing down Darla's neck and she's been relying on Jenny now that you're not here.

Nikki tried not to squirm in her chair as she felt the lash of guilt. Her absence and her actions had exposed her team to danger.

OK, WELL, I'M GOING TO GO NOW. SAY HI TO JENNY AND ELLEN FOR ME.

I WILL. WE MISS YOU.

MISS YOU TOO.

Nikki left the chat, double-checking that everything had been cleared and then exited the app.

Then she logged into her work email. It wasn't safe to do it. But hopefully by the time someone was suspicious it would be too late. She ignored the staggering number of unread emails and opened the *Saved Drafts* folder, scrolled to the bottom where there was on email that had been waiting for three years. The subject line read, *Looking Glass Protocol - V*, the body contained only a string of numbers. She took a deep breath and hit send.

"No phone now," said the stylist. "I must concentrate."

Nikki put the phone down and did as she was told, deciding to focus on her hair right now. Anything was better than thinking about any of the things that Jane had just told her.

Thirty minutes later, Val returned from the back, her skin glowing with the dewiness of a fresh facial.

"Well, Red, how's it going?"

"Not red anymore," said Mr. Tang, he stepped back and spun Nikki around to face the mirror.

"Woah," said Nikki.

"Holy shit," said Val.

AMSTERDAM X
JOLENE, JOLENE, JOLENE

"We can't show up here this many times," complained Nikki as they returned to the hotel De L'europe.

"What, you mean like the rest of the guests returning each day? How is that suspicious? Look, you just stay here. Give me a buzz if you see anything suspicious. I'll pop up to the fourth floor again and just climb up and leave the burner phone on your dad's balcony. It'll take me ten minutes—tops."

"It'll take you twenty," said Nikki with a shrug.

"I can't believe you're covering up your new hair with that hat, by the way," said Val, as she stripped the pre-paid cell phone out of the packaging. "It looks awesome."

"It does look awesome. It also looks about as noticeable as my original hair. And since we've already been here once today, I didn't want to be that noticeable." She didn't add that she couldn't believe she'd let Jane talk her into the new hair. Who was she kidding? She wasn't this bold.

"Whatever," said Val, dumping the debris into a nearby ash can, tucking the phone into her pocket and walking away.

"I need to stop cleaning up after her," said Nikki, taking the crumpled cardboard and plastic out of the ashcan and walking it to the nearest garbage can. She turned around just in time to see Petra Gilles walk through the front doors and head for the bar. "Of course," said Nikki and pulled out her phone.

MAARAVI'S GIRLFRIEND IS IN THE BAR. WAITING FOR MAARAVI?

A few moments later a response from Val plinged through.

GREAT. THAT WILL MAKE MY LIFE EASIER. TEXT ME IF SHE LEAVES OR ANYTHING.

Nikki chewed her bottom lip. On one hand, it was unnecessary risk. On the other, she did want to know more about Petra Gilles and what made her so *great* to Z'ev. With an almost invisible nod of her head, she went into the bar.

Nikki tossed her purse down next to Petra and took the adjacent seat. She glanced at the blonde, taking in the two fingers of whiskey over the uber trendy chilled whiskey stones. She looked sleek, not a hair out of place, and tasteful in a gray wool overcoat over black slacks and a pair of ankle boots that had the tiniest platform—just enough to make her tall without making her look like a stripper. Nikki liked the shoes, but she'd never actually seen a real cop wear them. It was like Petra was doing her best Hollywood version of a police officer. What to do? Play against that or with it? She flagged down the bartender. "I'm going to need a strawberry daiquiri," she said putting as much Valley Girl as she could into the inflections. "Like, immediately." The bartender winced, but went away to do his bidding. "Bartenders always hate running the blender," said Nikki turning to Petra. "It's why I make them do it."

Petra laughed, slightly breathlessly as if she hadn't expected Nikki to be funny.

"Don't you worry that he might spit in your drink?" asked Petra, her accent only lightly Dutch.

"Not really," said Nikki. "I flash a lot of cleavage, I tip well, and I usually make my dates order for me."

Petra laughed again. "That seems a bit Machiavellian."

Nikki shrugged. "It keeps dating fun. Because otherwise it's just some guy in a suit who thinks he's in charge. Honestly, if I date one more loser who thinks he's Christian Grey I'm going to scream. I mean, you can say you're into bondage all you want, but you might as well just stamp *mommy issues* on your forehead and be done with it."

"I don't know, sometimes a little rough can be fun," Petra took a sip of her whiskey and smiled a small, secret smile. It was exactly the sort of thing that Val would have said and Nikki would have been impressed by a few short years ago.

"As Gaga, the great one says, If it's love and it's not rough, it isn't fun. But I find that I have the most fun when they do what I want."

"And if they won't follow orders?" Petra looked amused.

"Who gives orders? It's better if they think it's their idea."

"So true," said Petra with an actual smile and a slight tilt of her glass in Nikki's direction. "Are you expecting some particular genius here tonight?"

"Ha! I wish. No, I'm hiding out here, avoiding my father and his latest girlfriend. What about you? Waiting on someone tall, dark, and adorably mentally impaired?"

"Yes," said Petra with a laugh. "But his issues are actually daddy issues."

Nikki shrugged. "Same dif. Only that means he probably thinks his mother, and therefore all women, are absolute saints. That can be fun."

"You seem to have thought deeply on this," said Petra frowning.

"I have a BS in Comparative Psychology," said Nikki making up something that sounded intimidating and awesome. "Where's my daiquiri? Seriously, he's, like, taking forever."

The bartender began a slow trudge back down the bar with

her brightly colored drink.

"Oh. And where did you get your degree?" Petra's tone clearly implied that it was probably an online university.

"Stanford," said Nikki. "Yay, alcohol!"

"I assume miss would enjoy whip cream," said the bartender.

"Miss would very much enjoy whip cream!"

He applied a dollop of cream and a mint sprig to the top of the drink and went away with an expression that said hell was reserved for people who ordered fruity drinks.

"Anyway," said Nikki, whipping off the mint, and taking a slurp through the straw, "the real question is, are you trying to get your dude to do something that's against his nature or within his natural inclination, but that he has chosen not to do. That's like spending too much money on something that he wants anyway. That one's usually pretty easy."

"It's the first one," said Petra. "But I think I've convinced him to think about it from my point of view." Again, she smiled her small smile, but Nikki could see the smug leaking out the corners.

"Job well done, then," said Nikki and raised her glass in salute. "Oooh, he's cute. Is that one yours?" She pointed to the doorway, where Z'ev was standing and looking pissed.

"No, that one works for me," said Petra sounding annoyed. "And he's a pain in my ass. Say," a gleam came into Petra's eyes, "you want to do me a favor? Give me a minute to talk with him and then come over and spill your drink on him."

"Sounds fun," said Nikki. "Is he solvent?"

"He's a government employee, so I doubt it."

"Oh, boo," said Nikki pouting. "Well, still could be fun for an evening. Just give me the high-sign and I'll come trip all over him."

Petra got up and walked toward Z'ev, who looked from Petra

to Nikki warily. Nikki gave him a headshake, and plunked down some bills for her drink with one hand, and texted Val with the other.

GIRLFRIEND IS ON THE WAY.

She watched with interest as Z'ev tried to converse with Petra and still keep Nikki in view. Petra was doing some very bossy posturing, nose up, arms folded. Trying to make Z'ev feel small and silly, Nikki supposed. It wasn't working and Nikki could have told her from experience, that it wasn't going to work. No response from Val had come through by the time Petra gave a slight head herk in her direction. Nikki counted to fifteen then tottered off the bar stool and walked towards them.

"Hey, um," said Nikki, then tripped and doused her drink down Z'ev's right arm as he instinctively reached out to catch her. "Oh gosh," said Nikki breathlessly, "I am so sorry." She pretended to struggle to stand in the slippery mess on the floor, forcing Z'ev to hold on even tighter.

"Really," said Petra. "This is why I prefer to do things myself. Just deal with this mess and let me do the real work."

Petra stomped out of the bar, turning at the last second and giving Nikki a wave and a wink. Nikki waited until she was out of view before standing upright, straightening her skirt.

"This is like the only warm jacket I have," said Z'ev, looking at the sleeve.

"But it's kind of ugly," said Nikki.

"I'm going to have it dry cleaned. I'll be wearing it tomorrow."

Nikki reached over and poured the last, sad remains of her daiquiri on his arm.

"If they can't get it out I will buy another one just like it," he said. "Only in puce."

"You don't know what color puce is," said Nikki.

"I will find out," he said.

"I'll just clean this up, then shall I?" asked the bartender arriving with an armful of bar rags.

"I'm really sorry," said Nikki. "It was a really good daiquiri. Can I help in some way?"

"You could stop standing in the puddle," suggested the bartender, throwing one of the towels down and pointing to it.

"You dumped your entire drink down my jacket and you apologize to him?" asked Z'ev, helping Nikki step from the puddle to the towel.

"I reiterate that it is an ugly jacket," said Nikki wiping her shoes.

"Well, now that I'm thinking of it, he deserves more than an apology. You're disrupting his workplace."

"He doesn't look that upset."

"It's OK," said the bartender, "I saw her tip. I figured I was in for it. I already sent the barback for the mop. There's a twenty-four hour dry cleaner around the corner if you're interested."

"Thank you," said Z'ev, beginning to pull of his jacket. "I am." He left the bar.

"Don't pout," said Nikki, following after him.

"What are you doing here, Nikki? Why are you following Petra?"

Nikki thought about correcting him, decided against it. "Petra is dirty," said Nikki.

"Oh, is she one of your Carrie Mae agents?

"Don't be ridiculous," snapped Nikki. "We're the good guys."

"Really, then come clean." He was striding briskly down the block, ignoring her shorter stride length, forcing her into an awkward jog to keep up. "What makes you think she's dirty? What evidence do you have?" Nikki ran through the evidence in her mind, trying to assess what she could or should share. "Well?" he demanded when she didn't respond soon enough.

"I'm trying to decide what to tell you?"

"So the truth is out of the question then?" He looked furious.

"No, but we already talked about this—it involves my dad. I'm trying to extricate him and make sure you get the bad guy."

"And you don't trust me enough to tell me your plan. Gee thanks a bunch."

"Well, when you don't believe me, it's a little difficult to want to share. Look, I think we can make it so that everyone gets what they want, but it's going to be tough with Petra being a bad guy."

"Petra is not a bad guy. She's the one who got Arjan in the first place! You're just making things up because you don't want me to arrest you, Val, and your father."

"It's also a little hard to trust you when you keep threatening to arrest me."

"You are breaking the law—you should be arrested," he said stubbornly. They had arrived at the dry cleaner.

Nikki looked around the street. The cobblestones were illuminated by the drycleaner's flickering neon and the glowing green cross of a pharmacy on the next block. Somehow, she couldn't believe her relationship had come to this.

"Petra asked me to help her ditch you. That's why I spilled my drink on you. I could have gone down the front; instead I went for the arm."

"You only a hurt me a little. Am I supposed to be grateful?"

Nikki's phone beeped. She checked the text; Val was on her way.

"No, I expect you to ask yourself why, if she's so awesome, did she ask a complete stranger to help ditch you. I have to go now. I don't want Val to know you're here."

"Nice to know you keep secrets from all your partners."

"Well, I don't want her to shoot you too," said Nikki as she walked away.

"Don't forget to check-in," Z'ev yelled after her, but she didn't respond.

THE PAST IV
HERE AND THERE

Lethbridge, Canada

"Why'd you leave?"

It was the only question on her mind, but for some reason Nikki couldn't make it come out of her mouth.

Her father was stretched out in the hammock, hands behind his head. The wind swept through the trees with a sound like a freeway in the distance and ruffled the hair that was so similar to hers, only his was now fading to blonde, gray creeping in around the edges.

The sun spread out over the rolling lawn like a felt blanket, heavy and hot. Twenty-year-old Nikki sat in the faded wicker armchair with her knees together, legs crossed at the ankles. Her black, square necked dress felt stiff and she could feel the zipper rubbing at a spot on her back. Her basic black pumps and black hat sat on the wicker coffee table. She'd already peeled off her pantyhose on the way back from the church and shoved them in her purse. His shoes and socks were scattered carelessly underneath the hammock and table and every so often he would wiggle his toes in the breeze. Grand-Mère would have disapproved.

"Whatever happened to that boy?" he asked suddenly, turning his head to face her. His English had become less accented, but it still had the faint ring of French. His grey eyes were paler than she remembered and there were a few more lines around them, but his face was still boyish. But perhaps that was simply his personality showing through. He also needed a haircut, she noted. His hair curled over the collar of his now unbuttoned dress shirt.

"Which one?" she asked, knowing which one he meant.

"You know the one..." he started to say.

"We just buried your mother," said Nikki. "Do you really want to talk about my ex-boyfriends?"

"No, I guess not," he said turning his face back to the trees. "So you're graduating this year."

"Another six months," corrected Nikki.

"But still it's coming up. What's that like?"

"You don't remember?" asked Nikki, laughing.

"I smoked my way through high school. I pretty much don't remember most things after September of grade twelve. I never did finish my higher education. I don't think. It's all kind of a blur."

"What about Mom?"

"Well, your mom is hard to forget. Lord knows I keep trying."

"Papa," protested Nikki.

"Sorry. No, I'd cut back by the time I met Nell."

"I thought the funeral was nice," said Nikki. "She would have liked the lilies."

"She's dead Nikki," said her Phillipe. "We don't have to be nice. She can't hear us and it's a pretty sure thing we're not getting any of the money."

"She was my grandmother!"

"Well, she was my mother, and trust me, she wasn't a nice woman."

"So she wasn't very... warm, but she did care."

"Nikki," he said, sitting upright and flopping his legs over the edge of the hammock, his bare feet dangling above the grass like a child on a swing, "I know the world equates grandmothers with warm fuzzies and baking cookies, but that isn't always the case. Just because someone occupies a role doesn't mean they are that role. You have to learn to see people for how they are, not how you want them to be. People rarely match their job description."

"Like you're not a really a father?" The words popped out of her mouth, faster than air escaping her lungs.

Phillipe grimaced, his sandy eyebrows drawing together and his lips twisting into a distorted line, as if she had wounded him. For a moment he looked every bit of his forty-something years, and centuries older than usual. In the distance, there was the sound of a church bell announcing something in a tone so big that it couldn't really be described as ringing, more like periods of sound that filled up the background of consciousness like a mountain filled up the skyline.

"Exactly like that," he said, the smile coming back to his face, the irrepressible light of irresponsibility beaming forth. "So you know what that means?" he asked leaning forward. The movement set the hammock to swaying.

"No," said Nikki, resisting the urge to reach out and slap him.

"It means that you and I will have to get to know each other like people. Like two regular people." He cast himself back into the hammock, flinging his arms out as if falling into snow. "We don't have to get trapped by titles or all the propriety that your Grand-Mère loved. We can just be ourselves!"

Nikki wanted to argue. She knew there was a flaw in his logic somewhere, but she couldn't pinpoint it. She was only aware of an over-powering sense of rejection. How could he think that being his daughter wasn't part of herself?

"Your mother and I never had that," he said, still staring up into the branches overhead. "She wanted me to be a businessman.

Wanted me to wear suits."

"You wanted her to be a free-spirited farmer's daughter," said Nikki, seeing the true split in her parents' marriage for first time.

"She was a farmer's daughter!" protested Phillipe, still sounding aggrieved.

"Just like you were the son of a wealthy businessman."

"Yes," he agreed, looking at her again. "We saw what we wanted to see and then after a while we couldn't avoid the truth anymore. But we never had the chance to see what was really there. Never had the chance to be friends with our true selves."

"That's because you went away," said Nikki, marveling at the coldness in her own voice. He shook his head.

"It was over before that."

Nikki shifted restlessly in her chair, wishing she'd never brought up the subject. She removed a speck of pollen off her skirt with short brushing movements of her hand. She glanced back up to the house where the wake was still going on.

"Where'd you go?" she asked. He twisted in the hammock as if searching for a more comfortable position.

"Oh, you know, here and there. I'd never gotten to travel much and there were so many places I wanted to go. Machuu Pichu and Easter Island, trekking the Andes. Angkor Wat, the Grand Palace of Thailand, riding an elephant in Vietnam." He sat up again, unable to speak of his passion lying down.

"Seeing the heat rise off the Sahara, fending off the shady camel dealers in Egypt. The townships of South Africa. The gambling dens of Macau. The world is full, Nikki, full of places and people and things that are so unbelievable that you can't really understand them until you experience them for yourself." His eyes were burned with the fervor of religion; only his religion was adventure. Nikki felt an answering excitement burn in her own chest, but she squashed it mercilessly.

"It's not all exotic people and purple vistas. You'll get mugged by the camel dealer, the elephant smells, and you'll lose your shirt gambling. Traveling is nineteen hours in a cramped metal tube full of recycled air and crying babies," she said and he laughed.

"That's just the price you pay to get there. You have to go test yourself against the world, then you'll know what you're made of."

"I know what I'm made of," said Nikki petulantly, as he settled back into the hammock.

"No," he said, "you never really do."

"Sure I do," argued Nikki because he wasn't letting her argue about the thing that was really pissing her off. "I don't have to go get eaten alive by mosquitoes to know I don't like them. I don't have to hike the volcano to know that I can hike. I already know."

"Sometimes you have to get burned to know the fire's hot," he answered cryptically.

"I know the fire's hot," snapped Nikki.

"But to know what hot really is, to know what kind of heat you can really take, you have to jump in feet first. That's what I mean."

"That's dumb," said Nikki, settling for childishness.

He turned his face away, looking down the lawn and across the road.

Silence lay heavily between them and Nikki frantically searched for a new topic. She wasn't going to apologize, but she felt a cold fear that he would simply stop talking to her.

"She left me her engagement ring," said Nikki, bringing up the first subject to occur to her.

"Did she? You've seen the will?" He raised his head to look

at her; his expression was mildly curious, tinged with skepticism.

"No, but she always said she would," answered Nikki.

"Well, we'll see then."

"You don't think she meant it?" asked Nikki, feeling a pang of doubt.

"I think she would rather die than give anything valuable to our family."

"She's not really dead for you, is she?" she asked.

"What?"

"It's hard to think she's dead because we weren't here to see her all the time. So now it's like she's only gone somewhere, but she's not really dead."

"And we're just sitting here, waiting for her to get back and yell at us to put our shoes back on," said Phillipe with a wry smile. "She always hated bare feet. Never knew why."

"She said it was undignified and spread germs. She donated a lot of shoes to children's charities over the years. She said new shoes gave you pride."

"Did she? I didn't know that."

"She didn't tell people."

"I hope you do get her ring," he said thoughtfully. "You'd probably actually wear it."

"I would," said Nikki, wondering what else someone would do with an heirloom ring, "she always said it was lucky."

AMSTERDAM XI
WORK B*TCH

"Are you sure we can trust Femke?" asked Nikki as they followed the GPS coordinates to their latest safe house. "That didn't really work out too well for us last time."

"She feels bad about that," said Val. "This one is free. And I don't know about your bank account, but free is about what I can afford."

Nikki winced at the truth of that statement. Living on the run wasn't cheap and Carrie Mae didn't exactly pay top dollar. She hadn't wanted to admit it to Z'ev, but tipping the bartender had put a dent in her finances. The salon had gone on one of Val's presumably stolen credit cards.

Nikki wedged into a spot on the canal side of the street. Her phone indicated that they had arrived.

"We're number 303," said Val looking at the tag on the key ring.

She got out of the car, while Nikki shut the car down and hid the wires she was using to turn the stolen car off and on.

"I don't understand," said Val, scratching her head. "The addresses are all even numbers. Where is 303?"

Nikki looked around. Val was right. The apartment building across the street was 306.

"Maybe we're on the wrong side of the canal?" She turned around to face the water, looking for a clue. This part of the canal was wide and a boat chugged through it, pushing ripples of bottle green water toward the stone walls. Nikki followed its progress through the waterway, waiting to see what would happen when it reached the bridge.

"We're in the right spot," she said, smacking Val in the arm.

"How do you figure?" asked Val still looking up and down the street.

"We were looking the wrong direction." Nikki pointed down to where a steep set of stairs led to a narrow walkway along the side of the canal. It was lined with boats tied to heavy metal rings cemented into the canal walls. Each ring had a number painted beside it.

"Femke might have mentioned," said Val, clearly annoyed.

They approached 303 cautiously. It was slate blue houseboat with brick red trim. They stepped aboard with guns drawn, cleared the rooms, and then swept for bugs.

"It looks clear," said Nikki with a shrug.

The boat was clean, mostly bare of furniture and contained zero art or knick-knacks. It looked unloved, but from Nikki's point of view, it was very reassuring. Hiding a bug or any other type of surveillance here would be difficult. She nodded to herself, tucked her gun away and looked up to find Val staring.

"What?"

"It's just so weird. I mean, I figured you would go brunette."

"It is brunette. Partially, anyway." She patted the top portion of her hair, which was a dark chocolate brown.

"Yeah, I just never figured you for the kind of person who would go for colors. It's just so different."

"You don't like the purple?"

Nikki walked into the mirror and stared at herself in the mirror. The stylist had done a masterful job. The brown was high-lighted with gold and then faded to a gorgeous peacock purple. The dye process had, as Jane had predicted, flattened out her curls a bit, taking them down to waves, rather than large spirals. She hadn't wanted to admit it, but it was the kind of curls she'd always wished she'd had. Val was right, it was different, but maybe different was what she needed right now. Not that Z'ev had even noticed or mentioned her hair at all.

"No, I love the purple," said Val. "It's just super weird. You look really different. Not bad. Just really different."

"Well, at least no one will confuse me with the red-head in the B.O.L.O."

"Truth. And now that we've got that taken care of, let's figure out what we're going to do about your Dad."

"Did you remember to give him our phone numbers?" asked Nikki, still fluffing her hair. Val was right, she looked incredibly different.

"Yes, I put them in the phone."

"And you're sure he actually got the phone?"

"Yes! Good grief, I've been doing this way longer than you. I do know how to run an op, believe it or not."

Nikki rolled her eyes, knowing that Val could see her in the mirror. "Then why hasn't he made contact?" she complained.

"Probably because he's either under surveillance or he has no reception."

"You know," said Nikki coming out of the bathroom, "I've been thinking about it. He had a computer in South Africa. He probably could have sent us an email or a message somehow. Do you think he didn't, knowing that we would come rescue him and that he could lure us into his cockamamie plan?

"I thought of that, but I'm sure his computer was monitored.

I wouldn't have sent email either, even if his computer had internet access. And to be perfectly honest, I'm not sure he's devious in that direction. I mean, he's plenty cunning, but it's just more directed at systems and outwitting *The Man*."

Nikki tried to remember the computer she'd seen on the desk in South Africa. Trying to remember if she'd noticed if it had internet access.

"Web cam," she said suddenly.

"What?" Val had her head in the fridge.

"That computer had a web cam. I bet that's how they were monitoring Dad. Because we checked the security set up and there weren't any cameras on the interior."

Val turned around, a frown on her face. "That's where they got footage of us together. Those things are ridiculously easy to hack. Damn it. We should have noticed."

"Or Dad should have noticed. If they saw us in his room, then they have to know he's up to something."

Val wrinkled her nose in discontent. "This Maaravi guy is starting to piss me off. How are we being beat by a glorified gardener?"

"Because we've been listening to my father," said Nikki. "We should really stop doing that."

"Hey, I know he kind of ran out on you as a kid, but he's a smart, caring guy. I'm tired of hearing you rag on him all the time."

"Seriously?" Nikki folded her arms across her chest. "Do you even know the last time I saw Dad before you turned up and dragged me on this little adventure?"

"He said you were in college," said Val with a shrug.

"Yeah, I was in college, but I had to take a week off to help my mom plan his mother's funeral. We weren't even sure he was going to show up."

"Well, no offense, but his mom sounded like kind of a bitch."

"Of course she was a bitch!" Nikki took a deep breath and let it out slowly, trying to return her voice to a normal volume. "You should know better than anyone that bitches get things done. Bitches survive."

"Bitches win," said Val. Nikki couldn't tell what her tone was—sarcastic, sad, bitter? Maybe all three.

"Grand-Mère was a hard ass. And maybe she could have been less of a hard ass on Dad, but you still show up for her funeral because she's your mom."

"You said he went," said Val.

"Yeah, he showed up for the funeral. Stuck around to eat the food at the wake and then disappeared again. My mom had to arrange everything. Mom and Dad had been divorced for like a decade. She and Grand-Mère literally hated each other. And yet Mom was the one who handled everything."

Val sighed. "Philippe's not very good at doing adult stuff."

"No, he's not. He never has been. He's a very fun person whom I love. But when it comes to his great ideas, we should not listen to him. We've been behind the curve this entire time because we've been worrying about him and what he wants. Would you have done that when you were working for Carrie Mae?"

"Ugh. No. Fine. You're saying we need to embrace our bitch-tasticness. I'm with you. What do you want to do?"

"We need to figure out what Maaravi wants and then we need to get there first."

"We know what Maaravi wants. He wants to get his dad out of jail."

"Does he?" asked Nikki. "Because I think a concerned son

would be draining company bank accounts and putting them towards his father's legal defense. I think he would be flying home the minute he heard of his father's arrest. I think he would be talking to his father's lawyer. Has he done any of that? No. As far as I can tell, he's been making out with his father's arresting officer and trying to pick up where his father left off selling guns."

"Maaravi may not know his girlfriend is the one who arrested his father."

"But he knows she has access to information about the police. He believed her when she told him not to go home."

Val walked the length of the room and into kitchen, chewing her lip. She absent-mindedly opened the fridge and looked in. "Beer. Of course, she provides beer."

"I didn't realize you hated beer so much."

"It's this damn city. They all love beer too much."

"You're a contrarian."

"If I had a world of my own…" murmured Val, still staring into the fridge.

"Everything would be nonsense?" It was a quote from *Alice in Wonderland*. Many of the pass codes in the West Coast Division were based on the book. Nikki's copy had become dog-eared as she looked up the new pass phrases for reference. She had not suspected that Val memorized any of them; it seemed like far too romantic a thing for her to waste time on.

"*Nothing would be what it is, because everything would be what it isn't. And contrary wise, what is, wouldn't be. And what it wouldn't be, it would.*" Val slammed the fridge shut. "That's one of the things I like about Philippe you know. His world is nonsense. He takes practically nothing seriously."

"Sometimes that's nice. But it leaves a bit of a mess for the rest us who can't live there with him. I clean up enough messes at work."

"I never did."

"Never did what?"

"Cleaned up any messes at work. I saved the day lots of time, but I always left the mess. I never cleaned it. Cleaning up messes was someone else's job. Probably one of the reasons I never got promoted."

Nikki gaped and then clicked her teeth back together firmly. "And you never felt guilty about it either."

"No, I never did. We got shitty pay. We got zero recognition. And we saved the world a lot. I figured, cleaning up messes wasn't part of my job."

Nikki sat down in one of the two chairs at the kitchen table. "We are such different people." She couldn't think of anything else to say.

"I know," said Val. "Which is weird because I really like you and generally I don't like responsible people—they make me itch."

"Val, if you really liked me, then why did you try to kill me on multiple occasions?"

"I like me more," she said with a shrug.

Nikki tried to dredge up some anger about this. Her mother would be angry. Any of the girls would be angry. You couldn't go around killing people just because they were inconvenient. That was wrong. Everyone knew it was wrong. But somewhere in the part of her brain that reminded her of a lizard, where everything was either an instant response to stimulus or a long calculation of odds, she heard the tiniest whisper of a thought. *I would have done the same thing… But I wouldn't have failed.*

"I wish we had ears on Dad," she said, reverting back to the original topic. "I want to know what Maaravi is planning on doing next."

"I think the question is, what are you planning on doing next?"

Nikki drummed her fingers on the table. She could feel the soft rocking of the water beneath them.

"I think I want to break into INTERPOL."

AMSTERDAM XII
CLEAR AIR

"I did not see that coming," said Val, sitting down in the other chair. "Why do you—Wait. Want to order Thai? There's a take-out menu on the fridge."

"I don't know. Are we allowed to order Thai after, you know… the thing in Thailand?"

"Look, if I crossed out a whole food group just because I killed a few people in that country there wouldn't be anything left to eat but Eritrean tsebhi. And I don't really like it that much."

"You never killed anyone in Eritrea?"

"Never did."

"Always something to look forward to, I guess. Anyway, yeah, I could eat." Nikki walked to the fridge and pulled the menu out from under the magnet. "What are you thinking? Curry and spring rolls?"

"Drunken noodles."

"We just had noodles last night."

"So sue me; I like noodles. Besides it's an entirely different type of noodle."

"OK, but I'm having curry."

"No one said you had to have the same thing as me."

Nikki shrugged and ordered. The restaurant appeared unperturbed about delivering to a house boat. As Nikki hung up the phone, Val's phone chirruped an incoming message.

"Femke?" asked Nikki.

"I doubt it," said Val, picking it up hesitantly. "Ha! It's Philippe."

"What does it say?" Nikki leaned over her shoulder, trying to read the text.

P HERE. M HAD ARGUMENT WITH GIRL AFTER YOU LEFT. SHE DOES NOT HAVE BOOK OF CLIENTS. M VERY UPSET—SAYS THEY NEED BOOK ASAP. M GOING TO VISIT A TOMORROW 10AM. HOPES TO GET BOOK LOCATION THEN. DON'T TEXT BACK.

"Maaravi's using her," said Val. "Got to be."

"I think it's the other way around," said Nikki. "I think she's the one in the driver's seat."

"I don't know," said Val. "What's her motivation to put his father in jail? Other than doing her job, of course."

"I don't know," said Nikki with a frown. She hadn't gotten that far. "Maybe she's in love. Maybe he's in love. Maybe they think they're the next Bonnie and Clyde."

Val rolled her eyes.

"You've been in love before," said Nikki. "I kind of think you're in love now. Why make fun of someone else who's got the same problem."

"Hush your mouth. And there's a big difference from being in love and being in love and having someone use that power over you to manipulate your decisions."

"No one likes to feel manipulated," said Nikki, wincing at the thought of Z'ev's angry face.

"Right. Now let's talk plan. Why—" But Nikki's phone rang cutting Val off. Nikki saw Z'ev's number and bit her lip. She had missed the Z'ev imposed call in time again. Working to someone else's time table was not going well.

"I'm going to take this outside," she said.

"Hey, I showed you mine," said Val, waggling her phone.

"I know, but it's my INTERPOL C.I. and she's super paranoid. If she hears anything, she'll freak out. I'll be back in a bit."

Nikki stepped out onto the deck and shivered in the chill blast of autumn air as she picked up the phone.

"When does the super spy immunity to poor conditions kick in?" she asked. "Like after five years?"

"What?"

"It's freaking freezing out here. I figured you've been doing this longer than I have and you never look cold. What's the secret?"

"Work in warmer climates and have more body fat."

"Be serious."

"I am serious. Why do you think I was so pissed about my jacket. This is the first time I've worked Europe in years due to the brown penalty and I'm wearing long underwear."

"The brown penalty?"

Z'ev sighed and she could hear him run a hand over the stubble on his head. "I'm brown and I speak Spanish, therefore I'm too Mexican looking and do not get assigned to Europe. I wouldn't even be here now if Peterson hadn't gotten sick."

"You don't look remotely Mexican. Seriously, have they ever met a Mexican? And besides, don't you always get stopped at the airport for looking too Arabic?"

"Yes, because all brown people look alike."

"Institutional racism aside, why wouldn't they use you in Europe? You're smart and super capable. Brush up on some Farsi and some German and you'd be an awesome European operative. Why shouldn't they use you?"

"Institutional racism," he said flatly. Nikki could tell she had managed to annoy him, but couldn't tell where it had gone wrong.

"It's dumb."

"Not disagreeing. You're late calling in, again."

"Yeah, we don't really do that kind of thing," said Nikki.

"What kind of thing? Report in on time so people know you're alive?"

Nikki felt a warm glow of smug. He cared if she died. It was a low bar, but she had still cleared it.

"Not on this kind of timeline. Our agents are allowed a lot more free rein."

"Well, bully for you," he said sourly. "We didn't finish our conversation."

"We weren't having a conversation. You were threatening to arrest me, ignoring everything I said, and explaining how super awesome Petra is."

"I never said she was super awesome."

"Yes, I'm pretty sure you said working with her was like existing in a Pantene commercial and you were all just the sunniest, bounciest happy family."

"I said I had no reason to be suspicious of her—that's hardly the same thing."

"But secretly you thought the thing about the shampoo commercial."

"Yes, but I happen to think that a woman's capability on the job shouldn't be judged by her hair."

"What about her shoes? Those are little bit ridiculous, right?"

"Are you jealous of Petra?"

"Pfft. No. Besides, she totally has a boyfriend. Did you find anything out about her?"

"No, I haven't found out anything about Petra! I'm not the

one providing information! You're supposed to be providing information."

"I am providing information! I provided the information that you can't trust Petra and that you should look into her."

"That is not information. That's just you picking on someone who can be honest about her job and has blonde hair."

"I'm not picking on her because of her hair. Jenny's hair is that good—I don't pick on her." Nikki clunked her head against the side of the boat. Why did she always focus on the trivial? Why couldn't she ever address the important things head on. "Z'ev, I swear, I'm not trying to be annoying. I really am trying to make sure we all get what we want, but I don't have all the pieces and if I tell you what I know you're just going to tell me I'm stupid."

"I would never call you stupid."

"I—" Unexpectedly, Nikki found herself getting choked up. He was right. He would never call her names. He was, he had been, a really good boyfriend. "I know." She finished on a sniff.

"Nikki, why are you crying?" She could hear the tenseness in his voice.

"I'm not crying."

"Nikki!"

"I'm really not. I just missed you suddenly."

"I'm on the phone with you right now." He was back to being exasperated.

"It's not really the same. Anyway," she rallied, "you really didn't run any background on Petra?"

"Don't be ridiculous. Of course, I ran background on Petra. She's ditching the team, putting out weirdly vague B.O.L.O.'s, she doesn't tell anybody what her plans are, and she dresses like a pretend cop."

"Yes, like she's got the role of a cop, but isn't actually one? It's weird, right?"

"Yes, but she's clean. Nothing pops. Financials look clean. No complaints. She was stationed in South Africa last year and Germany before that."

"Ah," said Nikki.

"Ah?"

"I'll explain in a minute."

"I've got no reason not to trust her."

"Except that your instincts say she's not right?" Nikki prodded, hearing something unspoken in his voice.

"She keeps reminding us to go by the book, but she doesn't follow procedure. She's lone wolfing it a lot. She disappeared for most of the morning and then again this evening when I saw you both at the bar. And after she came back this morning she spent ten minutes on the phone yelling at the CSI team on the phone. Apparently, they're not moving fast enough on the Meise evidence. And when I pressed her on why she put out the B.O.L.O. on you two, she said it was just a lead that hadn't panned out. But she didn't provide any specifics. Meanwhile, she's showing almost no interest in Hoek—the guy I picked up at your... I guess we're calling it a flop house for lack of a better term."

"Yeah, what you learn from him? What'd Val do to him anyway? She said she only shot his brother a little bit, but he seemed more pissed than that."

"Well, for one thing he thinks her name is Irene Adler."

"Apparently, he's never read Sherlock Holmes."

"Or watched any of the movies or TV shows, or run an internet search on her. Hoek is not the brightest bulb in the box. But basically, he doesn't know who you are and doesn't care. The way he tells it, he just went to a dangerous neighborhood to talk to his old friend *Irene* and he was, shockingly, beat up and arrested. Other than the guns his crew was carrying, we don't have a lot on him."

"That's suspicious. He should have a paper trail a mile long. Take a look at his guns for me. I pulled a standard issue Army 1911 off of one of his crew that looked too shiny and new to be surplus."

"Stop telling me how to do my job. Although, I guess, maybe I should take tips. The CSI team on the house turned up virtually no finger prints at the house. What did you do, wipe the place down before going to bed?"

"Yeah, it's S.O.P. on an op, you never know when you're going to have to leave unexpectedly. What did Petra do with all of that information?"

"She got annoyed and told me to keep working on it. But she didn't seem to care that much. Now, seriously, Nikki, tell me what's going on."

"South Africa," said Nikki. "It must have started when she was in South Africa."

"What started?"

"How did she get to Arjan? She must have had some sort of Confidential Informant, right? That gave her an inside tip on his operation?"

"Yes," said Z'ev suspiciously. "That's how the case went down."

"Then I think you should be asking yourself, who that C.I. is and why he would be providing information to INTERPOL when Arjan is well-known for having a take-no-prisoners and burn the bodies approach to business."

"Usually there's some sort of leverage or a simple fear of

going to prison."

"Yes, but that usually only works if an informant is lower level. But the kind of information Petra had couldn't have come from someone low level, right?"

"I see where you're going with this, but she scooped up 99% of his crew when she hit Arjan. No one is getting special treatment. I checked. Everyone's housed in Gen-Pop. No one is getting special meals. No one has had their trial unexpectedly delayed. She wants these guys in jail."

"Then you need to look outside of his crew."

"You obviously know. Why don't you just tell me?"

"Because if I just tell you, you won't believe me. You'll say I must be mistaken and to leave the spy work to the professionals. You may be working with the brown penalty, but I'm working with the boob penalty."

"That's not fair."

"Isn't it? I love you baby, but you've given me the *she's so cute when she's mad* pat on the head more than once. And even if I can make you listen, you don't believe me. I told you point blank this evening that there was something wrong with Petra and you didn't believe me."

"I'm still not sure I believe you," he snapped. "I've got no evidence that she did anything wrong. But I've got loads of evidence that you break laws all the time."

"See, it's better if I can get you to discover it for yourself."

"You are being ridiculous and completely unfair!" He kept his voice down, but he sounded absolutely furious.

Nikki felt like she was channeling Val through the wall of the houseboat as she shrugged. "Fair doesn't really have a lot to do with it. Anyway, Thai food's here. Gotta go. Love you. Bye."

She hung up the phone and stretched her arms over her head as she took a deep breath. It felt good to finally get that off her chest.

AMSTERDAM XIII
TIME FOR THE DOUBLE CROSS

"Come on Val, hurry up! What are you doing in there?"

"I'm changing, as per your detailed plan."

"My plan did not include you taking forever and hogging the only working restroom stall. When did you become shy? Besides, I've got to pee."

"Then you should have thought about that before you we left for the mission."

"Oh my God." Nikki yanked the knife she had clipped to her waistband out and flicked it open with a hard pop. Then she slipped it into the space between the stall frame and the door. The lock released immediately and Nikki hurried in, already yanking down her pants. Val was mid-change from *sanitation employee* to *lab technician*, and turned away from Nikki, buttoning her blouse with hurrying fingers.

Nikki watched her exit the stall and tried to pick what she would say next. If it were Jane, she would want something with feeling words. Possibly also hearts and flowers. If it were Ellen she'd want something that thoughtful and logical. If it were Jenny, well, Jenny would want her to skip the hearts, flowers, and careful approach. Jenny would just want her to cut to the chase. But it wasn't any of her teammates out there; it was Val. What worked with Val?

Nikki buttoned her pants and opened the stall door.

"I thought you said you were wearing Kevlar when Ellen

shot you." Direct assault? It might work.

"I say a lot of things," said Val without looking up.

"You didn't walk out of that river, did you?"

"No one walks out of a river, you swim and then you sort of stagger."

"Val, be serious."

Val sighed. And finished sealing their sanitation outfits into the faux evidence bag. "No, I was fished out by an ex-Viet Cong doctor turned Buddhist monk. He was very upset. My blood was luring the catfish away from his bait. I lost part of a lung and the bullet missed my spine by about half an inch."

"Mrs. Merrivel put a watch on all the hospitals and the borders, just in case."

"He took me to the infirmary of his monastery. By the time I could move again, they'd lifted the watch."

"Is that why you've quit smoking?"

"I didn't quit. I am not a quitter. I've temporarily suspended my preferred hobby due to your father's insistence that he can't date a smoker, and it's going to kill me, blah, blah, blah." She flopped the fingers of one hand against her thumb in a 'yap, yap, yap' motion.

Nikki snorted in laughter. "And the fact that you now have even less lung power to work with had nothing to do with it."

Val shrugged. "All factors were considered in the decision making process."

"You really like him, don't you?"

"I really do. And we sort of fit well together." She looked as if she were about to say more, but then shrugged and stood up. "But if we're going to be to bring up uncomfortable topics, do you mind telling me why you had them leave my name on the

Consultants of Note plaque at the office?"

Nikki crossed her arms, recognized it as a defensive posture and tried to decide which was more noticeable—holding the
position or immediately uncrossing them. She decided to hold.
"Where did you hear that?"

"I know people who know people. Does it really matter?
You're the only one who could have made them leave it up after I
died. Why did you do it?"

"Because Afifa Muhammad died in a car wreck."

Val stood up and leaned against the sink, scratched her head,
and then folded her arms to mimic Nikki. "Nope, sorry, I've got
nothing. You're going to have to slow walk me through that one."

"In Thailand, I asked you if that story about you extracting
five women out of Afghanistan was true. And you said that technically you had only saved one of them, because four of them had
just gone back or gotten in trouble, and the one you had saved had
only stayed safe because she was dying of cancer.

"So when we were going through your things, I looked them
up. Afifa beat cancer with a radical mastectomy, but died six years
later in a car wreck. She was an organ donor though; four other
people are alive because of her. Of the others, you were right. One
almost immediately went back. She raised funds and got her parents, her sister and brother-in-law out. They now live in Wisconsin
for some reason. The sister has three children. Of the remaining three women, one works for the UN, so yes, you're right, she
is frequently in dangerous forward military positions. The other
two were sisters who chose to leave when it was *decided* that the
thirteen-year-old should get married. The older one became a
nurse and a midwife. She routinely travels back to the region with
Doctors Without Borders providing health care for women who

can't or won't see male doctors. The younger one was just finishing up her residency as a heart surgeon when I checked. She had also gone on several trips with her sister. I don't know what the reach is for those three in terms of lives saved. I could probably have Jane calculate, but it seems safe to say that it's probably at least in the hundreds. I don't know how many women you have to save to be on the wall, but I figured that was enough."

"And what about the Thai women that I let be sold into slavery?" asked Val. "How do they figure into your calculations? Because I like the way you do math. If you keep going I'll be a goddamn saint in no time, but I don't think it quite pans out."

"Do you think we walked away from those women? We did not. We confiscated your boyfriend's books and his bank accounts and we spent a lot of that money funding recovery operations."

"Oh gee, thanks for cleaning up my mess." She shook her head. "It doesn't even out. You should have let them take my name off the wall. I should have pried it off the wall before I left."

"You're still not getting it! People aren't..." Nikki floundered for words. "We don't only save nice women, and we don't save women so that we can pop them into little boxes on a shelf where they can stay safe and tidy for all the years to come. That's some weird fairy tale bullshit. We save them so that they can get a chance to live their life the way they want. Because we need women out there living big risky lives, living well organized lives with matching sofa cushions, living tiny lives of infinite courage. The length of the life doesn't matter; the point is that we helped them live the life of their choosing. I left you on the wall because you lived, have always lived, the life of your choosing. You said it yourself—you make your decisions with purpose. You dive out the plane without a parachute in front someone you know kind of hates you and is carrying a gun, on purpose. Yes, you made some piss poor decisions that caused a lot of pain, but damn it Val, you lived and you mattered to a lot of people. Cautionary tale or hero, I thought you were noteworthy."

Val's lips pinched shut, and she looked away staring at the floor.

"But I'm not a good person," said Val at last. "I've never been a good person."

"I would be surprised if you had been. You don't really like good people. They annoy you," said Nikki and Val laughed.

"I don't think you're listening to me."

"And I don't think you're hearing me," said Nikki. "It's OK. Yeah, you suck. And half the time I spend with you I want to punch you in the face."

"Thanks for holding back."

"It wouldn't be productive. I know we haven't talked about what's going to happen after this—"

"And this isn't really the time."

"Well, if you stop selling women into slavery and trying to kill me, I think that when we come to the end of this, I could get my head around the idea of pretending I never saw you and Dad. We could all just walk away. Carrie Mae doesn't have to know you're alive. We can all just pretend none of this ever happened."

"Like your team hasn't ratted us out by now."

"Mmm… I don't think so. Mrs. M is on leave and her replacement isn't very…" Nikki hesitated for effect. "Let's just say she's not very well liked. I really doubt that my team has done anything. After all, they're *my* team. They wouldn't rat me out."

Val looked thoughtful.

"We don't have to talk about this now," said Nikki, picking up their bags. "After all, we don't really have time to decide anything. I'm just saying, stop trying to kill me, and things would go a lot smoother."

"Hey, I haven't tried to kill you once in the last week!"

"Thanks for holding back," said Nikki.

"It wouldn't be productive," parroted Val, with a grin. "I'm just saying, you've got to live in the now."

"I'm trying," said Nikki. "I really am trying. Now, let's stop talking about this touchy-feely crap and go see if we can't steal some evidence."

"Go team," said Val with a shrug and exited the bathroom. "I'm still not sure why," complained Val as they walked down the corridor, "We couldn't break-in as lab technicians. Why the costume change? It's annoying and now I smell a little like garbage."

"For the fiftieth time, because the officers at the gate know all of the lab personnel. And while we might have been able to bullshit our way in with proper credentials, we didn't have the time to make any and neither of us speaks Dutch, so you're just going to have to deal with the smell."

Val wrinkled her nose, and plucked distastefully at the sleeve of her lab coat. "But you're Carrie Mae. And didn't you say that Carrie Mae and INTERPOL share the evidence facility? Can't you just walk up and ask to be let in?"

Nikki rolled her eyes. "No, I can't. Carrie Mae Protocol is to put in a request in advance, so that the Branch Director can get you either credentials to enter the building or set up a cover story to enter as a guest. Sudden mysterious arrival, without any proper clearance? That would set off alarm bells at Carrie Mae and INTERPOL. I don't think we really need both of them gunning for us right this second, do you? Anyway, why do you always complain about these things after you agree to them? Can you just—"

A man in navy pants and a blue checked shirt stepped out of an office and began striding purposefully down the hallway toward them. He checked when he saw them, a small frown forming between his man-scaped eyebrows.

"Hoi. Ben je nieuw?"

Val smiled, then nodded. The man smiled back, clearly taken in by Val's show of humanity.

"Heb je nodig…" but trailed off as the cell phone clipped to his belt began to ring. Nikki and Val continued to walk as he picked up the phone. They reached the end of the hall with the locked double doors and stopped.

"This better work," she said through a clenched smile and waved at the man who was still talking on the phone. He smiled back and gave a small wave.

"It'll work," said Nikki, hoping she wasn't lying. She pulled out the key card Val had *acquired* the previous evening. Nikki had spent half the night logged into the Carrie Mae main frame as Jenny, to program the key card to Rachel White, head of the West Coast Divisions Research and Development department. It should get her into this facility. Emphasis on the *should*. Nikki held out the card to the card reader and prayed.

The door swung open.

"And cue *The Ode to Joy*," said Nikki. "Although, that would make me Hans Gruber and I don't want to get thrown off the Nakatomi Tower."

"What are you talking about?"

"You know, *Die Hard*? He opens the vault and the music swells?" Val's face remained blank. "No one gets my jokes."

"Has it occurred to you that perhaps your jokes aren't funny? And can we move it along? The metrosexual down the hall is coming this way and I don't really need a date for the weekend."

"I am a laugh riot," said Nikki stepping through the doors and allowing them to swing shut behind her. "Besides, *Die Hard* is a Christmas classic and a cultural touch-stone. How are you not getting the reference?"

"I have better things to do with my life than watch movies more than once."

"Are you serious?"

"Probably not, but you'll never make me admit it."

"Now who's a laugh riot? I'm going to make you plan whatever it is we do next, so I can complain the whole time."

"You know I like to wing it. Besides, you'd never let me plan," said Val. "You wouldn't trust me not to double cross you."

"You have... a... point." Nikki's pace slowed down as they rounded the corner into evidence warehouse. "It looked smaller on the plans."

"It looked a *lot* smaller on the plans," said Val.

Unlike many things in life, the INTERPOL Evidence Warehouse was exactly what it claimed to be in the title—a warehouse. Subdivided into two sections, one half being warehouse storage and the other half being lab and office facilities. A sheen of white paint did nothing to mask the cement block construction and defensible narrow windows placed high in the three story walls lit the interior of the building with a cold fall light. A chain link fence and desk blocked their forward path. Built at a standard six foot height, the fence appeared miniscule and ridiculous, dwarfed by the rows and rows of shelving rocketed skyward, crammed with white cardboard boxes.

A bored looking police officer looked up from the magazine that he was idly flipping through. *"Goededag. Bewijs?"*

"Ja." Val held up their faux evidence bag.

"Tekenen," he said smothering a yawn, and pushing a log book in their direction.

Val signed them in with names that Nikki was pretty sure were from Austin Powers, but she said nothing, smiled, scrawled an illegible signature where Val pointed and walked through the gate.

"OK, now what?"

"Did you pay attention to my briefing at all?"

"What? It was early and you yammered on for, like, ever." Val popped a piece of nicotine gum in her mouth and grinned. "Relax, Red, I'm just messing with you. We find the evidence library computer interface. We log in; we get the code for where they're storing the Meise evidence. Then we find Arjan's little black book and then we get the hell out of Dodge. Although, I'm still not sure how we're supposed to figure out where Arjan stashed his client list if the CSI team hasn't figured it out."

"I'm assuming we're smarter than they are."

"Seems like a stretch."

"All right, I'm assuming we're more capable of thinking like a devious bastard than they are."

"Much more likely. Computer's up ahead." Val pointed as they turned down another aisle.

Nikki hurried to log in. The less time they were here they less chance there was for everything to blow-up in her face. She typed in her, or rather Rachel's credentials, and hit enter. The search prompt appeared, just as Val pivoted around, suddenly tense.

"Did you hear that? The gate opening?"

Nikki hadn't heard it. Cautiously, she stepped away from the computer and went to Val's spot. They listened intently, straining against the silence. Finally, Nikki heard the low murmur of voices.

"Damn it," hissed Val and ran to the computer, typing furiously.

Nikki stayed where she was, listening. She was certain that the voices were speaking English, but weren't native English speakers. Whoever was talking was still a few aisles away, but she could tell that one was a man, and one was a woman. There was something familiar in the haranguing tone of the woman. She crept forward attempting to peer through the shelving to the speakers. Almost instantly she ran back.

"Hurry up," she whispered fiercely. "It's Maaravi and Petra."

"I'm trying!" Val whispered back. "This isn't as straightforward as it looks." Finally, a set of coordinates flashed on the screen. Val seemed to be memorizing them. Then she checked her watch, closed the program and logged out. "This way," she said jogging down the aisle and then to the right.

Nikki followed Val. They rounded a corner and Nikki slammed into Val's back as she came to a halt. Ahead of them the looming shelves of evidence had been removed to form a wide area filled with four six foot tables. Two of the tables were strewn with the flotsam of someone's office and Petra and Maaravi were bending over the table. Maaravi, his hands encased in rubber gloves, picked up a leather-bound book and flipped through it.

"Gently," snapped Petra. "We need these to be in the same condition when we're done."

Val pushed Nikki back and led the way through the maze shelving.

"Where are you going?" whispered Nikki. "They're clearly

going through the evidence on the table. We're too late."

"Maybe," said Val, checking the square placard on the end of one of the shelves for the number and letter that designated it's 'address'. "But that didn't look like everything to me. We should look at the shelves and see if they left anything."

Nikki looked back, undecided. Behind her she heard Val flipping open boxes.

"Val, I think we should just go. Let's not—" An explosion rocked the building and an alarm went off. "What the hell was that?"

"Could be practically anything," said Val still rummaging in boxes.

Nikki ran to a center aisle. A haze of black smoke could be seen through one of the windows. Nikki intended to return to Val, make her put the boxes back, and then run out the way they'd come in.

Instead she found herself floating through the twilight world of fireflies that comes right after getting hit on the head very hard. She had the same thought she had every time this happened to her: *this is going to hurt when I wake up.*

Another explosion shook her from soft liquid state into a hard world of concrete, blaring lights, and a head that felt three feet thick.

Nikki pulled herself upright, climbing up the evidence rack. At her feet, an upended evidence box showed where Val had taken her weapon. A second box had contents that Nikki recognized all too well. She took a step forward, and fell back down, tripping ignominiously on the very weapon that had felled her the first time—one half of a pair of ornately painted, heavy wooden clogs. She heaved herself back to vertical, clutching the clog and the back of her head. The entire room seemed to vibrate, ringing like a gong. The gong was punctured intermittently a high-pitched plinging noise. She shook her head trying to clear the sparkles. But the shaking only made it worse. She looked down the aisle, Val was a black, wavering silhouette that was rapidly disappearing. Nikki staggered after her.

The guard at the cage gate was unconscious. Whether from Val or other causes she couldn't tell. She attempted to pick up speed, but only managed to make herself want to vomit. Once in the hallway, she pursued a trail of slow closing doors to an exterior courtyard. Her hand was on the last doorway when a second explosion rocked the building. Yanking open the door she saw Val sprinting through a hole in the concrete block wall surrounding the building. The guards fired on a truck, but a blonde Viking looking dude, that Nikki could only assume was Anders Hoek, put down his grenade launcher to cover Val's escape with a spray of gunfire from an automatic rifle.

"Well," said Nikki as the truck peeled out, "at least she didn't shoot me." She looked around; guards were pouring into the courtyard. It was time to not be here anymore. She headed back toward the warehouse, pulling out her phone as she went. It was time to do what she didn't want to do—she dialed Z'ev.

He picked up on the second ring. "I was about to call you."

"Uh, yeah, hey. Um… We've got a little bit of a problem."

"Oh good. You already know," said Z'ev.

"I think this entire block knows," said Nikki glancing back at the blackened hole in the wall. "When did you let Anders Hoek out of jail? You couldn't have warned me?" She shoved her free hand in the pocket of her lab coat; her fingers were freezing.

"Anders Hoek? Who cares about him? I'm talking about

Arjan Meise."

Nikki turned her head, trying to hide behind her phone, as Petra Gilles ran by, her blonde locks bouncing like a Pantene commercial. She was dragging Maaravi by the arm.

"Slow down," Maaravi protested. "We have to go back. We didn't find the book."

"And we're not going to," snapped Petra. "You're trigger happy friend back there blew it! What the hell were you thinking having him come here?"

"He doesn't work for me!" Maaravi yelled.

"Then how did he get here?" The argument continued across the courtyard toward the parking lot.

"What about Arjan Meise?" whispered Nikki.

"He's being released from prison."

"What?" Nikki's voice veered toward Minnie Mouse territory.

"His lawyer just filed to have the case dismissed in court."

"How can that even be possible?"

"The lawyer legally changed his place of business to Arjan's house. He's been working out of there daily for the last month. He claims that INTERPOL was illegally surveilling him at his place of business while he was working on Arjan's case meaning that the entire case is based on illegal evidence."

Nikki took the phone away from her ear and stared at it. "That's ridiculous. It's legal fancy footwork to keep Arjan out of prison."

"Well, it's legal fancy footwork that's working because Arjan is getting out of prison *right now*."

Nikki avoided eye contact as another contingent of guards ran past her.

"Where is he going?"

"I don't know. Home maybe."

"Or maybe to see his son?"

"Possibly, but—" Z'ev cut off and she could hear the crackle of a radio. "Nikki please tell me that you didn't to the INTERPOL evidence warehouse."

"What? No! I mean, technically yes. But I'm not the one who blew everything up."

"Nikiki, what did you do?"

"I actually haven't done anything yet. That's part of the problem."

"Nikki, if you're caught, I can't get you out of this!"

"Relax. I'm not going to get caught. But I am going to go back in and get Arjan's client book before the uh…" She hesitated, not wanting to get into an argument over Petra right now. "The bad guys. I want to get the client book before the bad guys can steal it."

"Just leave it there! If it's in evidence, then the good guys have it and should stay where it is."

"Don't be ridiculous," said Nikki. "We need evidence. And between Petra," Z'ev sputtered, but Nikki ignored him, "and Arjan's lawyer, it won't be staying put for long. But I'm going to need you to do something while I'm getting it." She took a deep breath and leaned against the wall. She felt physically ill. This was quite possibly the worst moment of her life. "I'm going to need you to go arrest my father."

AMSTERDAM XIV
TOUGH DECISIONS

"Uh, say what now?"

"Hold on." Nikki put the phone in her pocket.

Guards were running out, guns up, suspicion clear on their faces.

"Que se passe-t-il?" Nikki tried French on the theory that anything was better than English. At least in French she sounded native to the European Union. Unless the listener were French, and then she sounded natively Canadian. She flashed her fake ID badge.

The guard's face puckered as he tried to think in a different language. *"Entrer dans. Ils nous attaquent!"*

Nikki widened in her eyes in faux terror and nodded. Running past the guard, she swiped badge at the door and ran back into the building. A few more similar encounters and some eyelash batting and she was back in the warehouse. The guard was still unconscious behind the desk. Nikki checked his pulse before letting herself back into the warehouse.

"OK," said Nikki, putting the phone back to ear and heading back to where she'd started. "Maybe not arrest. Maybe you could just go pick him up and sit on him until I get there."

"Did you just bluff your way back into the INTERPOL building?" demanded Z'ev.

"Yeah, I told you I need to get some stuff."

"You just walked back into the facility that you just broke

into by using French?"

"Yes. Now look—"

"That shouldn't work."

"Well, of course it works. Guards are like terriers; they chase things that run away from them. Don't run and you're half way home. Have an ID badge that gets you past the swipey thing and you must be OK. We really don't have time for this." She took a left and entered the Carrie Mae section, looking for Val's boxes. "Val just double-crossed me and escaped with Anders Hoek."

"Oh, there's a big surprise. How could you think she wasn't going to? Mr. M told me what she did to you in Thailand. Why haven't you put a cap in her ass?"

"Why does everyone try and define her by Thailand? That isn't the sum total of her life. She can be more."

"Yeah, well, she doesn't appear to want to."

"I know," said Nikki, righting the boxes Val had dumped out onto the floor and going through the contents. As described by the evidence catalog she had received three years ago, there was a random assortment of bits. The collected detritus of an agent who always meant to come back for that, but never liked to clean up messes. "And that is very disappointing. Plus, I thought we'd had a real moment there in the bathroom, that I'd gotten through to her, but apparently not."

"You don't sound terribly surprised," said Z'ev suspiciously.

"I'm not. After someone shoots you once or twice, you get the hint. Anyway, stop detouring me. We don't have a lot of time." She began to hold up evidence bags, reading the labels or squinting through the plastic at the contents. She paused occasionally to pull out useful items. "Val, I can handle, but I hadn't counted on Arjan or Anders Hoek being on the loose. I really need you to go to the Hotel De L'europe and pick up my Dad. If you could just bring him over to 303 Singel Street, I would be ever so grateful. Although, technically, it's not on the street due it being a house boat. Oh thank God." She lifted the black cashmere sweater out of the bag. There was a waft of Chanel, Val's signature perfume, but Nikki didn't care.

"Did you find Arjan's client book?" asked Z'ev eagerly.

"No, I stopped to grab some gear first. Picked up a sweater. Seriously, it's freakishly cold here. Why would anyone live here? It's not even Norway or anything. Let's never live in Norway."

"You don't know; Norway could be lovely."

"I don't know, and I won't know, because as soon as I'm back home I'm going to go sit on the beach for like, a week." She struggled to get out of her lab coat and pulled on the sweater. "Anyway," she said pulling the lab coat back on and yanking open the evidence bags she'd collected, "are you moving? Are you going to get my Dad? You're closer, so you ought to make it before everyone, but there isn't a lot of time."

"Yes, I'm going," said Z'ev, sounding annoyed.

"He's being guarded by one guy. He looks like he managed to get a lot of Neanderthal genes, but my money's on you. Just watch out that Dad doesn't pull a fast one. He's wiley."

"I'm getting the picture," said Z'ev.

"See you soon."

Nikki felt a sense of relief as she shoved bits of Carrie Mae gear into her pockets. It felt like coming home. She replaced the box lids and tucked them back on the shelves. Now for Arjan's items.

She found the Meise evidence still strewn over a center table under the fluorescent lights, but two lab geeks were cleaning up.

The girl had a hair clip with a butterfly on it. Nikki recognized it as being from the Carrie Mae Spring 2014 line. Nikki bit her lip. Leaving a digital trail from her ID badge was one thing. It would really only show up if someone were looking for it. Actually talking to people was a bit more than she'd planned on. Another item went back in the box. Sighing, Nikki stepped forward.

"Leave it on the table," she said holding out her badge to butterfly clip girl. The girl's eyes widened.

"There was a break-in. We're supposed to put everything back." Her accent was heavy Dutch, but perfectly understandable. The male lab tech looked from Nikki back to his colleague in confusion.

"There have been some changes in the case. We need to review this evidence now, before it has to be released."

"Agent Gilles didn't say anything about that," said the girl, still suspiciously. She took Nikki's badge and gave it serious examination. "Can you explain yourself?"

Nikki allowed herself a small smile of triumph. The passphrase question had been offered. "I'm afraid I can't explain myself," she replied. "Because I'm not myself, you see?"

"Ah," said the girl. "Well, they might have warned us you were coming."

"It was an unexpected detour," said Nikki. "Also, didn't expect the fireworks. Sorry. I'm Agent Lanier." She offered a hand to shake and the girl responded.

"I'm Sanne. What can we help you with?"

"Somewhere in this pile of evidence, Arjan Meise hid his client book. I need to find it before anyone else does."

The male tech asked a question in Dutch. Sanne replied, but he continued to look dubious.

"Is he going to be a problem," asked Nikki. She had reclaimed some knock-out powder from Val's belongings, but she wasn't sure what the lifespan or durability was. It had been in the cardboard box for awhile.

"No," said Sanne. "I explained that you're from Agent Gilles. She's been second-guessing us already, so I said you were a specialist she brought in."

"Well, I'm not here to win a popularity contest, so I guess that will probably work." Nikki approached the table and looked at the collection of goods. "What are the most likely places to find a client book?"

"Agent Gilles had us look through every single book," said Sanne, gesturing to the large pile of books. "There aren't any books that aren't what they appear to be. There aren't any books that have special marks or high-lighting. So if there is a hidden list in there... Then well, I guess he's better than us at hiding things."

"I find that unlikely. Plus, he has to use the list; it has to be fairly accessible on a daily basis."

"That's what we've been thinking," said Sanne nodding. "And Joost points out that it's unlikely to be stored on paper."

"So what we're looking for is an item that would be readily to hand, that could either store a memory card or stick."

There was a burst of Dutch from Joost and Sanne nodded. "Or it may not be here at all. He may use cloud storage. We both agree that seems unlikely due to the notorious vulnerability of cloud storage, but it's still possible."

"You've got someone going through his digital files, right?" asked Nikki and Sanne nodded. She looked at the table top and boxes. It was as though an office had been condensed into two six foot tables. She remembered standing in Arjan's office and she tried to picture where everything would go. "Do you have pictures of the office before you removed all the items?"

Sanne snapped something to Joost and he held up an iPad with pictures. The office looked as she remembered it—desk facing the door, built in bookshelves on the wall behind. Two chairs in front of the desk, their backs to the door. Only in the pictures, everything was decorated. The books were on the shelves along with knick-knacks and book ends. Two black and white photos hung on the wall. One of a stone gravestone angel and one of a church roof gargoyle. The desk was strewn with a few objet d'arte and the obligatory cup holding pens.

Nikki walked to the table and began arranging the knick-knacks to match the photos of the office. What was she missing? Maaravi had been here already and he hadn't found the files, and presumably he had a better idea of what he was looking for.

"We examined all the items for hidden compartments," said Sanne. "We didn't come up with anything."

Nikki looked at the items, then looked at Joost's photos again. She frowned. "We're missing something."

"I know, but I just can't figure out what!"

"No, literally, we're missing something. There's a pillow on the floor in the corner of this photo. Where is it?"

Sanne and Joost exchanged words. They both scrutinized the photo, then the table. "We don't know," Sanne said at last. "This is all the evidence that came in. Maybe it is still at the house?"

"I was just there. It's not." She stared at the photo. She was absolutely certain that the pillow on the floor hadn't been in the office when she'd been there, but it still looked familiar. Mentally, she travelled through each room of the house. Maybe it wasn't important anyway? She checked her watch and smacked a palm on the table in frustration. "I'm out of time."

"Sorry," said Sanne looking embarrassed.

"It's not your fault. Nothing else in this damn case has gone my way, so I don't know why this would be any different. Keep looking."

"We will. But um… be careful. I have seen the videos. He's not a nice man."

"What videos?"

In response, Sanne took Joost's iPad and poked around on it. He had the resigned look of someone who was used to being steamrolled. "His arrest videos." Sanne hit play and handed the iPad to Nikki.

The video showed a basic interrogation room. It was shot from behind the interrogating officer to get maximum coverage of the suspect's face. Arjan Meise was staring not at the officer, but directly into the camera, his craggy, aristocratic face set in an expression of bitter contempt. The INTERPOL officer nattered on at him in Dutch, but he ignored every word, continuing his staring contest with the camera.

"It goes on like that for twenty minutes," said Sanne. "Zoom ahead to minute 19."

Nikki did as instructed, dragging the play bar across the screen. Nothing appeared to have changed except that now the interrogator was louder and clearly more frustrated. He had pushed back his chair and was standing up, leaning on the table, speaking directly into Arjan's face. Then at minute twenty, the interrogator made a mistake. He emphasized whatever statement he had been making by poking his finger at Arjan's face. Nikki watched, fascinated as Arjan's focus shifted from the camera to the interrogator. But the officer clearly missed the subtle shift in Arjan's pale blue eyes and continued poking.

"This is going to hurt, isn't it?" asked Nikki.

"Yes," agreed Sanne.

The officer made his final mistake when he poked Arjan in the chest, making firm contact, thunk, thunk, thunk.

Arjan issued no warnings. He seized the offending finger, pulling it towards him while at the same time shoving the table back, knocking the agents' legs out from under him. With the man stretched across the table, he broke the finger with an ugly snap and then, still hand-cuffed to the table proceeded to repeatedly hammer the man's face with elbow strikes. Moments later INTERPOL agents rushed in to save their comrade. They pointed their guns at Arjan as they pulled their friend away, leaving a bloody smear across the table. Arjan simply sat back down and stared at the camera. But this time he was smiling.

"Broken nose, broken cheek bone, broken finger," said Sanne.

"Well," said Nikki, "I guess this is why they pay me the big bucks."

As expected, Sanne laughed. It was the constant Carrie Mae joke, that the agents were underpaid compared to other agencies.

"We'll call you first if we find anything," said Sanne, then a tad too eagerly, she pulled out a business card. "In case you need to call me, or... uh mention me in your report."

Nikki tried not to roll her eyes. Had she ever been that green and eager? She winced, remembering that yes, she had. No wonder Val had shot her.

It took awhile to get out of the building. There was a lot of shouting, and police, and reporters, but eventually she'd slipped out. The cab ride back to the house boat was quiet. She'd thought about boosting another car, but it seemed too likely to draw attention after the break-in at the warehouse. It occurred to her for the first time that Val might go back to the house boat. She really didn't think so, but her palms started to sweat wondering if she should have warned Z'ev.

She paid the cab driver and stood on the sidewalk looking down at the house boat. Nothing on the street moved. If she was right about Val, then the houseboat was perfectly safe. If she was wrong then Val would have a nasty surprise waiting for her. Nikki walked down the stairs, and along the promenade to the gangway. The door opened a sliver and she could see a gun barrel peak out.

"That's far enough," said Z'ev.

Nikki hesitated, one foot on the plank. "Everything OK?" she asked, holding her hands out to her sides, showing no weaponry.

"Nikki?" The door banged open. "What the hell did you do to your hair?"

"Oh," she said, dropping her hands, and walking across. "I forgot about that."

"You forgot? Your hair is frigging purple!"

"Not all of it," said Nikki patting her hair defensively. "I think it looks good. Besides you saw it last night. Didn't you notice?" Nikki suddenly felt put out. He really hadn't noticed.

"You had a hat on. I thought it was a wig."

"Well, other people think it looks good. They wanted to take pictures of it at the salon for their website. I said no, of course. But what else was I supposed to with an INTERPOL B.O.L.O. out on me?"

"It…" He seemed stymied. "It does look good. I think? It's just so not you. I mean, it's nice— Wait, you went to a salon?"

"What, you think I was going to *Legend of Billie Jean* it up in a bathroom sink or something? I think not. I'm Carrie Mae. We have standards."

"I wouldn't know what you're likely to do. You've been lying to me for the last three years, so how would I know what your job standards are or what you're willing to do? To be perfectly honest, I'm not sure I know you at all."

Nikki stared up into his dark brown eyes and felt a heart-chilling stab of anguish. He really felt like he didn't know her. He really felt like she had lied about everything. How was she supposed to repair that?

"Nothing to say? No words of reassurance about how I know you better than anyone? How everything will be all right?"

"You don't want me to lie," Nikki blurted out, and saw a flash of anger in his face.

"Your dad's inside," he said, turning away.

"I don't know if everything will be all right," Nikki gasped out, feeling like the words were squeezed out of her lungs. "If I knew it was going to be all right, I would have told you three years ago."

"I didn't know either, but I told you!"

"No, you didn't! I found out. You didn't have a choice but to trust me. And I have never blown your cover."

"You told your entire organization!"

"Of course I did. We weren't together when I found out and you were a threat. You still are a threat."

"Everyone, and I do mean everyone, from Jackson to the girls to Mr. M, made that perfectly clear. Which means it never occurred to any of our friends that they could trust me."

Nikki hadn't ever considered her friends to be Z'ev's friends too and she had no immediate response for that.

"I helped Jane move. Ellen calls me when she needs help with home repairs. How many goddamn times have I had to pick up Jenny after her car broke down?"

"I know. How is it that I drive the vintage automobile and she has all the break downs?"

"She doesn't take care of her vehicles. I don't think she knows what an oil change is. But my point is that you and I had a life and everything about it was a lie. You keep acting like it's no big thing and that I'll just get over it, but I don't see you offering a lot of suggestions on how I do that. It is a big deal. Personally and professionally, it's a huge deal to me. I wasn't kidding when I said I don't know you. I don't. I don't know anything about you."

There was a thump and a muffled squawk of pain from inside the houseboat.

"Well, you know for certain that this isn't my natural hair color, so I guess we'll have to start with that," said Nikki and pushed past him.

Her father was lying on his side, still tied to a chair. He was fumbling for his boot where Nikki could see the hilt of a knife.

"Nikki! Thank God you found me. Help me up, but be careful, there's a big guy running around here somewhere.

"Yeah, Dad, I know." Nikki took the knife out of his boot and cut through the ropes. She set the chair upright. "Don't worry about him."

"Don't worry about him? The guy is built like a mac truck. How are you planning on taking care of that?"

"I expect she'll just date me, move in with me, and then try and rip my heart out with a life altering, devastating lie," said Z'ev, pushing past Nikki into the kitchen.

Nikki cleared her throat. "Dad, meet my boyfriend, CIA

Agent Z'ev Coralles. Z'ev meet my dad, Phillippe Lanier, the smuggler."

"Ex-boyfriend," corrected Z'ev.

"Ignore him. I'm working on that."

"When are you going to learn that *no* means *no*?"

"Never," said Phillippe climbing to his feet. "If I have taught her anything it's that *no* just means you need to think creatively. And it's Extraordinaire."

"What?" asked Z'ev, pausing as he reached into the fridge.

"Smuggler Extraordinaire, if you please. I like my intro's to have a little more pizzazz."

"Really?" asked Nikki. "You're going to demand an extra special title? Because I thought I was being nice by not introducing you as the bastard who set me up."

THE PAST V

SURPRISE ME

Seattle, Washington

The rain was barely a mist, but Jackson insisted on walking her to the house anyway.

Eighteen-year-old Nikki laughed as he hoisted a lopsided umbrella over her head. "I think it's wetter in your truck than it is out here."

His truck was an ancient rust bucket Ford. Caitlin Barcourt made fun of it constantly. Jackson simply pointed out that he had paid for it himself, unlike John Weiman's Pontiac Firebird which had been a gift from his third stepmother. Nikki tried to pretend she didn't care about the rust water in her hair.

"Why do you think I'm walking you to your door? I thought it would be nice to dry off a little."

Nikki laughed. They had barely made it to the first step when the porch light popped on and the door opened. Nikki looked up, expecting to see her mother. Nell approved of Jackson just about as much as Caitlin Barcourt. Nell's dislike of anyone from Kaniksu Falls was absolute. It would be just like her to squelch any chance for a goodnight kiss.

"Well," said a man's voice, "*Quel surprise!* Here I was thinking about taking you out to dinner and someone has beat me to it. *Autres temps, autres mœurs.*"

Nikki blinked at her father. Other than being clean-shaven and having a little gray at the temples, he was exactly as she remembered. She struggled for words. Did she run in for a hug? She would have as a kid, but five years with only a handful of letters had left her uncertain of how things stood between them. Did she hate him? Did she love him? What was she supposed to say?

Beneath the umbrella, Jackson squeezed her hand and she remembered that she wasn't the only one there.

"Uh, Jackson, you remember my dad?"

"Um, yes. Nice to see you again Mr. Lanier." Jackson stepped up the remaining stairs to shake hands and fill in the awkward gaping moment. "Jackson Tyrell. We used to live in Kaniksu Falls. I went to school with Donny and Nikki."

"Oh, of course. Nice to see you again. Didn't quite place the face before, but I recognize you now." Philippe smiled warmly as he shook Jackson's hand and Nikki was shocked to discover that she thought he was lying.

"Where's Mom?" asked Nikki looking over Philippe's shoulder.

"I was going to ask you the same thing," he replied. "But come in, let's get out of the rain while we wait for her." Philippe went back inside, heading for the kitchen. Jackson turned to her looking uncertain.

"Don't leave me," Nikki mouthed and he nodded.

"You two look like you're just getting back in, but do you want to order pizza? I would kill for some pizza." He was already dialing the phone.

Nikki looked around the kitchen as he ordered pepperoni and black olive with green pepper. The spare key from the hollow rock in the backyard was on the table. A black back-pack with black electrical tape over the logo sat on one of the chairs. Nikki got a soda out of the fridge and handed it to Jackson, then poured water for herself and flavored it with half a Crystal Light packet.

"That's disgusting," said her father hanging up the phone. "Why aren't you drinking a real drink?"

"I have to lose five pounds," said Nikki. "I'm the top of the pyramid this year."

"I have no idea what that means, but I believe it to be full of *merde*," said Philippe.

Since his sentiments echoed Jackson's, Nikki ignored them. Men didn't understand these things. They all claimed to want a girl who wasn't obsessed with dieting, but that didn't make them magically like dating plump girls. They just wanted a girl who didn't *admit* she was dieting. She hated that her mother was right on this topic. Not that she would ever say that out loud.

"Does Mom know you're here?"

"I left her a message," said Philippe with a shrug.

"You're not contesting the divorce or anything weird are you?"

"What? No, that went through ages ago. Why would you ask that? Can't I just pop in to say *hello* to *mon petit lapin?* When did you get so suspicious? It's this living in the big city. It poisons people."

Jackson was looking at her strangely and Philippe looked sadly disappointed. Nikki blushed suddenly, embarrassed.

"Sorry, I'm just really surprised. It's been so long."

"I know! Too long!" He embraced her fiercely, picking her up off her feet and spinning her around. "I missed you so much! But! I brought you a present!" He set her down long enough to dive into one of the pockets on his bag and came back holding a silver cuff bracelet. It was a style that was so not in right now. It was a total hippy girl thing to wear with complicated Celtic knots carved in it. "Surprise! What do you think?"

"I love it," said Nikki, smiling and putting it on.

The front door banged open and Philippe reached for his bag again.

"Nikki!" yelled Nell. "You had better not be upstairs with Jackson!"

"We're in the kitchen, Mom!" Nikki yelled back.

Nell came around the corner, shaking out her rain coat and stopped in the archway, staring at Philippe.

"Um," said Jackson, finishing his pop in one gulp. "I think it's time for me to go."

"Chicken," whispered Nikki as he hugged her goodbye. He only nodded and pulled an apologetic face.

The door banged shut after Jackson and Nell still hadn't said anything. "Maybe I'll just wait out in the front room for the pizza guy," said Nikki.

"No!" snapped Philippe. "I mean, I think it would be better if Nell and I went out front and waited."

"OK," said Nikki. "I'm going to go up to my room now. *Papa*, do you want me to put the blue or gray linens on the spare bed?"

Nell's eyes seemed glued to Philippe's face.

"Either is fine, *chère*. Surprise me," he said.

"Your father's not staying," said Nell.

Nikki didn't respond, but went upstairs to change the sheets.

"It's not safe for you to stay," said Nell.

"It's perfectly safe," said Philippe.

Nikki shook her head. When were her parents going to learn to behave like adults?

AMSTERDAM XV
FALLOUT BOY

Philippe's jaw swung loose and he looked from Nikki to Z'ev and back again, as if looking for a clue about his next move.

"*Bebe*! What are you talking about? I would never set you up!" He looked wonderfully wounded. If she had been twelve she might have believed it.

"Oh, please. That letter, sent to my grandmother's house? You have always sent mail to Mom's. The only reason you'd change, is if you didn't want Mom to read it and immediately point out how full of shit you are. First the sob story letter, then getting yourself kidnapped."

"Now, that is not true. I really was kidnapped!"

Nikki continued on as if she hadn't heard him. "The knowing looks with Val in South Africa. We just have to meet you in Amsterdam? Anders Hoek happening to show up at the bar on the same day we arrive in town? Please, you wanted me in Amsterdam the whole time. You needed me to get Val into the INTERPOL storage facility. And maybe I could be OK with that kind of betrayal, but I draw the line at helping a man like Arjan Meise. You're going to tell me where Val is going next and you're going to tell Z'ev everything you know about the Meise operation, or so help me I will start blowing up your life in ways you didn't even know were possible."

Phillippe looked from Nikki to Z'ev. "Don't look at me," said Z'ev. "I had been assuming she was on your side."

"And why aren't you on my side?" Philippe tried hurt again. "I'm your father. You and I have been through so much. It hurts that you don't trust me."

Nikki took a step forward and stomped on his toe. He leaped into the air grabbing at his foot, hopping around the room in a way that set the boat rocking.

"A father would know that I'm not that stupid. Start telling the truth."

Philippe at last sat down in the chair that Z'ev had tied him to. "*Bebe*, you have to understand…" He drifted into silence, still rubbing his toe. "I'm dealing with certain realities."

"No," said Nikki, "you have to understand. I'm dealing with certain realities. I work for an international organization dedicated to helping women everywhere. We operate below the radar of most of the world's intelligence agencies. We care about helping women, regardless of politics, religion or race and I'm part of the lead Covert Action Team out of the West Coast division. Right now, Z'ev Coralles is the only active, male CIA member who knows about us. His knowledge is putting my organization at risk."

"OK, wait," said Z'ev. "Mr. Merrivel would be the inactive CIA member, but are you implying that there are female agency employees that know about Carrie Mae?"

"*Oui!* There was much that was unsaid in that statement, wasn't there?" agreed Philippe.

"And we're not discussing any of it right now," said Nikki. "We're discussing the fact that while I am here, dealing with my father, it means that I am not back at my job, dealing with the Z'ev situation and protecting him from the more militant factions of my organization."

"There are totally female operatives who know," said Z'ev.

Nikki ignored him.

"Since I love him deeply, and since I hold you and Val personally responsible for this situation, you can trust me when I say I am very annoyed. The only people who are going to be more annoyed than me, are every agent in my entire organization if they find out that Val is alive. Ellen may have taken the chest shot in Thailand, but you know, she was fresh out of the academy, and she was in a helicopter. I really think that she can make it a headshot next time. So unless you want Val's brains on the pavement and unless you want me to never speak to you again, you will start fixing this situation for me, right now."

"You shot her?" Philippe looked shocked. "She said you parted on bad terms, but she didn't say you shot her."

"I didn't shoot her," said Nikki. "Our friend Ellen shot her. After Val shot me and dumped me in the Chao Praya river."

"She didn't tell me that. Are you sure you're not exaggerating? I mean, she might have shot you a little bit, but she probably knew you'd survive."

Behind Philippe she saw Z'ev unfold his arms and straighten up from his slouched, annoyed slump against the wall.

"No," said Nikki. "Her plan's success pretty much depended on me dying."

"That's just not the Val I know," said Philippe defensively. Z'ev threw up his hands in frustration and disbelief. Nikki looked away; emotionally she couldn't handle the idea that someone else found her father as unbelievable as she did. She'd spent so long trying to convince herself that her parents were the crazies, that she was the sane one, that having exterior confirmation was disturbing to her equilibrium. It was like pushing against a wind that suddenly stopped.

"Well, that's the Val I know," said Nikki.

He was silent for a long moment and his expression conflicted. "If you think that's what she did—I'm not saying she did, but if you think that, then why would you come with her to get me?"

"Because I love you, and as much as Val is a sociopath with a horror story for a childhood and narcissistic tendencies, I love her too. And I think you're both capable of more."

He scratched his head. "I'm sorry I got you into this mess," he said. "I didn't think it would be this complicated. I just thought it would be fun to see you."

Nikki shook her head. That was exactly the sort of thoughtless statement that would have enraged her grand-mère.

"What was the plan, Papa? What were you and Val trying to do?"

"Val realized that her storage locker had been moved to Carrie Mae evidence storage, but she said that she couldn't get to it without you. So we decided that I would write you a letter. And then a few weeks later I would try to call you up and try and get you to meet me here in Amsterdam. And once here, Val's associate Anders Hoek would threaten us. And we were going to tell you that Val had evidence against him in the gear that was confiscated."

"And I would help get it to protect you. OK, what was really in that case book? And where does Maaravi Meise come into this?"

"Val has the account and password to a bit coin account that at the time was practically worthless, but now that bit coins are thing, it's worth five million dollars. And before you ask, no I don't know who it used to belong to. Val just said that no one would be claiming it. We were going to split it with Anders for helping convince you. Maaravi was never supposed to come into it at all. He wasn't even on my radar. I haven't seen him or Arjan since I split with Arjan over that thing with his wife. Maaravi really did kidnap me! He really did want me to help get guns into Europe to help get his dad out of prison."

"OK, and then Val and I showed up to rescue you and you saw the opportunity to put the old plan back in place?"

Philippe nodded. "Only now, I'm here and Val's not. I guess Val and Anders have the account number. So I guess that means I'm out of the picture."

"Not exactly," said Nikki. "As soon as Val opens her case book she's going to notice that it's not hers. I had it switched out yesterday."

"You knew she was going to betray you?" demanded Z'ev.

"I suspected," said Nikki. "I activated a Looking Glass Protocol when it became clear we were going to have to to the INTERPOL warehouse."

"What's a Looking Glass Protocol?" asked Z'ev.

"They're action plans for when things get weird," said Nikki. "For when the unexpected happens. You know, like in case Jane ever loses it and decides to take out the leadership of the Republican Party."

"Why would she do that?"

"I don't know. Maybe the Republicans figure out a way to repeal Roe vs Wade or maybe she just decides that transgender people should be able to pee in peace. I can't predict the inciting incident. Like I don't know why a house fire would start, but I know what my evacuation routes would be if I see flames."

"So you knew she was alive?" Philippe's forehead wrinkled in confusion.

"No, but we never found the body, and Val is not someone

who is easy to kill, so you know, Mrs. M and I put a few things in place, just in case."

"What's the Looking Glass Protocol on me?" asked Z'ev.

"Is this really the time?" demanded Nikki.

"Like I'm really going to get the opportunity to ask later," said Z'ev. Nikki wavered trying to decide which would annoy him the most: lying, avoidance, or the truth.

"Discredit and eliminate," she said at last. "But I'm really trying to prevent that from happening."

"Gee, thanks."

"Like the CIA wouldn't do the same to me in a heartbeat if they thought I was a threat." Z'ev didn't say anything in response, which was how she knew she was right.

"Enough!" said Philippe. "So you double-crossed Val before she could double-cross you, and then you had your boyfriend—"

"Ex-boyfriend."

"I'm ignoring that, per instructions," said Philippe. "You had him pick me up before Val could get to me. Which means that you thought that Val was going to try and stick to the original plan. How do you know that she won't just see that the book is blank, and cut bait? What makes you think she'll come back for me at all?"

"Well, I think she's in love with you."

Philippe blinked twice. "Yes! OK. That is so excellent. What do we do next? How do we make a swap?"

"Dad, my end goal isn't to make sure that you two ride off into the sunset together."

"*Oui, oui.* We all have needs that have to be met. But I know *mon petite lapin* will take care of her old man!" He beamed proudly.

Nikki tried to formulate something to say that would capture what she was thinking, but all that wanted to come out was a long scream of frustration.

"He's making your mom look sane," said Z'ev. "You know, I really thought that you didn't want me to meet your family because you had some problem with me, but I'm starting to think that it was because you know that they are all bat guano level wing nuts."

"Oh my God. Yes. I tried to tell you. I mean, come on— think back to when we first met. I went to dinner with you, a complete stranger who was packing heat, just so I could avoid my mom. People with normal families don't do that!"

"I don't even want to think about what you would have done to avoid your dad."

"Right!"

"That really hurts," said Philippe. "Anyway, what are you going to do about Maaravi, since I doubt he'll stop trying to get his dad out of jail, even if I'm not there to complete the sale."

"His dad's already out of jail," said Z'ev and Phillippe's face went pale. "He was getting out when I picked you up."

"Thank God you came to get me then, that guy is a monster."

"Well, maybe you shouldn't have slept with his wife," said Nikki.

"I didn't sleep with his wife," said Philippe.

"You said you split with Arjan after *the thing* with his wife," said Nikki.

"Yeah, a lot of us did," said Philippe. "When a situation turns bad and the only way out is to ice your wife, no one expects a guy to actually whack his wife. I knew Marit. She wasn't exactly a warm fuzzy person, but she was a hell of an artist with shotgun and she cooked a mean French onion soup and she didn't deserve to take two in the back of the head. If a man is willing to shoot his own wife, then he's not going to quibble over any of us. I'm a sup-porter of the people. I'm against big governments and corruption and I have no qualms about arming the revolutionaries that fight for their rights and their freedom. *Liberté, égalité, fraternité*, and all that. But Arjan... he's only in it for the money. After Marit died, I cleared out and kept my distance. Arjan Meise is just as corrupt as any of the dirty sleezeballs on Wall Street. Frankly, I don't know why Maaravi is even bothering to try and get him out of jail."

Nikki gave a deep sigh. "I'm such an idiot. I wish you'd told me this sooner, *Papa*. Of course Maaravi isn't trying to get him out of jail. He's the one who put him in jail in the first place."

"Noooo, I'm pretty sure that's not right." Philippe stopped and stared at Nikki. "Well, I guess, I mean, he did put most of his efforts toward securing a buyer for the guns. But he said that was because he needed the money for Arjan's defense."

"Has he ever called Arjan's lawyer?"

"Not that I know of. Which, I was fine with because that little bearded dude creeps me out anyway. Seriously, I know people say that lawyers have no soul, but I'm pretty sure that this one actually sold his. Anyway Maaravi spent most of his time making out with that girl, Petra, and trying to find a buyer. Meanwhile, Muggins here had to do all the work of getting the guns into Europe."

"Did Petra know about Maaravi's plans to find a buyer?" asked Z'ev.

"I'm really not sure. He didn't want me to talk to her. He was pretty clear on that. From what I heard, they spent most of their time discussing Arjan's client book, but, I'm really not sure what she did or didn't know."

Z'ev frowned. "That doesn't mean she's flipped," he said, seeing Nikki's expression. "It's possible that Maaravi's using her.

He fed her information to get his father arrested. She listed an anonymous source on most of the original warrants—that was probably Maaravi. Maybe she doesn't know about his smuggling plans."

"Then why did she take him to the evidence warehouse?"

"He was at the evidence warehouse?"

"Yes. He and Petra were looking at the evidence they got from Arjan's house."

"Well, maybe he convinced her that he would help her look for his father's client book?" Z'ev didn't sound entirely convinced by this theory, even as he said it.

"I'm sure that was the thinking, but even if her intentions were pure, having a sexual relationship with a source is still unethical. And giving him access to evidence is a real problem."

"Like you've got a lot of room to talk about unethical," snapped Z'ev.

"Hey, back off. You can complain that I've made bad decisions or that I've lied to you, but the decisions I make on the job are for the good of our clients and for the good of my organization. I have never betrayed my country or my co-workers."

"No, just me," he said bitterly.

"I never have!"

Philippe's head bounced back and forth between them, watching the argument with avid interest and expression that said he wished he had popcorn.

"You told everyone I was with the CIA!"

"I did not tell everyone. I told everyone at work. You may not have noticed, but we're pretty good at keeping secrets."

"You put me in danger and you didn't tell me."

Nikki sighed. "You're right, I did. I should have done what

they asked a long time ago and broke up with you. But I didn't. I tried to be loyal to you and I tried to be loyal to them. It turns out I didn't do very well at either. And it would be super great if we could have this argument sometime when my father isn't here. Also, can we focus on Petra? I'm telling you she's flipped."

"And I'm telling you; she's one of the good guys. She has to be working Maaravi to get to Arjan."

"Being with INTERPOL or the CIA doesn't automatically make someone one of the good guys," said Nikki.

"She's right," said Phillippe. "A lot of them are assholes."

Nikki held up a warning finger in his direction, but continued to focus on Z'ev. "I'm telling you she's gone."

"What makes you so sure?"

"Because I've seen it before," said Nikki. "I watched Val just… walk away from everything we believed in. It wasn't even that she stopped believing in it. It just wasn't enough anymore. The job took too much and didn't give enough back at some point. And when she met someone who she thought could give her what she needed, she left."

"There are other ways to leave," said Z'ev.

"Absolutely," agreed Nikki. "But that's not the decision that she made. And I don't think it's the decision that Petra made. But even if we assume her relationship with Maaravi is simply an error in judgement, can we really trust her judgement now?"

"You want me to take my team leader down?"

"I want you to focus on the mission and ask yourself what is the surest way to complete it."

Z'ev didn't respond. Instead, he went back into the kitchen and opened the fridge, staring into it with a grim face.

"Nikki's right, you know," said Philippe as Z've took Nikki's left-overs out of the fridge and opened the styrofoam container.

"What would you know about it?" asked Z'ev.

"If Petra's on the up and up, why haven't you heard from her? I don't know much about the other side of law enforcement, but shouldn't you be getting phone calls and texts and what not? Arjan just got out of prison; your case is falling apart. Shouldn't your team should be regrouping and forming a new strategy? But your phone hasn't made a peep."

Z'ev's phone, responding to a cosmic imperative, chose that moment to ring.

"It's the office," said Z'ev, looking smug.

AMSTERDAM XVI
DOWN BY THE WATER'S EDGE

"Dad," hissed Nikki, as Z'ev walked away, "can you try not to antagonize him? Things are bad enough right now without you throwing in your two cents."

"If he can't take the truth about his corrupt organization that has caused the deaths of countless thousands, then you should break up with him anyway."

"Can't handle the truth… Right. Because he's the one who can't handle the truth."

"It's hard to learn how the world really works, and I really admire you for working for an underground organization. I think it's awesome that you're fighting the system. I just think you should assess whether or not you and that big guy are really…" he hesitated as if trying to phrase things delicately, "compatible in your world view points."

"Dad, seriously, shut up. I can't eavesdrop while you're yapping."

Z'ev actually wasn't saying much. He was nodding and looking grim.

"I'll be right there," he said, hanging up the phone. "I have to go."

"Go where?

"Well, it turns out that someone put a bunch of holes in Anders Hoek."

"Oh," said Nikki, and knew instantaneously that her face had given away too much.

"Oh, that's too bad? Or oh, I know who did that?"

Honesty is the best policy, honesty is the best policy. Really, are we sure? Oh, what the hell.

"I'm pretty sure that he provided the distraction so Val could escape the INTERPOL warehouse."

"So you're saying that the last person we think was with Anders Hoek was Valerie Robinson and now he's dead? And we don't think she's a killer?"

"That's an unfair assumption! Hoek associates with a lot of unsavory people," said Philippe.

"Yes," agreed Z'ev pointedly, but Philippe seemed to miss the point.

"I'll come with you," said Nikki. "Maybe I can spot something that will confir... tell us who shot him."

"Yes," agreed Philippe. "Go show him how it wasn't Val."

Z'ev rolled his eyes. "You just want a chance to escape."

"Of course, he does," said Nikki. "Can't we just handcuff him to the radiator or something?"

"Well, no, because it's a boat and it doesn't have a radiator. But how about the stove?"

"Sounds great," said Nikki.

"No," said Philippe.

"You don't get a vote," said Nikki.

"Are you really OK with this?" asked Z'ev taking out a pair of handcuffs.

"Sure, why not? It keeps him safe. It keeps us safe. Sounds perfect."

"Except for the part where your dad is handcuffed to a radiator."

Nikki shrugged. "We're not doing it for fun and it could be worse."

"I fail to see how," said Philippe.

"I could handcuff you to the toilet," said Nikki.

"I can't believe you would even contemplate that."

"Well, I can't believe you'd contemplate lying to me and trying to use me to get money, so now we're even."

"That is really unfair. I was going to tell you the truth, just not right away. If I had simply written and asked you, you wouldn't have come. These things are better in person."

"So when were you going to tell me the real reason you left?" asked Nikki, hauling him to his feet and walking him to the radiator.

"That really is unfair. Your mother made it very clear that she didn't want me anywhere near you or to tell you the truth. And my mother said it would be damaging."

"And you're so well known for listening to both of those women."

Z'ev clicked the handcuffs in place and then held the door open for Nikki.

"I always knew we were letting you spend too much time with my mother!" he yelled after them.

"You're really OK with this?" he asked glancing back at the boat, as they exited from the gangplank.

"Exacting a little pain and suffering from my selfish, absentee father? Yes, I am. Oh, what? It's not like it's permanent. I'm not keeping him locked in the basement or anything. It's just an hour or two." She checked his face again. "You think I'm being a bad person?"

"No, I really don't. Just a little more hardass than I expected."

"He's probably right. I probably did spend too much time with Grand-Mère. But maybe if he'd been around, mom wouldn't have wanted the parenting break and wouldn't have sent me off to visit in the summers. So whose fault was it really?"

"I don't know. Honestly, I'm having a hard time talking to you in that hair."

"You don't think it looks good?"

"It looks good, but it's like your voice is coming out of a different person. It just throws me off. Anyway, come on, we can take my car."

"That's probably good," agreed Nikki. "Don't want to show up to a crime scene in a stolen car."

"I'm going to pretend I didn't hear that."

"OK," agreed Nikki.

Z'ev's car turned out to be a classic CIA black SUV with police plates.

"Were you trying for stereotypical?" asked Nikki settling in.

"It was what they assigned to me. I'm pretty sure they thought they were being funny. And I'd complain, but this one has seat warmers and a great sound system."

Nikki chuckled.

"OK, when we get to the crime scene, I'm not going to introduce you. Just walk in like you own the place, don't say anything to anyone but me, and if you've got sunglasses and gloves wear them."

"Basic CIA spook routine?" asked Nikki, fishing in her bag for sunglasses and gloves.

"Yes. If someone questions you directly, refer them to me. And since this is a crime scene, it should go without saying that you should try not to touch any evidence."

"Got it," agreed Nikki. "Do you go to a lot of crime scenes?"

"Depends on who I'm working with. I work with the DEA fairly often, so I see some of their stuff. Although, they do a lot of cartels, so most of the time I'd prefer not to see their crime scenes."

"Yeah, I've been doing a lot of work with the Tijuana branch lately. Those girls are fighting an uphill battle. I keep thinking that there's got to be a more systemic approach to fighting the cartels."

"Well, the US could try targeting the economic systems that support the drug cartels. We could stop targeting poor people, and start targeting the affluent buyers in the US. We could stop paying prisons to put people in jail. And we could also stop letting the CIA use the DEA and the drug economy to run foreign policy missions."

Nikki sighed deeply.

"What?"

"Everything you just said, sounds like we're going to have to do more recruiting for the legal department. They've been whining that they need more woman power to fight the rising surge of anti-ovary policies spewing out of the Republican hate hole. And it's a priority, it really is, but what am I supposed to do? Loiter around college campuses? I don't know. Maybe we could look at a targeted long-term strategy to undermine some of the cartel banking practices and work on public policy here. I don't know, more women in office? Or would more female police be better? I'll talk to Shirley. She's the public policy liaison. She'll have some thoughts."

Z'ev was staring at her.

"I was using the word *we* generically. I didn't mean that you should actually do something about it."

"Who else is going to do something about it? I wish you could talk with Shirley. It sounds like you have some good ideas."

"Those aren't ideas. That's me bitching about work."

"At work we say take the top three complaints and build policy or procedure around them. If there is that much consensus about what the problems are then we should be able to attack them."

"Carrie Mae has a lot of sayings."

"It was the founder. She was apparently very pithy and liked to cross stitch little sayings into things. Mrs. Merrivel has a framed pillowcase of the one about the .38 and mascara in her office—it was a personal gift."

"The founder?" he asked, distracted as he consulted his phone, looking at a map.

Nikki tried to assess if he was being purposefully obtuse, or was simply distracted. Everyone knew about the founder. "You know, Carrie Mae Robart, the heiress that turned down the fortune of father's tobacco money to start Carrie Mae Cosmetics in her garage?"

"Oh my God. You mean that Carrie Mae has been…" he waved a free hand at Nikki, "from the beginning?"

"Of course. Ms. Robart was inspired by the revolutionary movements of the time—the feminists and Black Panthers. She just thought that the overt statements of the Panthers led to targeting from the FBI; she didn't want to expose any of her ladies to that."

"She just wanted to help women?" Z'ev's tone implied disbelief.

"Yes, what's wrong with that?"

"Nothing's wrong with that. I just can't believe no one

noticed."

"Lots of people noticed. It's just that most of them weren't men, and if men did notice they considered whatever action had taken place a one-off. Because, you know, women couldn't possibly do that."

"Hm," said Z'ev, which either meant that he was trying to figure out directions or he thought she was directing her comments at him.

"Do you want me to navigate so you don't have to look at your phone and drive?" She held out her hand for his phone, but he pulled the phone further away.

"No, I've got it. We're almost there anyway."

He turned the SUV down a narrow alley and then another and another until Nikki was concerned about finding their way back out again. From the smell they were nearing one of the more tidal affected canals and the buildings were mostly old warehouses that looked on the verge falling down. Nikki reconsidered *verge* as they passed a building that had crumbled to one level. Z'ev drove on until at last he came out into an open space meant for big truck turn arounds. It was full of police cars with flashing lights.

"Remember," said Z'ev turning off the engine. "Don't talk to anyone. Don't answer any questions. Just point them all at me."

"Got it," said Nikki, putting on her sunglasses, and pulling on her gloves. "Don't worry, Ellen and I play it this way all the time. Silent is more threatening."

"Ellen I could see," said Z'ev. "Probably wouldn't work with Jane though."

Nikki snorted. "No, she gets too excited and can't stop talking. She can't help it. OK." She blew out a big gust of air. "Time to get my game face on." She looked at Z'ev and burst out laughing. "OK, no seriously, you cannot look at me when I'm doing this."

"Hey, I want to know what your game face looks like."

Nikki stuck out her tongue. "It's going to look like Blutarsky from *Animal House* if you keep looking at me."

Z'ev put up his hands like horse blinders and turned his head to the left. Nikki shook off a final giggle and tried to shake off a feeling of embarrassment. She consulted in other territories all the time. Doing it in front of her boyfriend shouldn't be that big of a deal.

Only, it's totally a big deal.

She pulled the collar up on her coat, tugged on her gloves and set her face to serious. She gave Z'ev a nod and he led the way through the cars and through an archway in a tumbled brick wall. The interior space was a warehouse that looked as though it had suffered a fire sometime in the last decade and never been repaired. The roof had collapsed in places. Glass littered a carpet of grass like deadly sequins. Here and there, pools of stagnant water collected among the rubble against the far wall. A cluster of police personnel marked their destination. A pathway had been marked out with police tape, but the police pathway diverged from a naturally beaten-down trail in the grass. A technician in white booties was walking along that trail with evidence flags and a camera. Nikki dutifully followed Z'ev, along the police pathway, keeping her expression set to bored behind her sunglasses.

Z'ev ducked under the police tape and held it for Nikki. Nikki stood up and looked around the demarcated crime scene. She'd never been to an active crime scene. She'd only ever caused them before. Anders Hoek was lying face up, eyes open to the sky, a bullet hole in his forehead and one in his chest.

It was not her first dead body, but she found that she was feeling awkward about making eye contact.

"Coralles! Good you're here. He's just where you said he'd be. Too bad we didn't get here earlier." The officer or agent or whatever INTERPOL had, was Asian with close cropped hair and a heavy wool pea coat.

Z'ev was responding, but Nikki ignored them, squatting down to look at the body trying to pretend he wasn't a person— that he was just a problem that she needed to solve. The bullet hole in his forehead had powder burns around it and there was stippling in the face. She wasn't an expert, but in her experience that meant that the gun had been ridiculously close to his face. Which also meant, that since very rarely does someone let a gun get that close to their face, whoever had shot Anders Hoek had shot him first in the chest and then in face. Nikki scanned a little farther and saw the gun, a .38 revolver marked with an evidence flag on the far side of the body. The gun had an electrical tape wrapped handle and a short three inch barrel. From this angle, Nikki could see that there were bullets left in the cylinder.

Nikki looked around the scene. A six pack of beer was resting on a chunk of concrete, but two of the slots in the cardboard carrier were empty. A set of car keys sat next to the beer. She looked in the grass and spotted two bottles behind the rock. Nikki knelt down for a closer look at the bottles. They were La Trappe and had a cathedral on the label. Both beers were about three quarters down.

"Yah, we spotted those," said the man talking to Z'ev, pivoting away to focus on her. "We're waiting on photography."

Nikki ignored him and kicked out into a plank position to smell the grass at the mouth of the bottle. There was the barest hint of hops and a stronger whiff of mud and oil. From her prone position she could see that there was a smudge of lipstick on the glass.

"His phone is gone?" she asked.

"We haven't found it yet."

"You had him in custody. I'm assuming you got his number. You're going to be able to pull his logs if you haven't already?" She stood up and realized Z'ev was shooting her death rays of fury.

Right… Not talking to anyone. That was one of the rules. Meh. It was a stupid rule.

The INTERPOL officer looked at Z'ev and then back at Nikki. "He didn't have a phone on him when we arrested him and he doesn't have one registered to him."

Nikki nodded. Ever since the incident with Z'ev in South America, Nikki frequently had the team leave phones behind before going out on mission. It made sense that Hoek would live off burners and follow a similar protocol.

"Who's asking?"

"She's with me," said Z'ev, sourly. "Don't worry about her."

"I am worried about her. I'm worried about her contaminating my crime scene."

Nikki looked up and around the grounds. Anders had picked a spot not far from parking, under the last remaining bit of roof with relatively comfortable seating.

"Don't worry about me," said Nikki. "I've seen what I need to see. Z'ev I'm going to make a phone call. I'll meet you back at the car. You might as well look in his car for his phone. I don't think you'll find it, but you might as well look."

She walked back along the path, already pulling out her phone. It took her a moment to find the number of the bar she'd been to with Val and even longer for Femke to pick up the phone.

"Femke, this is Val's friend."

Femke groaned. "Not another problem with accommodations?"

"No, the houseboat is fine. I want to ask you about Anders Hoek."

"What did that asshole do now?"

"What no colorful Dutch swearwords? I've been trying to work *bokkelul* into a sentence for days."

"You don't work it in—it is its own sentence. And Anders doesn't rate creativity. He's just a *gemiddelde* jerk with a Viking complex and a good beard."

"Did he have a girlfriend?"

There was a pause Nikki interpreted as surprise. "Yah? I think. Hold on." There was a muffling of the phone. "Hey! Anders with the beard... *Heeft Anders een vriendin?*" There was a reply that Nikki couldn't hear. Then Femke came back on. "We think so. But she never came around. He just talked about her. Espen thinks she was away a lot, but maybe also kind of a bitch."

"Any physical description?"

"No, sorry."

"No problem, thanks. Hey, if you hear from Val, tell her to call me."

Femke sighed. "I'm not a messaging service, and I don't get involved."

"Didn't ask you to involve yourself. I've just misplaced her. If you happen to see her in your capacity as bartender, tell her to call me."

"Mm. Maybe."

"Thanks again," said Nikki and hung up the phone.

"Well, Sherlock," said Z'ev approaching with a quietness that was annoying in someone that big. He should make more noise. "Do you have it all figured out?"

"No, but I'm making progress." She tried to assess if he was still mad. He didn't look mad.

"I think you gave me street cred. Van Bergen was really annoyed by your little performance and kept calling you my CIA spook friend."

"It wasn't a performance. I was trying to figure out if Val killed him. The Asian guy's name is Van Bergen, really?"

Z'ev shrugged. "It's the Netherlands. What else would he be named? What did you find out?"

"I think he was shot by a woman," said Nikki. "I just don't think it was Val."

"How is there time to wedge another woman into this? You know she was with him only three hours ago! You just don't want to admit Val killed him."

"It's true, I don't want Val to have killed him. I want my father to be dating someone nice, but I'm not delusional, I know who Val is. I honestly don't think Val was here."

He paused, lips pursed as if holding in his next comment, and assessing his options.

"OK, walk me through it. Why do you think that?"

"Two beer bottles, one had lipstick on it."

"Confirmation a woman was here. CSI also found high heel prints. No reason it couldn't have been Val."

"True except the lipstick was in the coral family. Val doesn't go any brighter than merlot—she likes her lipstick to be red, red, and more red. Also, the beer was La Trappe, a local brand, and had been drunk. Val hates beer. Not that she's incapable of drinking it, but since being in Amsterdam she's espoused nothing but hatred for their love of beer. I don't think it's likely that she'd suddenly change her mind."

"The bottles were lying on the ground. They could have been spilled."

"I smelled the ground. I don't think very much spilled out from either of the bottles. They were mostly drunk."

"Not definitive," said Z'ev.

"Then there's the gun. It's clearly a drop piece."

"An illegal piece. Why wouldn't Val use it?"

"All of Val's guns were illegal. Most recently she was carrying a Ruger she took off of Anders. She wouldn't need to drop the gun she used. Also, not for nothing, but she prefers larger guns. She says .38's are for pussies. Then there's the location. This place is obscure."

"If she knew Anders then she'd been here before. Val could know the place."

"But why would she? If she'd been with him since she fled the warehouse, why go here to kill him when she could just dump him in an alley and be done with it?"

"You said it yourself; this place is obscure. She probably wanted to be away from traffic cams."

Nikki shook her head, unconvinced. "She has been to Amsterdam before, but she wasn't a regular. Of course, it is possible that she'd been here with Anders, since he had clearly been here multiple times. You're right, it's a long distance from traffic cams, but also once inside, he picked a spot protected from the elements and with a place to sit. That's not something you do on a whim."

"So?"

"He's a native to this city. Who is he meeting out here, routinely, that he couldn't meet in a pub or someplace else?"

Z'ev shrugged. "OK, fine, I'm thinking about it. What about the phone? Why did you ask about the phone?"

"Val wouldn't need to take his phone. She's been using nothing but burners for weeks. You can pull his LUDs all day long, but it won't give you anything that links to her. She wouldn't need to ditch his phone. All she'd need to do is ditch hers. So why is his phone missing?"

Z'ev was wearing the hostile expression that was a definite hallmark that she was making a point that he didn't want to hear.

"So who shot him then?" he asked.

"That's a good question—probably his girlfriend. I put out a feeler on that, but couldn't get a description. But the question I'd actually like answered is how you knew Anders would be here?"

AMSTERDAM XVII
THE GIRL CAN'T HELP IT

For a microsecond Z'ev's expression froze in place then immediately slid into something polite and casual.

"What do you mean?"

"You told INTERPOL to come here to look for Anders."

Z'ev grunted and dropped the calm expression for annoyed.

"I was hoping you hadn't heard that."

"Hope springs eternal in the human heart. Sadly, from my experience, that hope is often crushed. How'd you know where he was?"

Z'ev shifted uncomfortably. "I tagged him. The Agency got these cool little GPS microtags and I had a few with me. I ran Hoek's guns through the system, but I kept getting delays. And then I heard he was getting released on a paperwork technicality, so I ran down to evidence and I stuck one on his wallet. He bounced around the city for a little bit, went to the INTERPOL warehouse, made two stops and then came here. I figured that the warehouse gig had to have witnesses or be on surveillance which should have been enough to pick him back up on suspicion of blowing crap up or whatever. So when he hadn't moved for about forty-five minutes, I told the INTERPOL crew to go pick him up. But apparently there was a reason he hadn't moved."

"He was dead. What's the deal with delays on the guns?"

"I don't know, some sort of system error. I finally gave up and just had them run the serials through Langley. That may not get anything, but I was tired of wanting to punch a computer."

"Fair enough. OK, well, you might not be convinced that Val didn't do it, but I am. That means he dropped her at one of his previous stops. Can we pull up where he went? Maybe we'll catch a break and find a spot labeled *Val's Hideout*."

Z'ev shrugged and pulled out his phone.

"Oh my God. You have an app for that? Must be nice having government sized budgets."

"When you can't be morally pure it helps to have gobs of money."

"OK, here's INTERPOL. From there he—"

"Coralles!"

Van Bergen yelled for Z'ev, waving at them from the bumper of Hoek's car.

"I'll be right back," said Z'ev, handing her the phone.

Nikki opened her own phone, using the map app to look at the location after the INTERPOL warehouse. Z'ev's app only showed coordinates. It didn't show anything useful such as addresses, neighborhood, or street views.

Location one, post-warehouse, was a hotel in the red light district. Location two was a bodega—or whatever the Dutch equivalent of corner grocery mart was—probably his beer buying location. Location three was near the city's port. Val could have exited at any one of those locations. Nikki looked at Z'ev's app in frustration. It didn't give her enough information. How long had Hoek stayed at any of these spots? Had he been to any of the locations previously?

"The girls could fix this in no time," Nikki muttered to herself, staring at the screen in annoyance. She looked for a menu button. Maybe she was missing something? There didn't appear to be any dropdowns. Why have an app if it wasn't user friendly?

The phone began to ring. The caller ID showed a Virginia prefix. She walked quickly over to Hoek's car where Z'ev and Van Bergen were deep in conversation.

"Big brother is calling," she said, shoving the phone at him.

Z'ev grunted, took the phone and walked away, leaving her staring at Van Bergen.

"We can't find his phone," said Van Bergen leaning toward her aggressively. Nikki shrugged. Van Bergen's English was good, but also Americanized, which was unusual. Most Europeans learned English in an English style, where phones were *mobiles* and attitudes were reserved. "But you knew we wouldn't. Anders Hoek was moving up the slime ball ladder. We can't have the kind of guy who can kill a guy like Anders Hoek loose in this city. If you know something you need to tell us."

Nikki tried not to smile. Van Bergen had learned his English from Humphrey Bogart movies. Under the amusement, she also felt a pang of guilt. This was something she never had to encounter with Carrie Mae. Being under the radar meant she didn't spend a lot of time with police. She hadn't realized they could be quite so passionate.

"I'm working on a tangential matter," said Nikki, carefully. "I really don't know who killed him. But the missing cellphone would indicate to me that he probably knew his killer and she probably didn't want to leave that evidence behind."

The least she could do was point him in the right direction.

"But the file on Hoek doesn't mention a girlfriend. The only mention of a woman is that Irene Adler he was looking for and come on, we all know that's an alias."

"And we all know files don't have every detail. My sources say he had a girlfriend."

"That doesn't scan. What kind of girlfriend meets you out here?"

"Good question," responded Nikki. "You could always work the problem backwards."

Van Bergen's face adequately expressed confusion.

"You have a location and a time frame. See if you can get a cell company to give you every call made that match those parameters. See if anything pops."

"That's potentially thousands of unrelated calls. I don't think I can get a warrant for that."

"Show the cell company some dead body pictures and ask for their help," suggested Nikki with a shrug. Van Bergen looked thoughtful.

"I'm going to make some calls. You available for drinks later? We should touch base and compare notes."

"No, she's not," said Z'ev.

"Sorry," said Nikki, ignoring Z'ev, "that tangential matter has some explosive properties that need to be kept in check. Maybe next time I'm in town." She smiled sweetly and walked back to the car, leaving Z'ev to deal with whatever happened next.

She had barely settled into the seat when she got a Snapchat alert.

Hey Rita Hayworth! You there?

Nikki could practically hear the giggle that followed that. The screen name was Jayne Mansfield.

Hey Jenny. I'm here for a couple of minutes. At least until Z'ev kills me with the daggers shooting from his eyes.

What'd you do now?

Managed to turn the course of his investigation and

GET HIT ON BY A CUTE INTERPOL DETECTIVE.

HA! WELL, AT LEAST HE'S TALKING TO YOU? I JUST HAVE A QUICK QUESTION—THE M'S ARE AT THE HOSPITAL FOR A FOLLOW UP, SO I DON'T WANT TO INTERRUPT. MELISSA KANE JUST RELEASED THE MANUAL FOR THE GIRL'S CENTERS—MEANING THAT HER PORTION OF THE HOMELAND INITIATIVE IS FINALLY OUT OF BETA.

THAT'S AWESOME!

Nikki gave a small fist pump of elation. Melissa Kane was running Carrie Mae's very first center for underprivileged girls in Detroit. It was the first cohesive program that openly carried the Carrie Mae name; up until now everything had either been lobbying, donation, or covert. Nikki was happy to know that she and her team been a small part of getting the center off the ground.

YES, IT REALLY IS. THREE GIRLS SUCCESSFULLY LAUNCHED INTO COLLEGE. SHE THINKS SHE'LL DOUBLE THAT NEXT YEAR. REALLY EXCITED FOR HER. BUT IN THE MANUAL, IT HAS A BUDGETARY LINE ITEM FOR SECURITY AND INSTEAD OF PUTTING A NUMBER, SHE PUT 'SEE MRS. MERRIVEL FOR PERSONALIZED SECURITY PLANS' AND GIVES THE LA DIVISIONS CONTACT INFO. WHICH, ON ONE HAND IS HILARIOUSLY AWESOME. ON THE OTHER HAND, SINCE THE MANUAL IS THE OFFICE EXCITEMENT OF THE DAY, IT MEANS THAT DARLA IS MOMENTS AWAY FROM DIALING MY NUMBER AND ASKING ME ABOUT IT. WHICH WOULD BE FINE IF I COULD REMEMBER IF THAT WHOLE INCIDENT WAS ON OR OFF THE BOOKS.

ON. THE FILE SHOULD BE AVAILABLE TO DARLA. I THINK IT ORIGINATES AS A SUPPORT REQUEST FROM MELISSA, SO IT SHOULD BE UNDER HER NAME, AND MARKED AS APPROVED BY MRS. M. IF DARLA DOESN'T ASK, BE SURE TO FIND A WAY TO BRING IT UP. THE TEAM COULD USE THE PR.

ON IT. HOW'RE YA'LL DOING OVER THERE?

Um, let's see… My dad, who is currently handcuffed to a houseboat radiator, is dating my nemesis, who tried to double cross me and is currently on the loose in Amsterdam and suspected (by my boyfriend) of murder. My boyfriend is still mad at me for lying to him for our entire relationship. There's also an arms dealer who may or may want to kill my dad. And then there's his son, who kidnapped my dad originally, and is also trying to sell weapons, and he's mixed up with an INTERPOL agent who I swear is dirty, but no one will believe me.

So it's Thursday?

Possibly. I literally cannot remember. I'm trying not to freak out.

Don't freak out. We don't need another Nicaragua.

That's unfair. That taxi deserved it.

Yes, it did. You'll figure it out. You always do.

I think you mean— I always get lucky. I can't rely on that.

Fortune favors the prepared. You get lucky because you put in the work. You've put the work in with Z'ev. He's a bit thrown right now, but tell him what's in your heart and you two can pull through. Meanwhile, uncuff your dad and tell him just what kind of skank he's dating. You need him to start being on your team for once.

I tried, but I don't think he believed me. And actually, I kind of think Val might be in love with him. I guess it will depend on whether or not she comes back for him.

We'll find out then. On the arms dealer front, I don't know… Shoot them? Blow them up? Whatever seems appropriate at the time, honey.

Nikki smiled at her phone screen. Even through text she could hear Jenny's Southern twang reminding her to do the appropriate thing regarding illegal weapons dealers. Z'ev startled her by opening the driver's side door.

"Good news?" he asked looking from her to her phone.

"Melissa Kane just pushed the Girl's Center out of Beta. It's going National," said Nikki.

Z'ev's back. Gotta go.

"I don't know what that means."

Good luck! We love you!

"You remember me telling you about the Detroit Center? Carrie Mae put together a program headed up by a social worker, Melissa Kane? Easy access, combined services, education assistance, one location, free help for any girl who needs it."

"You went down there for a few days, didn't you? Something about coordinating some sort of kick-off event?" Z'ev started the car and then seemed to put the pieces together. "There was no event, was there?"

"No, there was a little issue with some gangs. We sorted it out. Anyway, the program is going National! It's super exciting. That's real, long term change for women's lives!"

Z'ev was staring at her.

"What?"

"I thought…" he stopped.

"Thought what?"

"I thought when you said—when I found out about Carrie Mae—I guess I just figured that all this hoo-rah, up with girls, yay Carrie Mae stuff was part of the act. But it's not, is it? Carrie Mae is really out there doing it, aren't they?"

"Doing what?"

"Trying to save the world."

"Who's got time to save the world? No, we're just shooting for *Helping Women Everywhere*," laughed Nikki, repeating the original Carrie Mae slogan.

"Right," said Z'ev, shaking his head. "OK, what now? Back to get your dad out of handcuffs?"

"I guess. If we have to," replied Nikki, with a sigh.

"Probably should," replied Z'ev. "Also, and just for the record, no matter what else happens, you are not allowed to date Van Bergen."

"I can date whoever I want," snapped Nikki automatically. "What's wrong with Van Bergen?"

"Nothing's wrong with Van Bergen! It's just not OK to make him stop hating you in the space of one phone call and then start dating him while I'm standing right there!"

"Oh, that. I was just trying to be helpful. I'm not going to date Van Bergen. Besides you were standing right there. *Tres* awkward."

"It's like we're not having the same conversation," said Z'ev, maneuvering the car to go back through the alleyways.

"What are you talking about? I'm totally agreeing with you."

"Yes, but you're agreeing with me because you think so, not because I say so."

"Well, when you're right, you're right."

"And when you disagree with me, I'm wrong."

"Yes? Maybe? No? I'm sorry, but I can't argue any more until you tell me what we're arguing about."

"I find you very… frustrating sometimes," said Z'ev.

"OK," said Nikki.

"That's all you're going to say?"

Nikki floundered slightly, not sure how to respond. "Ellen

once told me that she had a severe rough patch with one of her daughters when she was about twelve and she finally just took her to a therapist. And after a few times the therapist stopped her in the middle of a session and asked, 'Are you aware that every time your daughter expresses an emotion you correct her?' And Ellen said, 'Well, she shouldn't feel that way about Great Aunt Ruby.' And the therapist said, 'Emotions aren't right or wrong, only actions are.' When she told me that story, it was like a little light bulb. My mom does that to me all the time. I'm not going to do that to you. If you feel frustrated and angry, then you are. What am I supposed to say to that?"

"I'm hurt Nikki. All those other things are because I'm hurt."

"And I can't argue that either. All I can argue is whether or not I'm going date Van Bergen or find Val or catch Arjan Meise. Those are the only arguments I can win."

He was silent, apparently concentrating on driving.

"There are other things besides arguing," he said. "You could try talking to me. Everyone else has tried it—your ex-boyfriend, the girls, Mr. M. You're the only one who hasn't given it a go."

"That's not really my skill set," said Nikki. "Besides every time we try, we get interrupted or you threaten to arrest me or my dad."

"Yeah, well, those are the only arguments *I* can win."

But I'm not in jail yet, so you're not really winning, are you?

Nikki bit back her retort as it occurred to her to wonder how much Z'ev really wanted to win those arguments. Perhaps, discretion might be the better part of valor in this instance.

She cleared her throat. "OK, well, if we can stop the Meise's… Can I call them Mice?"

"No."

"If we can arrest them or whatever, and manage to figure out what to do about my father and Val, with the usual caveat of, you know, living through it, then I think we should probably consider talking to each other. About stuff."

"I would like that," he agreed in his most civil, getting along tone.

Nikki was afraid to talk again for the rest of the trip in case it ruined the moment.

AMSTERDAM XVIII
DEAL

Her father, when they arrived back at the house boat, was half-way out of the cuffs. Nikki confiscated his two bent paper clips and unlocked him.

"I knew I should have stayed in better practice," he said, without a trace of resentment as he flexed his fingers. "Lock-picking skills go rusty if you don't use them."

"Could be the tools," suggested Nikki. "Bobby pins do work better than paperclips."

"Sadly, I don't travel with any bobby pins handy. What did you find out?" he asked plumping himself back into a chair as Z'ev investigated the kitchen.

"Anders Hoek is dead. I don't think Val killed him."

"Opinions vary," said Z'ev taking the left over Thai food out of the fridge. Nikki couldn't read his mood—his emotions had folded back in on themselves.

"Other opinions are wrong," said Philippe firmly. "Hoek wasn't a nice guy. From what I hear he and his weird girlfriend were trying to move serious cargo."

"What kind of cargo?" asked Z'ev.

"You know, he didn't say come to think of it. I just assumed it was drugs. I don't touch that kind of smuggling, so I didn't inquire. But it could have been weapons, or people."

"What do you know about his girlfriend?" asked Nikki.

"Nothing. Just that she was really pushing him to step up his game. That's why he took the gig with us. He needed the cash for some scheme his girlfriend came up with."

"So you never met her?" asked Z'ev. He was searching the kitchen, after a few minutes he gave up and finally settled on washing the chopsticks Nikki had left in the sink.

"No. Which I thought was kind of weird. I mean, we were doing an informal interview kind of thing, to see if we were a good fit to pull off the plan, so it wasn't really socializing. But still, it seemed weird that she didn't show."

"Any clue what her big plan was?" asked Nikki.

"No. And I didn't ask. None of my business. Just got the impression that it was a stretch for him. Some people aren't meant to be The Big Boss, *tu comprendes*? Really felt like this girl was pushing."

"Hm," said Z'ev.

"So that's out of the way. What have you heard about Val? Have you called her?"

"Believe it or not, *Papa*, Val is not my primary focus. We need to stop Maaravi and Petra and the stupid arms deal you set up."

"Yes, but Val could help with that. We should call her."

"We're not going to," said Nikki.

"You're not being sensible," said Philippe impatiently.

"How do you know she didn't just leave town, or that she didn't get killed like Hoek?" asked Z'ev.

"Val wouldn't get taken down by some girl," said Philippe rolling his eyes. "But it's true, Nikki could have scared her off. That's why we should call her."

"I actually meant that she could have just cut her losses and left you here," said Z'ev.

"She wouldn't do that," said Philippe, but Nikki caught a whiff of uncertainty.

"Well, that's great for you," said Z'ev. "But I don't really need her. I'm trying to stop an arms dealer and his son. Frankly, I think she's a complication we don't need. I think we should forget her and focus on the task at hand."

"Nikki," gasped Philippe, "are you going to let him talk like that?"

Z'ev paused, chopsticks full of drunken noodles half-way to his mouth, and looked at Nikki in disbelief. Nikki made a gesture that was half apology, half resignation.

"We don't need to call her," said Nikki soothingly. "She's going to call us."

"Why?" said Z'ev.

"We have what she wants. We have her case book and we have my dad.

"Did you know that Arjan sells guns to Boku Haram?" asked Z'ev, discarding the basil from the take-out food container.

"I did not," said Nikki. "But I assumed that, as an arms dealer, he wasn't selling them to nice people."

"Also Al Quaeda and Daish. Cutting off his pipeline of weapons would hurt a lot of people who spread terror."

"I'm with you."

"No you're not. You're worrying about Val and your dad. I'm thinking about the mission. This is all personal stuff. You have your dad. Let Val do whatever Val's going to do. You want to prove that you're one of the good guys, then this is your chance. Stop messing around with them and help me stop Arjan Meise. Let's call in the rest of the INTERPOL team and give them what you've got on Maaravi."

"Well, what I've got on Maaravi is also what I have on Petra. But you seemed to think that I shouldn't be besmirching her name.

And if I give them that information they're going to ask where I got it. Which, oops, means Dad and I end up in jail. So I would prefer not to go that route. I am also thinking about the mission. And I would be an idiot to ignore a heavy hitter like Val or think that she's simply gone away. Also, since I'm an operative without a back-up team, I have to rely on the resources I have at hand—which in this case is Val."

"How is she a resource?" demanded Z'ev.

"If I'm right, she is going to want my dad back. She would have discovered almost instantly that the case book was a phony. So why has she taken so long to get in contact?"

"Because she left town?"

"No, because she needed time to strengthen her offer."

"What offer?"

"I'm telling you, she's going to call. And when she does she's going to offer a trade. She's going to offer me something I want, in exchange for something she wants. Since she knows I want Maaravi that will probably be what she offers me. The real question is, which one is she going to ask for in return—my dad or the book?"

"Really? It's going to be me. Of course, it's going to be me." Nikki and Z'ev ignored him.

"We could still use INTERPOL back up."

"No," said Nikki firmly. "They're not going to listen to me. I mean, Van Bergen might. But I can't date everyone just so they take me seriously. And honestly, they'll just get in the way."

"They'll just get in the way, or you work better alone?" Z'ev asked sarcastically.

"No, I work better when I've got support from Jenny, Ellen, and Jane. But since I'm currently off-grid, I don't exactly have that luxury."

"They may not listen to you, but the INTERPOL task force will listen to me. What's wrong with letting me lead?"

"Hey!" Philippe exclaimed. "Stop trying to turn the ship here. Nikki's the one with the plan. You wouldn't even know about Petra and Maaravi if it wasn't for her."

"You just want her to solve your love life."

"If she hadn't sent you to grab me, my love life would have been fine. She broke it; she needs to fix it. Really *chère*," Philippe said, giving her sad, disappointed eyes, "I appreciate that you've got problems, but couldn't you have looked the other way just this once?"

"Dad," Nikki ignored his question, "what do you know about Maaravi and his guns? Did he ever find a buyer?"

Philippe looked distinctly uncomfortable.

"Dad? What do you know about Maaravi's gun deal?"

"You have to understand, that I'm an *artiste*. It is not enough to come up with the system. I have to know that it works."

"What did you do, Dad?"

"Nothing, nothing. But I did tell you that I offered to connect Maaravi to some people I know, and so when he couldn't find the client list... I did."

"Oh my God. You said he turned you down!"

"He did at first, but I mean I had everything set up. We were just missing a buyer, so when he couldn't get his dad's list...I made an introduction."

"When is the deal going down?" demanded Nikki.

"Oh. Well, I don't know exactly. Sorry."

"What do you mean you don't know?" demanded Nikki. "You just said you brokered the deal."

"No. I didn't broker anything. He forced me to smuggle guns into the country under his flower shipping business and when he said he needed a buyer, I just introduced him to some very nice Chechen independence fighters. I thought maybe their needs could meet. But once I made the introduction and showed them the set up I was uninvited from the party. So no, I don't know."

Nikki stared in disbelief.

"Try kicking him in the shin," suggested Z'ev.

Nikki's phone suddenly buzzed with an incoming text and they all jumped slightly as it rattled on the table.

I WANT PHILIPPE. YOU WANT MAARAVI. I KNOW WHERE HE IS. LET'S TALK.

"It's Val," said Nikki, showing the text to Z'ev.

"I guess you'd better call her," he said closing up the take-out container.

The phone picked up on the third ring.

"You swapped out my goddamn case book."

"I'm also wearing your sweater." Z'ev moved to stand next to her, so he could hear Val's half of the conversation.

"The black cashmere? Damn it, I knew I should have taken that with me."

"What can I say, after someone shot a bunch of holes in the building, it got kind of drafty. I got cold."

"You know, you could have just said, *Val, I know what you're doing and I've already had the case book swapped out for someone's recipe collection.* This whole thing could have been avoided."

"And if I'd said that, you would have denied it. And then you would have come up with another way to get what you want."

"Probably true. Although, I am totally going to try the Spicy Mussels with Chorizo and Wine. Out of curiosity, where is my case book?"

"Looking Glass Protocol has it being couriered to the LA branch. It's probably being dropped off with Mrs. M right now."

"Damn it, Red. Do you know how hard it is for people like Philippe and I to retire? I have certain lifestyle needs and I really would like to stop shooting people and go sit on a beach."

"And while I'm sympathetic to that, I don't think you should be able to sit on a beach after blowing up my life and enabling terrorists."

"You know what your problem is?"

"I'm sure you'll tell me."

"Your problem is that you make too many things your problem. You can't save the world Nikki. Why do you even care?"

Nikki didn't have a good answer for that.

"Because someone has to," she said. "And today it's me."

"OK, fine. Well today, it is not me. Today, all I care about is the beach. And my beach would be a lot more fun with Philippe. I want him back."

"Let's hear your offer."

"You want Arjan and Maaravi. I know you do. You think if you can tie the Arjan situation up in a bow, your boyfriend won't rat Carrie Mae out to the CIA."

Nikki avoided eye contact with Z'ev.

"There's just a couple of problems with that plan," Val continued. "One, Arjan just went into Maaravi's hotel room and he was packing a little more than an extra sweater under his coat, if you know what I'm saying. He's figured out that the kid double-crossed him."

"Is Maaravi still alive?"

"Yes, Petra got there a couple of minutes before Arjan did.

You know, I might have gone with your theory about Petra being the one in charge, if Maaravi hadn't cold-cocked her and dumped her in the trunk of his car."

"Where are they now?"

"Ah, you would like to know that, would you?"

"Yes, I would," said Nikki, reining in her temper.

"Well, I want Philippe, a beach, and," there was the sound of pages flipping, "a Coconut Shrimp Salad with a Mint Margarita Slushie."

"And how do I know that you won't give us crap information, take Dad and disappear?"

"I'm not really out to screw you kid. I just want what's mine. It's the Aalsmeer Flower Market. You've got one hour. Don't be late."

The phone clicked off.

"What'd she say?" asked Philippe.

"She said she wants a margarita," said Nikki.

"Really? That's so unlike her. She usually prefers her drinks to be a little less fluffy."

"And she wants to go to the beach."

"Are you sure you were talking to Val. I mean, she's got the pallor of a vampire. We fight over the sunscreen. We go through vats of it really. She says sun damage is the number one cause of aging skin."

"Nikki says that too," said Z'ev.

"Proper skin care is extremely important," said Nikki defensively. "Sunscreen, waterproof mascara, and a silenced .38 will take you just about anywhere you want to go in life." It was one of the Carrie Mae Academy's mantras, and as soon as she said it, she regretted it. There were some things that men just didn't understand.

"I hadn't really…" Philippe trailed off. "You know, I'm not really sure where to go with that statement, so I'm going to pretend it didn't happen. What's the plan—are we meeting Val or what?"

"We should call in my team," said Z'ev.

"And tell them what?" asked Nikki. "Your girlfriend's father's girlfriend says that Maaravi Meise is at the 21 Flavors, oh sorry, I mean the Aalsmeer Flower Market, preparing to sell guns to some very nice Chechens?"

Z'ev rubbed his head. "If Maaravi has Petra— By the way, I would like to have it noted that dumping her in the trunk of his car, doesn't sound like she's flipped to me."

Nikki shrugged her acknowledgement.

"Then we have a serious cause to go pick him up. We should have back-up."

"Any back-up exposes Carrie Mae to more risk," said Nikki. "I can't have that. Besides, he probably only has a couple of guys. That's a cake walk. You're all the back-up I need."

"And how do we know Val isn't waiting across the street with a rifle or, you know, a silenced .38?"

"Dad, would you continue to date Val if she killed me?"

"What? No! I would be very upset. I need grandkids. Which, by the way, none of us are getting any younger. I'm just throwing that out there."

"I can kick him in the shins if you like," suggested Z'ev as Nikki gaped, mouth open, at her father.

She shook her head, trying to clear it. "Somebody should. Look, you heard Val. Arjan is on the warpath. If we can nab Maaravi, rescue Petra, and stop the weapons exchange, then you can call INTERPOL. They can swoop in and stop Arjan, and you'll have saved the day."

"And what will you be doing while I'm saving the day?"

"I will be… dealing with Val."

"What does that mean?"

"I'm interested in that one too," Philippe added.

Nikki vacillated. "I don't know what it means, OK?"

"Nikki, they're criminals. They need to be locked up," said Z'ev.

"You know, comments like that will get you disinvited from Christmas dinner," said Philippe.

"Dad, you haven't been home for Christmas since that one time when I was in high-school. And now that I'm thinking of it, I'm pretty sure you were on the lam and hiding out."

"I try not to live in the past," said Philippe.

"You mean, you try not to remember things that make you look bad."

"If we're doing this, we need to go," said Z'ev. "We don't have a lot of time."

He looked like he was about to say something else, but was interrupted by Nikki's phone.

Nikki checked the number, swiping her thumb to answer automatically, and heard Z'ev exhale loudly. "OK, so I got the documents translated," began Jane, as if they had only been talking moments ago. Nikki blinked, trying to recall what documents Jane was talking about. "They appear to be an appeal for the release of Arjan Meise based on illegal surveillance. I ran background on Meise: Dutch arms dealer with a nasty reputation and a long history of doing bad things."

"I'm afraid you're a little bit late to the party," said Nikki. "We already know about Meise, and he's actually already been released from prison."

"Oh. Sorry. I would have been faster, but it's surprisingly hard to find a freelance Dutch translator who can do all the legal mumbo jumbo and tell you what it means."

"Not your fault," said Nikki. "But thanks for calling." She made an apologetic face at Z'ev, and mouthed the word *Jane*. He nodded.

"Do you know if he got reimbursed for the dog food?"

"I don't, um, what? What does that mean?"

"Well, from what you sent it looked like they were demanding that the court reimburse him for having to have someone take care of his dog while he was in prison. But it's possible that someone edited that out. It got a little hard to decipher at some point with all the red lines all over it."

"Dog bed. It was a dog bed in the photo. He has a dog. Dad, did you know Arjan has a dog?"

"Wouldn't surprise me," said Philippe with a shrug. "He always had some sort of useless little dog running around. He used to threaten to feed people's ears to his dog. Which wouldn't have been that frightening, except that Dustov swore he saw him do it one time."

"Hey, you found your dad!" exclaimed Jane.

"Yeah, except I lost Val."

"That's not good," said Jane.

"She's not lost, lost. She hasn't left town or anything. We're not sending for Ellen just yet."

"So you're working on it?"

"Yes, I'm working on it."

"Well then I won't worry. Meanwhile, why the fuss over the dog?"

"Where do you hide something when you know the police will take everything out of your house?"

"Not in my house obviously."

"Obviously. Talk to Z'ev for a minute. I need to make a call. Here," she handed the phone to Z'ev. "Give me your phone for a minute. I need to call INTERPOL." She ignored the tiny sound of outraged Jane, as she took Z'ev's phone and dug in her pocket for Sanne's business card. The evidence tech answered on the third ring, sounding formal and professional.

"Sanne, it's Agent Lanier. Do you have the original evidence notes from the Meise case?"

"Yes, why?"

"The arresting officers, did they note who else was present at the time of the arrest?"

"Yes, but it was just his lawyer and a neighbor. The neighbors have been fully investigated, but they only moved in a few months ago, so apparently any suspicions against them have been dismissed."

"Which neighbor was it? The one on the right or the left?"

"I don't understand the question."

"If I'm looking at the Meise house, which neighbor was it?"

"I'm not sure. I only have the address. Hold on." Nikki switched to speaker as Sanne read the house numbers off, so that she could dial up the address in map app on Z'ev's phone. She zoomed in for a street level view and smiled.

"Does that help?" asked Sanne.

"It helps a lot," said Nikki. "If I'm right, INTERPOL will have Arjan's client list by nightfall."

"As long as," Sanne cleared her throat, "no one else needs it first."

"Don't worry about it," said Nikki. "If I do this right, everyone will get what they want. Thanks." She hung up and looked around for Z'ev.

"Hopefully, that includes me," said Philippe, grinning.

"I'm not making any promises," said Nikki. "You and Val still have a lot to answer for. Where'd Z'ev go?"

"Out on deck. I think he was arguing with your friend."

Nikki frowned. "He'd better not be yelling at Jane."

"Or what, you'll stomp on his toe too? Would he even feel that? Seriously, what does this guy do—spend all his free time in a gym?"

"He's very health conscious," said Nikki.

"He eats a lot of vegetables, doesn't he? He probably flosses too. I mean, he just seems like that guy, you know? Why are you with him, Nikki? He seems like a total buzzkill."

"I thought you wanted grandkids."

"Well, sure. But is he really parent material? You said it yourself, he's a threat to your job and he clearly disapproves of it. So, obviously he therefore disapproves of you."

"He's never said that."

Phillippe's face was a picture of skepticism. "Have you asked him what he thinks?"

"Well, I might have, if I'd had a chance to talk to him, but instead I've spent the last week chasing around after you and Val. And for your information, he likes dancing, steak, really good Malbec, and he makes me laugh. And most of all, not that you would understand this, but most of all, I trust him."

"Except with the truth," said Philippe.

"Well, that's on me," said Nikki. "That is because of my issues, not because of anything he's done. And honestly, Dad, considering that you're dating Valarie Robinson, I hardly think that you have any room to comment on my love life."

"Well, if being your father weren't enough, I would think the fact that I am maintaining a stable, loving relationship with a woman who I view as my peer would give me all the room in the world to comment."

"Oh shut up!" Nikki yanked open the door and stomped out on the deck.

"Dude, I'm telling you," said Z'ev. "It's purple. Like purple, purple."

"And I like it!" yelled Nikki.

"And she likes it," repeated Z'ev. "But I'm guessing it's time to go." They exchanged phones, and Nikki glared at him suspiciously.

"My hair looks good," said Nikki, putting her phone back to her ear.

"He said it did," said Jane soothingly.

"I'm an adult and I can do things with my hair."

"Yes, you can," agreed Jane.

"This was your idea anyway."

"Yes, it was."

"I have to go stop an international arms dealer now."

"Go get 'em tiger."

Nikki glanced nervously at Z'ev who was now ushering her father off the gang plank.

"Did he say anything else?"

"We had a conversation," said Jane.

"That statement lacks clarity."

"It was personal," said Jane.

"I didn't count on him being mad at all of you too."

"I would say, that none of us took into account how much

he has been a part of our lives," said Jane. "He pointed it out. I felt like a horrible human being, and then I tried to explain slash apologize without undermining your position. We are currently at detante. You know, until you two sort things out or have him killed, whichever comes first. Which was totally awkward, by the way. I can't believe you told him that."

"I'm hoping a current policy of100% honesty will make up for the previous three years of lying. Jane, in case I don't get a chance to say this in the future, I love you and I appreciate every-thing you do."

"Ahhhhh! What are you doing. Don't say shit like that! Saying shit like that is what gets people killed. You take that back!"

"All right, I take it back. I find you annoying and take your work for granted."

"That's what I thought. Now go get your arms dealer."

"Yes, but first I have to stop and see a man about a dog."

AMSTERDAM XIX
FUNSKE

"Are you sure about this?" asked Philippe from the backseat.

"Yes!" said Nikki for the third time. "Arjan's client list is in there." She hoped. "I just need to go talk the people who live there into giving him, or it, or whatever, to me."

"Do you want us to come in too?" asked Z'ev.

"No, they're total non-combatants. Their house looks like IKEA barfed on it. I'll be less threatening on my own."

"OK," said Z'ev reluctantly. "But IKEA furniture doesn't mean they're safe people. I once knew a guy who got stabbed with a Grundtal."

"Jumbo is right. I knew a guy who killed someone with a Gnarp."

"You both spend too much time with the IKEA catalog," said Nikki and got out of the car.

The front door was opened by a woman with brown hair and real wooden clogs. In the hall behind her, a blonde man, wearing a black turtleneck was sorting the mail.

"Hi!" said Nikki, and smiling brightly, wishing that she planned ahead for these sort of things. The moment between her opening gambit and when the lies fell out of her mouth was worse than jumping out of a plane without a parachute.

Twenty minutes later, Nikki was exchanging cheek kisses with Nina when the doorbell rang.

"Now, who is that?" wondered Dietr, reaching for the door

handle. The door opened and on the front steps stood a dapper little man with the pointed white moustache and goatee. He was dressed in a charcoal gray, single breasted suit, with thin lapels and tiny threads of pinstriping. His shoes looked to be Italian leather loafers and he wore a gold pinky ring with a yellow diamond. Nikki recognized him as Arjan Meise's lawyer. He recognized the dog in Nikki's arms. She glanced outside; behind him, two muscular gentlemen loitered by the car.

"Wie ben je?" he demanded stepping across the threshold.

"She's the new dog sitter," said Dietr, frowning and looking from Nikki to the lawyer.

"What new dog sitter?" repeated the lawyer raising his eyebrows.

Nikki considered her situation.

Pros: her main opponent was a smaller gentleman of bookish extraction who didn't know who she was or what she was capable of.

Cons: they were in a very narrow hall. There were two XXXL sized gentlemen in plain view through the door. She had two innocent by-standers—one of whom was standing between her and the door, as well as her opponent to contend with. And she was working with the handicap of having a small dog under one arm.

Option 1: bluff and attempt to talk her way out.

Option 2: attempt to relocate the battlefield outside.

Option 3: attack.

Apparently, she hadn't been the only one considering her options. The lawyer punched Dietr in the face. Dietr stumbled back and sank to the floor clutching his nose. So much for bookish.

"Nina," said Nikki, "run."

Nina didn't move. She stood paralyzed with shock, staring at her husband. The lawyer advanced.

"Give me the dog," he commanded.

Nikki grabbed Nina by the arm and ran down the hallway. At the first open doorway, which turned out to be a hall powder room, Nikki shoved Nina inside and slammed the door shut.

She turned to face the lawyer, slightly too slowly as it turned out because he kicked her in the chest and she went sprawling. Funske barked as he went sliding across the perfectly polished white pine floor and into the kitchen.

"Funske, come." The lawyer stalked over Nikki's legs, ignoring her as he made for the dog. Nikki rolled her eyes and climbed to her feet. Funske had retreated under the kitchen table, barking furiously.

"I don't think he likes you," said Nikki, as she picked up a cold tea kettle off the stove. He blocked her swing at his head in the nick of time, managing only to douse himself in water as the tea kettle came to an abrupt halt above his head. His moustache quivered in anger at the indignity.

He punched twice, aiming for her mid-section, Nikki blocked and retreated, before retaliating with a tea kettle to his chest, knocking him back into the kitchen table. He kicked out in a flurry of kicks, forcing Nikki to dodge backwards. The seams on his suit never even protested. Considering that she'd once split a pair of pants doing a simple front kick, Nikki found this impressive.

"You will give me the dog," he barked, pushing up his sleeves and advancing toward her.

"Your tailor is amazing," said Nikki. His footstep faltered.

"Thank you. I don't know who you are, but you can't have the dog. I will take the dog."

"Yeah, no." said Nikki and threw the tea kettle at his head.

He blocked, but it gave her cover to dive in with a kick of her own. They traded blows, but Nikki ended the exchange with a knee to his gut that sent him reeling back into the counter. Nikki reached up into the hanging assortment of copper cookware over the stove grabbing for a frying pan, just as the lawyer picked up a kitchen knife, and launched himself back at Nikki.

"I don't have time for this!" yelled Nikki, yanking down the first object that came free and blocking a wild swing of his knife. It turned out to be a colander.

"Make time," he hissed, slicing at her again.

She blocked the knife, the blade making a classic sword fighting sound against the metal of the colander. Beneath the table, Funske made a counterpoint to the clanging of metal with sharp furious barks. The lawyer stabbed at her stomach, and with both hands on the colander, she blocked sharply downward and then swung the colander up into his face. He staggered back against the stove, shaking his head, round circle marks on his cheek. Nikki dropped the colander preparing to attack, but with impressive speed the lawyer swung the knife in a wide arcing cut toward her face. Nikki feinted back, then launched in as his arm came toward her again on a back swing. Grabbing his wrist and upper arm, she planted one foot and spun him around and into the floor. She adjusted her grasp to a wrist lock and cranked the wrist until he yelled in pain and dropped the knife. It clattered to floor and Nikki kicked it away as Funske launched himself from under the table and at the lawyers face.

The lawyer yelled in panic as Funske clamped on to his ear.

"*Haal hem van! Haal hem van!* Get him off of me! Get him off!"

"Funske!" Nikki dropped the lawyer's arm and grabbed the

dog. There was a tug of war over the lawyer's ear. He writhed on the floor, flailing as she attempted to unlatch the dog's teeth from his ear.

Nikki finally freed the lawyer from the dog and stood up. "Funske! Bad dog! Ears are not treats!"

The lawyer staggered to his feet, blood dripping down the side of his head. He leaned against the butcher block looking dazed.

"Nikki," said Phillippe walking into the kitchen, and picking the copper frying pan out of the array hanging over the stove. "What is taking you so long?"

"Phillippe Lanier?" asked the lawyer staring at Phillippe in disbelief.

"That's right," said Phillippe, encouragingly, adding his trademark winsome smile.

"But what are you—" The lawyer's question was cut short as Phillippe hit him with the frying pan. The lawyer sagged to the floor, unconscious.

"Dad, I was getting to that!"

"Really, because it looked like you were playing with the dog. Can we go now?"

"Just a minute!" Nikki rummaged through the kitchen looking for Funske's treat bag. "What about the lawyer's two goombah's outside?"

"Your boyfriend took care of them. I think the wife's losing it in the closet though."

Nikki realized that the annoying noise in the background was Nina crying. "Bathroom," she corrected, finally locating the treats. She fished one out and fed it to Funske before reaching for his collar and Phillippe rolled his eyes. "What? Like I want him clamped onto my ear? Here," she shoved the bag of dog treats at him, "you feed him while I look at his collar."

Philippe shook his head, but did as instructed. Nikki spun Funske's collar around until she saw the small neoprene bag strapped around the dog tags. Gently, she opened the bag, trying not to disturb Funske's ravenous devouring of treats.

"Ha! I love it when I'm right." Reaching in tiny neoprene sack, she fished out a memory card and held it up.

"Isn't that kind of memory chip just for cameras? Are you sure that's what we're looking for?"

"Data is data," said Nikki. "The computer doesn't care if it's pictures or spreadsheets."

"Huh. You know you could sell that for a lot of money."

"Or I could give it to my boyfriend and he could go have all these people arrested."

"That's just such conformist thinking. Where did I go wrong?"

Nikki found herself with so many answers that they all formed a blockade in a rush to get to her mouth.

"Hey babe," asked Z'ev leaning into the kitchen. "Am I letting the woman out of the bathroom?"

Nikki blinked at him, trying to focus on the problem. Z'ev looked from Philippe to Nikki. "Philippe, why don't you go wait in the car?"

"OK," said Philippe, putting down Funske and ambling from the room.

"You really want to punch your dad, don't you?" Z'ev asked.

Nikki gestured with a furious disbelief and finally made a sound. It might have been *meep*.

"It's going to be OK," said Z'ev soothingly, approaching

slowly.

"No," said Nikki, "it's not. He just told me I was a conform-ist thinker."

"Has he met you?"

Nikki clunked her forehead against his chest. "I can't take this. I really can't. Maybe I should have just let him be kidnapped? I mean, he's an adult—sort of. He could probably have gotten himself out of the situation. Val could have gotten him out any-way. Why didn't I just stay at home with Grandma and the girls? I could have been eating pie right now."

"She does make good pie," agreed Z'ev. "But you know, your mom was there, so probably we wouldn't have stayed too much longer anyway."

"Oh my God," said Nikki looking up at him as he put his arms around her waist. "What's worse? This or a week's vacation with my mom?"

"I'm sorry, but I'm going to have to say, this. Your mom might be a tad overbearing, but she has your best interests at heart. Your dad, however, is insane. He tried to coerce you into breaking into an INTERPOL evidence warehouse, he's dating Val Robinson, and he's involved in international crime. Your mom wins."

"You're just saying that because mom likes you."

"Yes, she does. She thinks I'm a snazzy dresser with a good career and future. Meanwhile, your father keeps calling me Jumbo and implying that I'm not good enough for you."

Nikki wrinkled her nose in dislike. "I'm sorry. I have Arjan's client list, though." She held up the memory chip. "You can have it, if you want."

He hesitated, then sighed and tucked it into the interior pock-et of his jacket. "But we're still going to the flower market?"

"We need Maaravi," said Nikki. "This little assault will get us the lawyer, the client list will get us Arjan, but to make it a clean sweep, I want Maaravi and Petra."

"And what about Val?

"We'll cross that bridge when we come to it."

"You two never made it across the bridge last time," said Z'ev. "You dropped her off of it, remember?"

THE PAST VI
JOINT STATEMENTS

Vancouver, Canada

They were smoking a joint and Nikki felt stupid. At nineteen, she knew marijuana was supposed to be the cool, college thing to do, but Nikki wasn't feeling the cool yet. She was supposed to be due a little mindlessly destructive behavior. She'd arrived back at college. It was supposed to be enjoyable. Instead, Nikki sat on the floor and felt stupid.

She had arrived back at school and at the rental house she shared with her three roommates, broken hearted. She and Jackson were supposed to have driven back together. Instead, he'd avoided her phone calls, cleaned out his apartment and then dumped her over the phone. It was as if he'd calculated the best possible way to rip open the scars of her father's absence and also crush her heart at the very same time.

Her roommates had assured her that what she needed was a weekend away. A weekend where anything went. A weekend that was all about her. They were going to take care of her. They would take care of everything.

They had driven to Vancouver for a weekend of partying and now they were sitting in a hotel room smoking a joint. Nikki felt a restless twitch run down her spine.

"We could have done this at home," said Nikki, forgetting that her mouth was attached to her thoughts and speaking out loud. "Could have saved ourselves the cost of a hotel room."

"Yeah, but Vancouver is different," said Kimmy.

"How can you tell?" asked Nikki gesturing at the pastel print décor.

Kimmy's eyebrows rose, but her lids stayed firmly lowered to half-mast.

"You're upset," said Kimmy. Kimmy was majoring in chemistry and pulled straight As, while managing a pot habit that was recreational in the same way that Olympic athletes were amateurs. "You're not supposed to be upset. That's why we came here, so that you wouldn't be upset."

"Sorry," muttered Nikki.

"Yeah, man, you're bringing the party down," said Thang Vu. He was majoring in Engineering to please his parents and minoring in music to please himself. He kept threatening to switch to music full time, but sadly for his rebel impulses he was only a fairly good musician, but a rock-solid Engineer. He spiked his thick black hair, wore band t-shirts and a guitar pic on a string for a necklace. Thang plucked at an unplugged electric guitar and it made muted twanging sounds that even Nikki could tell were out of tune.

Victoria flitted around the room lighting candles and incense. She was getting her bachelor's degree in Education and Nikki could tell that her nose ring, purple hair, and alternative persona were six months of student teaching away from being non-existent. She was already starting to disapprove of Kimmy's drug habit. And although she hadn't actually used the words *drug* or *habit* to describe what the roommates generally referred to as Kimmy's oral fixation, Nikki was betting it was only a semester and a class on child development away.

Nikki looked at her friends, took a deep breath and choked

on the mixed smell of incense and pot. Vicky leapt up and went to the bathroom. A grating sound and a cool breeze indicated she had opened the bathroom window. Through the open door of the bathroom, Nikki could see one of Vicky's bits of underwear, a black thong, draped over the towel rack. The thong had 'pussy' and a picture of a very cute kitten printed on the front. Nikki took a moment to ponder what would happen to the exotic underwear after the hair color went? Would pussy stick around or would it be grandma panties in two years? Thang would work nine to five, rip off his tie and rush to band practice. Kimmy would go to rehab, find religion and be the most successful woman in the office with a criminal record. Either that or she would go to work for a drug cartel and use her degree to build a bigger, better marijuana plant. Could go either way. And Vicky would have her underwear collection, and feel secure in the knowledge that none of her students would ever know. Even Victoria would have her secrets.

"I don't have a secret side," she said mournfully.

"What?" asked Kimmy trying to talk, but not let the smoke out of her lungs just yet.

"You all have some sort of rebel identity," explained Nikki. "You're a pot head, Thang's a guitar boy, Vicky's a riot grrrl and what am I?"

"You…" said Kimmy, exhaling in a long stream, "are a Stepford Wife, and I am not a pot head. I am a Marijuana Enthusiast. Pot heads cannot manage their habit. I control the pot. The pot does not control me."

"My secret side is an uptight Barbie?" asked Nikki, ignoring Kimmy's side trip into denial.

"Stepford Nikki, Stepford Nikki," sang Thang strumming in time with his guitar.

"You know how in the movie the women seem like…" Kimmy paused, playing maestro to Thang's guitar, waving the joint like a baton, "they're repressed in person, all button blouse and starched skirts, but it always seems like they'd be a tiger in the sack?"

"Stepford Nikki, tiger in the sack…" There was more strumming, and mournfully Thang plucked out the next bit, "starch in the skirt, but is that all? Stepford Tiger Nikki."

"Sorry, what?" asked Nikki.

"Your wild side is in there…" said Kimmy inhaling again. "You're just going to have to kill the evil alien."

"Striking fear in the hearts of evil aliens everywhere," quavered Thang. "Stepford Tiger Nikki."

"Evil alien," repeated Nikki. "What evil alien? I don't think there was an evil alien in that movie."

"Wasn't there?" asked Kimmy.

"I should really write this down," said Thang, repeating the last chord.

"I could have sworn there was an alien," said Kimmy.

"Stepford Tiger Nikki, beautiful and repressed, waiting to be unleashed." Thang was jotting notes down on the back of the pizza menu.

"I'm not repressed," snapped Nikki.

"Vicky," called Kimmy, "what was that Stepford movie with the aliens?"

"You're thinking of the one with Frodo."

"Am I?"

"Stepford Tiger Nikki, tiger in the sack." Thang was back-tracking now, trying to figure out what he'd already composed.

"And they took speed?"

"That's the one," confirmed Vicky.

"Starch in the skirt, but is that all? Stepford Tiger Nikki."

"Thang, I'm going to break your fingers if you keep singing that." Nikki's head was beginning to hurt.

"And the aliens didn't like water?"

"No, the aliens did like water," corrected Vicky impatiently.

"Right, but they didn't like things that dried them out."

"Someday she's going to snap and the evil natured aliens will die. Stepford Tiger Nikki, no you won't let those aliens win."

"Yeah and they threw the alien into the pool with the chlorine and the drug dealer speed freak hooked up with the hot teacher."

"Now that sounds like a good movie," said Thang pausing to write down his latest lyrics.

"Yeah, Stepford Kids, Frodo, and the water aliens, that was good," agreed Kimmy.

"I am not repressed," repeated Nikki, knowing that they weren't listening. "I'm in control."

"But do you want to be?" asked Kimmy. "You know, it's ok to not be in control once in a while. You can let go. Look at me, I'm letting go, right now." She handed the joint to Nikki.

"If let go, I'd make you eat this joint," muttered Nikki as Kimmy wandered into the bathroom, dropping trou without bothering to close the door.

"I think," said Vicky, stepping out of the bathroom and firmly closing the door, "that there's nothing wrong with you. It's this break-up that's got you confused. I know for a fact that Harrison Pierson wants to ask you out. He's captain of the lacrosse team."

"Sounds like a Stepford Wife would be right up his alley," said Thang.

"Don't be so classist," snapped Vicky. "He's a really nice guy."

Nikki's wager shifted. The nose ring was going to be coming out in less than a month. Vicky was on her way to dating the captain of the lacrosse team.

"Anyway," continued Vicky. "Everyone get dressed—it's time to go out."

"I don't really want to," said Nikki.

"Dumped people always say that," Thang. "We're not going to listen to you."

"No one ever does," said Nikki gloomily.

"Shut it, Eeyore," said Kimmy coming out of the bathroom. "And give me my spliff back."

AMSTERDAM XX

FLORES PARA LOS MEURTOS

"So what is this place exactly?" asked Nikki.

"The Aalsmeer Flower Auction is the largest flower auction in the world," said Philippe from the backseat.

"Yeah, but what does that mean?" asked Nikki, pivoting around to look at him. "They sell flowers or something?"

"No, no, no. They do not sell flowers. They're like the middle man of flowers. Growers bring flowers to the auction. A sample of the flowers are loaded on a tram and driven through the buy room for inspection. In the buy room, the flowers are sold in what's known as a Dutch Auction."

"What's a Dutch Auction?" asked Z'ev maneuvering around a large truck.

"The auctioneer starts at a high price and then the price is lowered at set intervals until someone accepts the price. It's fast and efficient, and they sell about a bajillion flowers a day. And they're security is surprisingly good. It took me awhile to set up the sale."

"I thought you said you didn't know where the sale was?" said Nikki, spinning around in her seat.

"Uh, well, yes, but you see, technically the sale has already happened. They just need to take possession of the guns."

"What?"

"I told you, I shipped the guns in with Maaravi's flowers. Then I set up the Chechens as flower buyers and told them which price to take the flowers at—slightly higher than market value, so no one else would buy the lot. Then they transferred money to Maaravi's account through the flower auction. So that money is totally laundered! The problem, of course, is that guns cost more than flowers. Well, most flowers anyway. So they're going to pay the overage in cash and collect the weapons sometime today. If I had a little longer I bet I could have figured out how to ensure that no one ever had to meet face to face. I could have made it totally foolproof." Philippe shifted position and caught sight of Nikki's face. "What? Come on, you have to admit that's a pretty good plan."

"It's a pretty good plan," said Z'ev, from the front seat.

"See? Even Jumbo thinks it's a good plan."

"His name is Z'ev! And he's right; you do belong in jail."

"Hey, I didn't want to do this job. I literally had a gun to my head. But I believe that if you're going to do something, you should do it right. I am responsible to my craft."

"Well, at least it shouldn't be too hard to find Maaravi," said Nikki. "I mean, he's probably with his flowers in a warehouse somewhere, right?"

"I like the theory," said Z'ev with a shrug.

"Um, well, yeah," said Philippe. "There's a slight problem with that." Nikki raised an eyebrow at her father. "The Aalsmeer Flower Auction is literally the largest building by footprint in the world. It covers about 128 acres."

Nikki felt the muscle in her eye twitch. "Are you messing with me?"

"Nikki, *chère*, when did you get so suspicious? I would never mess with you."

"Except for the time you lied to her for her entire childhood," said Z'ev from the driver's seat.

"That was different," said Philippe. "It was for her own protection and honestly, that was mostly Nell."

"Or the time you bailed on helping in your own mother's funeral," Z'ev continued. Nikki glanced surreptitiously at Z'ev. She'd forgotten how much he knew about her life.

"Or the time, you said you'd show up for her college graduation, but didn't. Or what about, it was so hilarious, you remember that one time you teamed up with a woman who tried to kill her in an attempt to trick her into getting you into a secure facility to steal five million dollars? And you ended up putting her in the crosshairs of an international arms dealer. Gosh, that was a hoot."

Philippe looked affronted. "I don't think you were invited to this discussion. And there are perfectly reasonable explanations for every one of those things."

"I think you mean excuses," said Z'ev.

"You know, I thought you wanted to be the ex-boyfriend. What are you even doing here?"

"I like listening to deranged Canadians," said Z'ev.

Nikki tried to smother a chuckle.

"Laugh if you want, but I believe he was talking about you," said Philippe.

"I'm certain he was; that was why I was laughing. Dad, do you really not know where they were meeting?"

"No, I really don't. Aalsmeer could have assigned them to any of the warehouse facilities and only employees, owners and owner's representatives would have access. I might have been able to help you if you'd left me with Maaravi." He said that last part as if Nikki had made a very poor choice.

"Or, you might be dead because Arjan showed up and shot

you."

"Well, yes, there is that."

"OK," said Z'ev, "but then how are the Chechens getting in? They're not employees or owners."

"They're buyers. Once they have bought, then they're owners. I mean it's unusual, but they could probably talk their way into going to inspect the shipment or something. That really wasn't my problem. Maaravi set all that up."

"Aalsmeer is straight ahead," said Z'ev. "What do you want to do?"

"It looks like there's a guard at the gate directing traffic," said Nikki, squinting through the windshield. "I want you to pull up and say we're employees of the Meise Flower Farm and that we're meeting Mr. Meise on site. Dad, do you remember any of the specs on the shipment? Lot numbers or anything?"

"Yes, of course."

"OK, Z'ev is going to say all of that in Spanish. When the guard doesn't understand it, you're going to repeat it all in French and include the lot numbers."

"And when he doesn't understand French?" asked Z'ev.

"Then I'm going to get out of the car and repeat it all in French, bad English, and boobs."

"I'm just not comfortable with hearing you say that," said Philippe.

"Ditto," said Z'ev. "You really think this is going to work?"

"It usually does," said Nikki with a shrug. "I mean, usually we use Jenny's boobs, but I'm pretty sure I've got the technique."

"I don't think it's going to work," said Z'ev. "I'm thinking this is a total package kind of thing, and I can't blush like Jane and he's no Ellen."

"So few of us are."

"Well, if it doesn't work," said Philippe. "we can always just go buy tickets for the next tour of the building and sneak in that way."

"I'm not sure why, but that seems vaguely embarrassing," said Z'ev.

"That's because a fourteen year old could do it," said Nikki.

"There's nothing wrong with the classics," said Philippe and flopped back onto the upholstery looking disgruntled.

Z'ev pulled the car into line and slowed down as he approached the guard at the parking lot entrance. "Spanish?" he asked looking at Nikki.

"When in doubt, sound foreign," said Nikki with a shrug. Z'ev rolled down the window.

"Buenos días. Estamos cumpliendo con el Sr. Meise Meise de Granjas. Creo que aquí es donde comprobamos en?"

The guard leaned down to listen to Z'ev. Mentally, Nikki tried to prepare herself for the role of vacuous French secretary.

"Ah, si. La Sra Adler dijo que estaría aquí . Aquí hay tres pases. Aparcar en el verde. A continuación, siga la franja de pintura amarilla para almacén trece."

"Um… *Gracias,*" said Z'ev, taking three badges from the guard and putting the car in gear.

"OK, I give," said Philippe. "What did you say? That was amazing."

"I didn't say anything," said Z'ev, tossing the name badges at Nikki to distribute. "These are compliments of Val. Unless, of course, there's a second woman using the completely ridiculous pseudonym of Irene Adler running around."

"That's my girl!" said Philippe clipping on his badge with a grin.

Z'ev and Nikki exchanged glances of shared worry. "Tell me you've got something up your sleeve," said Z'ev. "Because right now, she knows exactly where we're going to be and when."

"Not really," said Nikki.

"Well, you've got from now until we get to the Green Lot to figure something out then."

"Umm…"

There was the sound of the car door opening and then slamming closed. Nikki and Z'ev both spun around in time to see her father sprinting across the parking lot toward the nearest building.

"He's got a good turn of speed," said Z'ev.

"He always said he enjoyed jogging," said Nikki. "Although, I'm pretty sure in retrospect that he also enjoys pot brownies, but from his form, I'll believe there's been some jogging."

"But what the hell does he think he's doing?"

"I doubt he's thought that far ahead. He's really more of a fly by the seat of his pants kind of guy."

"That seems accurate. Well, what do we do now?"

"Park the car?" suggested Nikki.

Z'ev found an empty spot, and turned off the engine. "How long do you think it will take him to call Val?"

Nikki checked her watch. "As long as it takes him to find a phone with an outside line or a handy cell phone."

"About five minutes, then. OK, well any chance that Val gave that guard accurate information? We could try beating him to Warehouse Thirteen?"

"Worth a shot," said Nikki with a shrug. "Are you going to get fired for this?" she asked as she got out of the car.

"I doubt it," said Z'ev. "I don't work for INTERPOL. I work

for the CIA. And if I can catch Arjan and prove that Petra was having a relationship with his son, well that's only going to make my stock rise at the Agency."

"They're going to be pleased that you made another agency look bad?"

"Oh yeah, they'll love it."

"That seems… weird."

"Welcome to inter-agency cooperation at it's finest. And are you really telling me Carrie Mae doesn't have any cat-fights?"

"Oh no, we have territorial battles and an on-going culture war, but when it comes down to it we put the mission first. But that aside, your plan to not get fired does rather assume that we live through this, and that we catch Arjan," said Nikki, scanning the buildings looking for a clue on which direction to go.

"He said follow the yellow paint stripe to Warehouse Thirteen," said Z'ev pointing down.

"Warehouse thirteen, like that's not a bad omen or anything."

"What did you mean, my plan? Did you just try to Jedi mind trick me into thinking that this was my plan? This entire affair has been your plan. I'm just here because you have a startling inability to believe the word *no*." He was moving to the fastest speed possible while still looking casual.

"I wouldn't call it a plan," said Nikki, working to keep up. "It's more just me trying to jiu-jitsu my life back into sanity."

"And what does sane look like to you? I'm serious," he said glancing down at her. "I'd really like to know."

"Sane looks like waking up next to you and then me going to a job where I help people every day and get to work with my best friends."

Z'ev stopped walking. "That's what you want?"

"Yes, that's what I want."

"And what else?"

"Nothing else. That's literally everything I want. I mean, I also want my mother to only call me on holidays and my father to be a normal parent and Val to disappear off the face of the planet. But I don't think any of that is realistically achievable. But you, me, the girls, and our apartment, I had that. I think I've got a shot at that. I think that's worth fighting for."

"Really, the apartment? You don't think a condo would be better?"

"I can't process that statement right now," said Nikki.

"Fair enough. Warehouse thirteen is right there. Let's go see if we can't stop an international arms deal, save an INTERPOL agent from herself, and arrest a flower salesman."

"No problem."

He laughed. "Glad you're so confident."

"Well, the way I figure it, we've always been at our best when people are trying to kill us, so we just have to go in there and do what we do best."

"Bicker and punch people?"

"You got it."

AMSTERDAM XXI
WAREHOUSE 13

The warehouse was a clanking whir of machinery. Two semi-trucks were parked in front of wide open doors. The back end of one was open, showing bins and stacks of flowers. They were being loaded onto large containers that lowered from an overhead system of tracks. But no workers were present and the machinery carried bucket after empty bucket around the loop of the warehouse and out through a breezeway. Near the second truck was a parked tram that looked like a luggage carrier at the airport. Maaravi's car was parked further into the warehouse next to a stack of containers. He was standing by the front bumper talking to a group of teenagers. She and Z'ev crept through the door, guns drawn, keeping low and moving from one giant container of flowers to the next.

Peeking around a pile of Hyacinths, Nikki revised her assessment from teenagers to dangerous teenagers. She wasn't sure what she'd expected from Chechen independence fighters, but somehow green Adidas track suits and machine guns hadn't been it.

"Those are the Chechen's? Aren't they a little young to be buying weapons?"

"War is a young man's game," whispered Z'ev. "Who did you think was going to be buying guns?"

"I don't know; old guys in serious sweaters. Not some teenager with a Run DMC fetish." Z'ev shrugged. "OK, well, how do you want to play this?"

"Wait until they've made the deal," said Z'ev taking out his phone. "Get it on video. Then bust it up."

"OK," agreed Nikki. "Let's move in closer. When it's time to move, I'll cover Maaravi and the guy closest to him, you've got the other three?"

"Right," agreed Z'ev, and moved ahead of her. Nikki took a small personal moment to admire his ass as he ran at a low crouch to the next container. He waved to her to move and she followed him. Z'ev hit record, flipped the phone around and managed to hold it steady while still keeping his gun held in the right direction. It was a small thing, but Nikki was impressed.

The Chechen at the back of the group, a dark haired youth wearing a soccer jersey and skinny jeans, came forward. He was carrying a briefcase. Maaravi pulled out a set of keys, and gestured to the second semi-truck. There was a shift in the group as everyone focused on the two objects of desire. Very slowly and with a clear placement of hands, Maaravi and the kid exchanged the briefcase and the keys.

There was a screech of brakes and a gray Land Cruiser pulled to a stop in front of the semi. Arjan Meise stepped out of the driver's side, pulling a gun with him. The Chechens fired first, diving behind and into the tram. There was explosion of daffodils as Arjan fired back.

"That is a Tommy gun," said Nikki. "I cannot believe he's actually carrying a Tommy gun. Who does that?"

Maaravi wasn't waiting to observe his father's gun preference, he was sprinting for the exit. Arjan fired after him and Nikki saw Maaravi flinch as he went to ground behind some machinery. The Chechens took the opportunity to make a break for it in the tram, chugging away from the scene at top speed.

Arjan was hunting Maaravi among the containers.

"Go get the Chechens," said Nikki.

"No," said Z'ev.

"Yes, that's the whole point of this thing. Get all the bad guys. Arjan's looking in the wrong direction. I'll get Maaravi and get the hell out."

Z'ev looked from the quickly disappearing Chechens and back to Nikki.

"One guy I can handle," she said. "What am I supposed to do with four disgruntled youth. Go get them."

"I'm calling INTERPOL," he said, kissing her and running toward the semi truck.

"Swell," she muttered, and ran after Maaravi.

She found him hiding under an overfilled container of baby's breath, panting and trying to staunch a dripping gash in his arm.

"Should have zig-zagged more," she said conversationally. Maaravi jumped slightly, entangling himself in baby's breath.

"Who are you?" he gasped.

"I'm the one who's not actively shooting at you, which pretty much makes me your only friend right now. Guess you shouldn't have tried to take over your dad's business, huh?"

"I didn't! I just wanted him in jail."

"And what, you accidentally happened to bump into some Chechen freedom fighters and thought well, shoot, they need some guns?"

"No, that was Petra's idea. She convinced me that I had to get rid of his guns immediately or they could take my farm. I didn't want to do it, but I can't lose my farm. But this whole time, she's been planning to take over my dad's business."

"And that's why she was so desperate to find his client list?"

"Yes! Wait, who are you? How do you know?"

"Never mind that. Come on. Let's go before you father realizes he's gone the wrong direction. And don't forget the briefcase." She grabbed him by his uninjured arm and Maaravi clutched the briefcase in the other arm. She headed toward the door she and Z'ev had come in. They broke through into the open space and she saw her father wearing an oversized jacket, standing awkwardly by the door.

"Papa what are you doing?"

"Uh, Nikki," said Philippe.

"Did you find Val?"

"Philippe!" yelled Arjan. "Heel!"

Sadly, Philippe turned and walked over to Arjan as he burst through the hyacinth.

"Dad!"

"Ce n'est pas à quoi il ressemble."

Arjan grabbed Philippe by the collar and yanked him closer.

"Well, Philippe can we assume that this is your spawn? She's a cute little thing. Don't really understand the new generation and their hair though."

Nikki kicked the back of Maaravi's knee, sending him sprawling. The briefcase, presumably full of money spun out of his grasp. She kept her hand on his shoulder, not letting him topple forward.

"Do you really think I won't shoot him, little girl?" asked Arjan, pressing the Tommy gun tight against Philippe's side.

Nikki took a quick glance around the room. Still no Val or Z'ev. Time to stall.

"I have absolutely no doubts that you will," she said calmly. "This isn't me testing your willingness to commit violence. This is me testing your willingness to negotiate."

"Ah, I see. An eye for an eye. You give me my son, and I give you your father."

"That's the general idea."

"And what makes you think I want him back? He just made a rather good attempt at a *coup d'etat*. You may not have noticed this, but I did just try to give him a little ventilation."

"If you kill him, you can't get the money he just made from selling your guns," said Nikki.

"What's to stop me from shooting all of you and just taking the briefcase?"

"The briefcase is just the overage. The majority of the money is in Maaravi's bank account."

Maaravi looked up at Nikki, surprised. "How do you know all this?"

"Look," said Nikki, "I'm not suggesting that killing family members doesn't occasionally sound like a great idea. After all, my father lured me to Amsterdam to help him steal five million dollars and he's dating a woman who shot and tried to drown me. Bullet shaped solutions had crossed my mind. But if you want the money, which considering your assets are still frozen, I'm assuming you do, you have to be practical."

Arjan laughed.

"Nikki—" Whatever Philippe was about to say was cut off as Arjan nudged him with the gun.

"Practical considerations must prevail."

"Besides, it's hard to make them suffer if they're dead," offered Nikki.

"So true," agreed Arjan. "I'll tell you what, why don't you send Maaravi over, I'll also take that briefcase over there, and if you and Philippe get out of town fast enough, I won't shoot you."

"Mmmm," said Nikki, shaking her head. "You should re-think that offer."

"I think that's my best offer," said Arjan. "I think maybe you should think about taking it."

"It's always nice to hear your opinions," said Nikki. Behind Arjan she saw Z'ev slither into the room. Overhead the contain-ers of flowers, continued along the conveyor belt, a purple scarf fell out of one and fluttered to the floor. "However, I think that what we should do is exchange our various relatives, Papa will take the briefcase, and you will get out of town before I decide to be annoyed."

"She's feisty, Philippe," Arjan laughed. "What have you been feeding her?"

"Ears," said Nikki. "Funske says hello by the way."

Arjan stopped laughing and took a step forward dragging Philippe with him. "And what would you know about Funske?"

"Everything there is to know," said Nikki.

"You're lying. Funske is with my lawyer."

"Small dude, white beard? Fast kicks, and exquisite tailoring? I actually didn't catch his name before Papa hit him with the frying pan. But regardless, I'm sure by this time he's in police custody. I hope poor Nina and Dietr aren't too upset about the mess we made of their kitchen."

Arjan seemed frozen. "Nikki!" hissed Philippe, only to have Arjan clunk him with the gun again.

"So," said Nikki, drawing the word out, hoping to give Z'ev time to get into position, "did you want to rethink that offer or did you want me to just go ahead and ruin your life?

"You have my client list?" asked Arjan.

"You have his client list?" repeated Maaravi, trying to turn around and look at her.

"I have your client list," confirmed Nikki, poking Maaravi with her gun.

"Then we don't need either of them," said Petra. She was carrying a tire iron in one hand and a snub nosed .38 it in the other.

"Petra, don't do anything stupid," said Maaravi.

"Shut up, Maaravi," said Petra witheringly. Then she looked at Nikki, and shook her head. "Do you know how long it's taken me to get him into this position? He really wanted to grow flowers. Like that's a real job."

"Who is this?" demanded Arjan.

"This is Petra Gilles, the INTERPOL agent, who apparently put your son up to his little *coup*, as you called it. You almost nailed it, Petra," said Nikki. "Too bad you couldn't stick the landing."

"You're right. I hadn't quite planned on his lawyer being that good, or Maaravi getting a sudden burst of conscience. And I really hadn't planned on the interference of a certain smuggler's daughter, but it could have gone worse."

"Really? How? Because currently, I have all of your evidence, the Chechens have all of your guns, Maaravi has all your cash, and INTERPOL is two seconds away from figuring out that you're dirty. I don't see how you could have screwed it up any more." Nikki tried not to sound smug. She knew she had been right about Petra. "You're stuck."

"I don't think so," said Petra and shot Arjan.

Philippe dove for the floor, possibly coincidentally in the direction of the briefcase. Arjan jerked back, seeming only offended by the single bullet hole in his jacket, and fired back. Val dropped from the flower conveyor, snatched the briefcase, grabbed Philippe by the elbow and pulled him behind a container tub. Nikki pushed

Maaravi over as Arjan sprayed bullets indiscriminately before running from the room. Petra ducked and then chased after Arjan. Maaravi rolled over, looked from Nikki to Petra's retreating back, and then got up and sprinted after them.

Nikki was about to give chase when Philippe began to rip off his jacket.

"Dad, what are you doing?" Nikki demanded, feeling a sudden chill. Why weren't he and Val heading for the hills about now? This was the perfect opportunity.

Philippe threw the ugly jacket on the ground. "Because," he said, stating what was now obvious, "I'm wearing a bomb."

"I cannot get a break," said Val.

"Welcome to my world," said Nikki.

"Ladies, I don't like to think myself an arrogant man, but honestly, right now I think this should be all about me."

"How did you even get into this situation?" demanded Val, stepping closer to inspect the bomb, strapped to Philippe's chest.

"The tooth fairy. How do you think? I ran into Arjan on my way here. Look, it doesn't matter. Val, here's a briefcase full of money. You need to leave now."

"Philippe, I say this with love—shut up."

"Arjan has a remote switch Val. I don't know how long we've got. Just be smart for once—take the money and go."

"No. Nikki, help me. It's got a clip switch here and I don't see the remote receiver. What do you see on your side?"

"Val!"

"Hush now, dear, adults are talking."

"It connects in back," said Nikki. "It's got a dummy switch up front, but I'm guessing the main mechanism is in the back."

"Fabric straps," said Val, tugging gently at the contraption.

"Probably a converted back-pack. We might be able to cut those and have him simply wiggle out."

"That looks like the best option to me," agreed Nikki.

"Hey, running gun battle headed for the next warehouse," Z'ev arrived in a rush. "Does anyone—oh. That's a problem."

"Arjan has the kill switch," said Nikki.

"Then we should probably go get him."

Nikki reached in her back pocket and handed Val her pocket knife. "Watch for wires hidden in the fabric."

"Hurry up," said Val jerking her head.

Nikki and Z'ev ran toward the sound of gunfire. Dodging amount the clanky machinery and damp, dripping buckets of flowers and water.

"I see Petra," yelled Z'ev.

"I've got eyes on Arjan. I'm going after him!" Nikki was about to launch in Arjan's direction when Z'ev pulled her back around and pointed her at Petra.

"You get Petra!"

"What? Why?"

"I can't punch girls!" Nikki looked at her boyfriend in disbelief. "Just humor me!"

Nikki rolled her eyes. "Fine. Just don't get shot and if you have to shoot Arjan, aim for the head, he's wearing a vest." It was Z'ev's turn to roll his eyes. He seemed about to say something, but instead pointed at Petra as she ran into the next warehouse.

Nikki gave chase, bursting through a wide doorway covered with hanging plastic slats, only to find herself in a refrigerated warehouse. The conveyer belt of flowers rattled overhead and the floor was stacked with container after container. Sightlines were non-existent and Petra was gone.

A forklift was trundling in her direction. The driver saw her and started yelling in Dutch. Probably something about hard hats. It didn't matter. Nikki jumped up onto the driver's seat and then out onto the forks, the driver's eyes widened to outrage, and there was more yelling as she hopped from the forks onto one of the shelving units. She climbed higher and then jumped to the next rack of shelves, hoping that they were bolted securely to the ground. The shelves swayed precariously, but didn't tumble. She jumped to the next one and then the next, leaving the angry forklift driver yelling below in the continuous mist that sprayed from water hoses on the shelves and onto the flowers. The warehouse was half the size of a city block. The shelves she dangled from were stacked with containers of flowers, and sloshing with water. Dangling from one of the supports she surveyed the floor. Beneath her, the clanking chain of flower buckets moved like a snake around the warehouse and out another door. Her fingers were icing up and she could hear the forklift driver shouting for help. Just as she was about to give up she spotted Petra, sneaking up on Arjan who was hiding behind a massive bank of roses in a startling shade of lavender purple. She saw Z'ev enter from another door. He wrenched a forklift driver out of his forklift and climbed into the driver's seat.

"That should go well," she muttered to herself. Climbing down one shelf, she timed the next batch of flowers as it slid along the conveyor belt. She felt a little bad as she jumped into the garbage can size container of chrysanthemums crushing most of them, but forgot about them moments later as she saw Petra grab an Aalsmeer employee and bash him in the face with her gun. She counted the clanks of the machine as it brought her closer to Petra's position. She readied her gun in one hand, and reached into her pocket for some Carrie Mae weaponry with the other. Petra moved forward and Nikki counted down to her destination.

Four, three, two, and… one!

Nikki dropped out of the bucket and onto Petra. They landed on the floor in a tangle. Petra's gun skidded away from her, and Petra rolled over and did the smart thing—grabbed Nikki's hand, bashing it against the floor. Trying to get her to drop the weapon.

With her free hand, she flipped open the compact full of knock out powder she'd taken from Val's belongings and slapped it across Petra's face. Petra reeled back, but didn't give up or pass out. Instead she punched Nikki, and used the impact as an opportunity to strip Nikki's gun from her hand. Still blinded by the punch, Nikki kicked out and up, landing a kick square in Petra's gut. Petra doubled over with an audible gasp. Nikki grabbed her by the collar and toppled her onto the floor, rolling with her until she was on top and Petra was on the bottom. She reached for the gun, but found that Petra had lost it sometime between the kick and the floor. She looked around and found that someone had already picked it up.

"Get off of her," demanded Maaravi. His teeth were chattering slightly either from nerves or the cold air, Nikki couldn't be sure.

Nikki did as she was told.

"What are you doing Maaravi?" she asked. Petra staggered to her feet, shaking filthy floor water out of her hair. "Petra has been using you to take over your father's business."

"No, I love Maaravi," said Petra, wiping her face. Nikki noticed that her lipstick was smeared. It was a rather distinct shade of coral.

"Really, is that what you told Anders Hoek before you shot him?" asked Nikki.

She could tell from Petra's sudden stillness that she'd scored a direct hit.

"What are you talking about?" he demanded.

"Anders Hoek, a smalltime crook here in Amsterdam. She's been using him for the last year to sell guns captured in INTERPOL raids," said Nikki. "Only when he became inconvenient, she put two slugs in him—head and heart." She gestured to where the bulletholes had been.

"The last year?" repeated Maaravi. "But you were with me?"

"But she wasn't with you all the time, was she?" asked Nikki. "Lots of trips home."

"Shut up," snapped Petra. "Don't listen to her Maaravi. She's making things up to get inside your head. You and I are together. We've got to bring your father down."

"Maaravi, she doesn't love you. She's been using you. You know it. That's why you locked her in the trunk of your car."

"I just want to raise flowers. I don't want to warehouse my dad's shit. I don't want to sell guns. I just want—"

"Of course you do," said Petra soothingly. "But we've got some problems. Her for starters. Let's just deal with her—get her to tell us where your father's client list is and then we can take care of him. Everything will be tied up neatly."

She took a step toward Maaravi and staggered slightly. She shook her head as if to clear it.

Nikki edged forward, angling away from the gun. Maaravi was watching Petra. There was a lot of distance to cover between her and Maaravi.

"Everything will be tied up when my father is in jail," he said firmly.

"Yes, of coursh," said Petra.

Nikki inched forward again. Far too far for knees or elbows. Punches would be a stretch.

"We just need the clientsh book." She blinked her eyes.

"No, we don't!" yelled Maaravi. "You just want to use it. She's right, you're using me. You've been using me all along!"

Perhaps it was the yelling, but for a moment it looked like Petra might rally. She pulled herself upright, and glared. "Shut up," she said and fell over.

Maaravi stared at the crumpled pile of Petra on the floor in disbelief. Nikki adjusted her stance, took aim, and kicked him in the face. The effect was satisfying. There was a solid whunk sound as her foot met his skull, his hands flew up in the air, tossing the gun up, and he dropped down beside Petra unconscious. Nikki reached out and caught the gun.

Why don't these things ever happen when someone is looking?

"Damn," said Z'ev, coming around a flower bin, dragging an unconscious Arjan. "That was badass."

Nikki shrugged and tucked her gun away, trying to pretend like this was an everyday occurrence. "What can I say? I'm totally badass."

Z'ev laughed. "You can't say you're badass. That's like saying you're breezy."

"Oh. Shoot."

Z'ev chuckled again. "We've got to work on your swag, babe."

"I'm never going to have any swag or street cred or whatever," said Nikki, shaking her head. "I'm Canadian. What do we do now?"

"Van Bergen's on his way. Let's find someone to help take these guys out of this freezing hell hole and wait for them."

"Did you find the detonator?"

"Got it," said Z'ev patting his jacket pocket. "Turned off. Any chance your dad and Val are still on the premises?"

"If they got Dad out of the bomb harness, I'm pretty sure they're not in the country," said Nikki.

"Well, as you are fond of saying, *c'est la vie.*" Three warehouse employees came around the corner carrying crowbars and looking serious. "Hi," said Z'ev taking a badge out of his pocket and flashing it at them. "Glad you're here. Anybody speak English?" One guy nodded cautiously. "Great. We could use some help carrying these guys out front and waiting for the rest of the police to arrive."

The English speaker pointed and directed his friends to help. Moments later they were all standing in the weak fall sunshine outside the warehouse. Arjan, Maaravi, and Petra stretched out on the pavement in front of them. Sirens could be heard in the distance. Z'ev turned toward the sound and Nikki caught sight of her father coming out of the warehouse opposite them. She glanced at Z'ev and then made frantic waving motions, pushing her father back by sheer will power. He stepped back into the shadows and then cautiously leaned out and blew her a kiss.

Z'ev turned back around. "I'm going to walk over and meet the cops. You've got this?"

"I've got three guys with crowbars. What could possibly happen?"

"Famous last words," he laughed. "I'll be right back. I'm going to walk back to where we started though. I want to make sure they didn't just leave that bomb jacket lying around."

"OK," said Nikki with a shrug, as though it didn't matter. He had been gone about thirty seconds when Val and Philippe jogged up.

"Job well done, *chère!*" exclaimed Philippe beaming at the unconscious trio.

"It looks like you've got everything handled," said Val, nudging Petra with her toe.

"Z'ev and I took care of it," said Nikki. "How'd it go with the bomb?"

"Fine," said Philippe with the microseconds pause of someone who prefers to live in the now. "Val handled everything beautifully!"

Val popped some nicotine gum in her mouth and shrugged. "I swore at it and sawed it off. If that counts as beautifully then, sure."

"I'm assuming you're here to say goodbye and make off with the cash?"

"Yeah, that's the basic plan," said Philippe. "But you know, I wanted to make sure you were… OK."

"He feels bad that he's ditching you," translated Val.

"Do you feel bad?" she asked Val, who looked surprised.

"What are you talking about? Leaving is the nicest thing I'll have done for you all week."

Nikki laughed. "Yes, it really will be. Also, please don't show up at Christmas or my birthday."

"*Chère*, that hurts," said Philippe, but Val grinned.

"I'll shoot you an email at some point. Oh, also here." She reached in her pocket and pulled out the fake case book. Ripping out a page, she handed it to Nikki. "It's the best I can do." Nikki looked at the page which was a recipe for *Chocolate Cherry Apology Cake*. "I'm keeping the rest. There's some good shit in here. And now that I'm retired I might take up baking."

Both Philippe and Nikki hesitated on a response.

"That sounds… lovely?" tried Philippe. He and Nikki exchanged looks and Nikki shrugged and nodded. Sure, lovely, could work.

"Your support is overwhelming. Nikki, it was nice to see you doing so well," she leaned in for a brief, Chanel scented hug. "Try not to do anything hideous to my car."

"I'm painting it pink when I get back."

"I hate you."

Philippe watched them, visibly confused. "I… *lapin*… Are you going to be OK?"

Nikki stared at her father, trying figure out what he was really asking. "Of course."

"She's going to be fine, Philippe," said Val. "Come on."

"But I feel like I should be doing something," said Philippe.

"Then you should have done something ten years ago," blurted out Nikki.

"*Bebe*, I feel bad about that. But I've explained; I couldn't come back."

Nikki took a deep breath and looked at Val. "He's never going to hear me."

"Probably not like you want him to," said Val. "Doesn't mean you shouldn't give him the opportunity to try."

"We don't have time for this," said Nikki, shaking her head. She reached over and hugged Philippe. "You two need to go."

"I don't know," said Philippe, but Val took his hand and began to walk away.

"*Au revoir, Papa*," said Nikki, waving. "Be good."

After a moment, Phillippe gave into momentum and followed Val, leaving Nikki with a half-hearted wave. Nikki sat down on an upturned flower bucket and watched the low-lifes while waiting for the police to arrive.

AMSTERDAM XXII

WHEN YOU'RE FINISHED
WITH THE MOP

Nikki laid down in the back of Z'ev's car. Her head still ached from where Val had clocked her with a clog. And Petra hadn't exactly been punching at featherweight. She closed her eyes for a moment. Z'ev and Van Bergen were dealing with things. She didn't need to be doing anything, right? Her phone bonged.

With a sigh, Nikki held it over her face and looked at the screen. Morticia Addams wanted to talk. Nikki opened the app.

WE JUST GOT A REPORT FROM DARLA THAT YOU MAY HAVE BROKEN INTO TO CARRIE MAE/INTERPOL WAREHOUSE IN AMSTERDAM?? MRS. M REQUESTS CALL ASAP.

Now?

NOW WOULD BE HELPFUL.

Nikki sighed and dialed the number.

"Nikki, dear," said Mrs. M, picking up on the first ring. "It's so good to hear from you. How are things on your vacation in Amsterdam?"

"Um, I think," she pulled herself up to briefly peer over the dash at Z'ev and Van Bergen directing a crush of people in official clothing, "I actually think it's going pretty well." She collapsed back down onto the upholstery. The seatbelt dug into her back.

"Really? Because I heard that possibly you had run into a bit of trouble."

"Nothing big. I just assisted in the arrest of an international arms dealer and a corrupt INTERPOL agent."

There was a surprised pause on the other end. "Well, that sounds very nice. How are you feeling about our information leak?"

"Currently, due to the arrests I mentioned, I'm optimistic that the situation can be resolved without any official action," said Nikki.

"Mm-hm. And the Robinson situation?"

"Uh," Nikki hesitated. "What Robinson situation? I don't recall having seen anything on that situation cross my desk."

There was a long pause on the other end of the phone. Nikki felt her hands go clammy and her knee pits start to sweat.

"You know, I also must have been mistaken," said Mrs. M. "Now that you mention it, I also can't find any paperwork on that particular problem. Of course, if we did have anything like that we would have to do something about it."

"Of course," agreed Nikki. "But I haven't seen anything."

"Well, then it appears we can expect you back at work on Monday."

"Naturally," said Nikki, calmly.

"Good. I'll let Darla know you'll be putting in a report about the Amsterdam situation next week."

"Thanks. Give Mr. M my love."

"Of course, dear. Good luck." The line went dead and Nikki dropped the phone back down to her chest.

"Doing OK in there, slugger?" asked Z'ev opening the door.

"Mrs. M just told me I have to be back at work on Monday," said Nikki, looking at him upside down from her reclined position.

"Bummer."

"Yes? I think? What day is it?"

"Thursday," he said.

"Oh. That's not too bad." She rubbed her head. The goose egg really was quite large. How had she not noticed that before? "I really wish Val hadn't hit me with that clog."

Z'ev's eyes narrowed. "I should have arrested her when I had the chance."

Nikki nodded, because what else was she going to do?

"How's it going with Van Bergen?"

"I convinced him to leave you out of it. It'll be a bit tricky when it comes to the suspect statements, but I think a quiet word with Arjan's lawyer will convince him that admitting to putting a bomb jacket on someone is not what he wants to do. Maaravi, I've already talked to—he would like to plead out and is happy to maintain a bit of discretion when it comes to admitting he kidnapped your father, so that means he also won't be mentioning you either. Petra's the only one I haven't talked to because she's still unconscious."

Nikki checked her watch. "She probably won't wake up for another three to four hours. Although, considering the age of the powder I'd err on the three side."

"You Carrie Mae'd her?"

"I helped her apply some face powder."

"Violently and at speed?"

Nikki lifted her hands palm up in a gesture that managed to encompass the idea that this was a possibility, but that she admitted to nothing.

"Swell. OK, well I'm going to be stuck here for several more hours. Plus, I still have to go retrieve the Chechens from the security office. What do you want to do?"

"Go back to the house boat and pass out?"

Z'ev scratched his nose. "Really?"

"God, yes. Do you know how hard it is to get a good night's sleep with Val around? You have to sleep with one eye open. Not to mention all the travel and time zones and jumping out of planes and fist fights. I want a nap."

"No, I meant—really, the houseboat? You do realize that I have an entire actual hotel suite with real plumbing and sheets and probably room service, if you wanted it."

Nikki sat upright, and glared at him suspiciously. "You're making this up."

"Making up the Marriott? That seems unlikely." He held up a room key card with the blessed Marriott logo on it. Nikki reached for it, but he pulled it back. "There's a catch."

Nikki flopped back against the seat. "Of course."

"You have to still be there when I get back."

"Sure. I told you; I don't have to be back until Monday."

"You have to be there because I still want to talk."

"Oh. Right. That." Nikki rubbed her forehead. "Yes, I will still be there."

He handed the card over with a skeptical look, then jogged away as Van Bergen called for him.

Nikki exited the car, and then the flower market. A short wait for a cab later and she was on her way to the Marriott. She sat in the back seat of the cab and tried not to fidget. She considered redirecting the cab to the airport when they stopped at the house-boat to pick up her bag, but didn't. She thought about getting her own hotel room at the front desk, but didn't. She had half an impulse to put her room service order on her own credit card, but ignored that one easily.

Laying in the bed post meal and shower, Nikki knew she

should be able to fall asleep, but instead found the events of the past week rolling through her head on a loop. She woke up at midnight, startled to find that she'd been asleep, reaching for her gun on the bedside table.

"Where am I?" she demanded of the darkened room.

"You're in the hotel," Z'ev said, his voice extra gravelly with sleep.

"Right," said Nikki, letting go of the gun, her heart pounding. The tiny line of light from the the curtains and the glow of the bedside clock only seemed to make the dark more dark. She felt Z'ev roll over. Ordinarily, this would be her cue to roll over herself and snuggle or hold hands or accidentally elbow him in the ear or something else basic and simple and intimate. Now she felt like that would be inappropriate. It was like she was in bed with a stranger.

"Do you think," said Z'ev, "that Val and your dad will really retire?"

Nikki sighed. "Honestly? I have an extremely deep fear that they will do something ridiculous like try to steal the Mona Lisa. I mean, I really believe that they *think* they want to retire, but having actually met them? It just seems sort of…"

"Against their nature."

"Yes."

"You do realize that you can't keep covering for them. I'm trying to be OK with letting them wander off, but I'm having to work pretty hard at it. I really believe people should be held accountable for their actions."

"Yes, I do too. The first year or two on the job was spent cleaning up the mess Val and her boyfriend made of people's lives. She can't really ever atone for that. Maybe if she'd died, that would have been justice. But she didn't. What is she supposed to do now? Does she deserve to just get thrown away? She did a lot of good as an agent. And as far as I can tell, she got divorced, got depressed, freaked out, met a guy and decided to just throw everything in the crapper and stop caring. And having been doing her job for a few years now, I see the bullcrap she had to wade through. It doesn't justify anything, but I understand it. I think Val's right; maybe there's no making up for some things, which means my options are forgiveness or punishment."

"So you forgive her. That's great, but you're not the only person she hurt. How do they feel about it? And what about your dad? He can't just go around smuggling things."

"There's no point in being mad at him," said Nikki. "He won't get it."

"But Nikki, you are mad at him. Don't you think he should…"

"Should do what?" The bed bounced slightly as she threw up her hands in frustration. "Understand that he's a monumentally childish, selfish individual? What if he gets it? What then? He can't make up for an entire childhood of not being there."

Z'ev grunted angrily. "He's getting a free pass because you're too nice to tell him he's a jackass." He sat up and the bedside light flicked on. "Like I said, I'm trying to be OK with letting them go, but it's kind of hard."

Nikki twisted her head to look at him from another angle. She thought he'd been mad from a literal justice and law point of view. She hadn't considered that he would be mad because of how they treated her.

"My mom and I fight all the time, and I absolutely wish she'd been a little less undercutting and clingy throughout my entire childhood. But as crazy as she is, at least she was actually part of my childhood. Dad was just a phantom that lingered over everything I did. And now, I don't know, I just feel like, I can finally move forward. I don't have to wonder why he left me. I know why. He's an asshole. Question answered. And frankly, as long as he doesn't pop up like some sort of illegal mushroom, having him disappear off to wherever is nice. Having him in prison would mean that I'd have to concern myself with his defense, and write him letters, and think about him regularly. This is so much more convenient for me. Plus, at least with Val around I know he'll have someone to look after him. I'm not saying letting them go was justice. It wasn't. And I'll totally feel bad about that at some point. But I'm enough of my father's daughter that right now, I just feel...relief."

"Hmm," said Z'ev. He got up and poured himself a glass of water with a bottle from the mini-bar. "We don't talk," he said.

"Huh?" said Nikki.

"We each get home from missions and we have our life, but this is the first time in months that we've actually talked about anything that mattered."

"Well, in my defense I didn't actually know that Val was alive or that my dad had been to prison or was apparently a world-renowned smuggler. So I couldn't have talked about it, even if I wanted to."

"But you didn't want to," he said with a sigh. "Talking about your dad has always been off limits. And I admit I assumed it was because you didn't want to talk about the prison thing. I didn't realize that you didn't know. But even if you'd known, would you have wanted to?"

"No," said Nikki honestly. "Talking about emotional stuff, or stuff that matters, is really hard for me. Jane always wants me to be introspective and deep and emotionally honest. I just want a cocktail and to not have to think about this shit."

He leaned against the dresser, glass still in his hand. Nikki wondered if she should relocate or stand up or move to a more protected position. But her robe was somehow entangled in the sheets and moving would be such an obvious admission of discomfort.

"Is that why you didn't tell me?"

"Tell you what?"

His hand jerked convulsively, splashing water on to the carpet. "Nikki," Z'ev rubbed his hands over his face, "seriously, just be honest. Why didn't you ever tell me about Carrie Mae?"

"I have been honest with you! I was under strict instructions not to."

"Bullshit. People give you instructions all the time. You only ever follow the ones you agree with."

"That's not true. I follow lots of orders I don't like. I mean jeez, I've been flying to Mexico like every other week because Mrs. M's temporary replacement had her head up her ass."

"That explains the frequent flier miles email I got. Look, we both know that you could have told me at any point in our relationship and you didn't. Bottom line is that you don't trust me."

"No! That isn't it." Nikki sat up, attempting to fling the covers away, but ending up battling them like an octopus. She was a neuron's firing away from stomping her foot by the time she managed to get free of the bed.

"Then what is it?" he asked, making no move to help her.

"I was scared."

"Of what? Of what I would do?"

"Well, yes, on the basic question of whether or not you would tell the CIA. I was very concerned about that. But I mean from our relationship point of view…" She waffled, unable to articulate what she was trying to say.

"What did you think I would do? What were you scared of?"

"I was scared that you wouldn't… I mean, you've met my dad. What if you just decided it wasn't worth it?" Nikki couldn't string her thoughts together in a coherent way.

"You thought I'd just ditch out on you like your dad? I've met your mom and I didn't leave. I can't spend a lifetime making up for his stupidity!" He clunked his glass down on the dresser in frustration.

"No! That's not it. I mean, my dad is like this thing in my life, like a road I don't want to travel down. I don't want to go there."

Z'ev was staring at her with the slightly open mouth of someone trying to understand gibberish. He hitched up one side of his underwear and scratched his head.

"I'm not really sure where we're going with this, but I'm nothing like your dad."

"You're not like him at all. And every day that we've been together I've have been so, so grateful that you're not. You're honest and trustworthy and I love you and even if you…" her voice broke on a sob, "even if you never want to see me again, I'm so lucky to have had that. But what if I explained about everything and you just didn't, you couldn't take that? I know people say, *oh, you want to know what your wife will be like in twenty years, just look at the mother.* I think they mostly mean in the ass department, but genetics applies to both parents." Nikki knew she was rambling.

"Oh my God," said Z'ev, his expression clearing. "Val's right. I'm a total idiot. You're not worried that I'm your dad. You're worried that you are your dad."

"All my life, people keep saying that I'm going to snap, that someday I'm just going to lose it like my dad. That I'll just run off and do something crazy. My mom, Grand-Mère, that's all I ever heard—*don't be like Philippe, but oh, how you're just like him.* What if one day you wake up and I'm just gone?"

Z'ev leaned forward squinting at her in disbelief as if she was performing the worst kind of mime. "You mean like last week?"

"What? No, I mean—"

"Or that time you broke up with me, broke your phone, disappeared off the face of the Earth and then showed up on the cover of a Canadian tabloid kissing a rockstar?"

"I didn't break my phone! Kit's bitchy mom broke my phone."

"And there weren't any other phones anywhere? You could have called."

"You just canceled our Christmas vacation plans! I was not about to— No, I'm not having this argument again."

"Really? Because I'm planning on having it least eight to ten more times. I figure somewhere around then it'll start to get funny."

Nikki opened her mouth then closed it again. "What?" she asked weakly.

Z'ev laughed. "Nikki, you like flipping out. It's kind of your thing."

"I really don't," protested Nikki. "Things just happen and then I have to deal with them."

He nodded, but continued as if she hadn't spoken. "When people like Ellen lose their nut, we all worry. It's big, it's unpredictable, it's splashy, it's a problem. That's why you were so upset when she killed that guy. You were surprised. Then there's people like your dad. He's never actually gone berserk. He just creates problems—cannonballs into the pool and climbs out while the rest of us are still getting hit by waves. But what I've realized this week, is that you're good at those people. You see it coming, you predict the ripples, and you ride the waves. The rest of us are wondering what the hell just happened and you're surfing away."

Nikki bit her lip, not sure what to say. "Jane says I'm good at unpredictable situations because I'm a stable instability."

"Yes," agreed Z'ev.

"Some people would find that hard to live with," she offered.

Z'ev leaned forward and looked around as if telling a secret. "Yes, but I like it," he whispered. "I mean," he pushed away from the dresser, stepping closer to her. She found her heart rate speeding up. "I don't like being lied to. And I don't like it when you run out on me, but do you know how many girls I dated that couldn't argue, that couldn't be spontaneous, that had no secrets? Don't you understand how boring that is? Every dinner, every moment, was predictable. But when I'm with you every boring moment is a precious gift from the gods because I know damn well that in two minutes you're going to get in a fist fight or someone will probably be shooting at us."

"Why do people always do that?"

"I don't know, baby," he said, pulling her into him. "It's probably because they don't know who they're messing with."

Nikki looked up at Z'ev and smiled. It seemed like there was million things she should say, but she was tired of talking. So she kissed him.

CALIFORNIA I
RETURN TO ME

Z'ev had been a lot more relaxed since their *talk* in the hotel room. Sex had that effect. Also, his work seemed extremely happy with the fact that he'd arrested an INTERPOL officer, so that was probably helping. They had spent most of the weekend doing mop-up for their respective companies. She had even managed to commend Sanne in one of the reports, much to Sanne's delight. And Nikki was delighted to find that they could actually book the same flight home. But they had barely landed at LAX when her phone burbled with incoming texts.

"Mrs. M wants us to come to dinner," said Nikki, looking up at Z'ev.

"Good," he said, nodding. "I want to talk to John again. And I want to meet some of the CIA employees who are working with Carrie Mae."

"They're not going to let you do that," said Nikki.

"Yes, they will," he said confidently. "They want me to keep my big mouth shut. Plus, Mrs. M will think that I could be an asset. She'll want to persuade me."

"Or maybe she'll think you're a threat!" said Nikki. "I already feel like I'm getting away with a lot. Can we maybe not push it?"

He hefted their bags of the carousel, easily shouldering both of them. "No," he said. "I've decided that you're right."

"About what?" demanded Nikki. "Because I'm pretty sure I didn't advocate anything that would get you shot."

"Well, what I've learned from this week is that I shouldn't just let things go and hope I'll get what I want. It doesn't work with you and it's not going to work with my career."

"Oh God, please tell me you're not planning on blackmailing Carrie Mae into helping your career? Because that will not work."

"No! Of course not! I'm saying that I should start looking for opportunities that let me do what I wanted to do when I first joined the CIA—help people. They keep sending me out on these bullshit DEA missions, which I'm good at, and it's fine, but killing drug dealers isn't really what I signed up to do. I wanted to help the world be better. The stuff I've been doing lately feels like I'm fighting the tail of the dog. And I don't really know what's going on with Carrie Mae, but it seems like they're helping people. Maybe we could work together."

"But you're a man," said Nikki.

"So men can't help people?"

Nikki chose not to answer that, but she wasn't sure what to say instead.

"Anyway," he continued, as they exited out to the loading area, "I think I could use more career mentoring. John can help and I bet your ladies in the CIA could to. You said it yourself—we're both working against penalties. It just seems like I could learn a lot and we might make good allies."

Nikki tried to work her head around the fact he was considering getting mentoring from her organization. She loved him dearly, but he'd always tipped the chauvinist meter just a little. On the other hand, if she'd learned anything about him it was that he was situationally adaptable. Apparently, he was deciding to apply those skills here.

"Also," he continued," I think we should buy a condo."

Nikki stopped walking. "What?"

"I told you, I'm going to stop waiting around and hoping I get what I want. You obviously respond better to full frontal assault. What do you think about buying a condo? Our apartment's nice, but we're dumping money down the drain. We could be building equity. Also, it would allow us to do modifications, like put in a gun safe and security systems. Which, with our careers and your relatives, seems like a good idea."

"But a condo…"

"Or a small house. I'm not picky. I just don't know much about yard maintenance."

"But you would look hot mowing the lawn with your shirt off," said Nikki, which wasn't at all pertinent, but it was all she could think of.

"Will you wash the car in a bikini?"

Nikki felt like she'd walked off the map of this conversation and she had no idea how to get it back to someplace that she recognized.

"Yes?" she offered.

"Then yeah, houses with lawns are on the table. But seriously, the next weekend we're both home, let's start looking."

"I think we should look at getting pre-approval first," said Nikki, practically. "Make sure our credit is in order."

"Meh," said Z'ev, signaling for a taxi. "Can't Jane just fix that?"

"Well, yes, but… Z'ev?"

"Yeah?" He signaled again and then glanced at her.

"You're really sure?"

"Yeah, my brother does my financial planning and he's been recommending that I buy for years. It's just never made any sense with me moving around and being out of town so much. But I've really been thinking about it the last six months or so and I think we should really consider it."

"I mean, are you sure you want to buy property with *me*?" asked Nikki.

He set the bags down, leaned down and kissed her. Nikki felt her stomach do flip-flops as his arms slid around her waist.

"Do you love me?"

"Yes! I've been trying to tell you for like four days now!"

"Oh, I got the message," said Z'ev. "I mean last night at the hotel was pretty clear."

"Shut up," said Nikki, blushing.

"So if you love me, and I love you…" He kissed her again. "Why shouldn't we be able to work everything else out?"

Nikki had doubts. The CIA and Carrie Mae were not meant to be allies. There were constraints and different cultural approaches and a startling lack of understanding on feminist theory from the CIA.

His kiss lingered on her lips.

Maybe they could make it work.

As long as her father didn't try to steal the Mona Lisa, her mother stopped calling her twelve times a day, and no one tried to shoot them—maybe they had a chance. Maybe.

"I think," said Nikki, smiling up at him, "I think I would like a house. With you. You know, with the usual caveats."

"Yes, yes," he said, smiling, "no dying. But we've come this far, baby. I think we're going to make it."

LOOKING FOR MORE ACTION PACKED ADVENTURE? WHY NOT TRY...

The Shark Santoyo Crime Series

When twenty something Shark got out of prison and made a deal with Geier, the boss of his old gang, he knew he'd be walking into trouble, but he never expected to meet the teenage crime savant Peregrine Hays. The knife-wielding beauty may fuel his dreams, but Peregrine has secrets of her own, and soon Shark is swept up in a whirlpool of murder, revenge, and love. Both streetwise and crime-hardened, Shark and Peri seem like a perfect bloody team as they battle crooked federal agents, sex traffickers, and gangs in search of vindication. But when Shark is faced with an enemy that knows him better than anyone else, he and Peri learn that their options may be staying together OR staying alive...

Shark's Instinct Sneak Peek...

SHARK'S INSTINCT

MONDAY ~ OCTOBER 16

1
7

Shark: Rolling Thunder Lanes

Shark Santoyo rubbed a hand over his prison buzz cut, and considered his options. They appeared to be death or accounting.

He wondered if he could make it to Mexico before the FBI caught up with him. His jailhouse college degree had given him a basic understanding of American History, Psychology, Criminal Justice, and a hatred for the *Grapes of Wrath*, but higher-level accounting had not been part of the curriculum.

That was unfortunate, since his current mission in life was to find where Big Paulie had put Geier's money, and Big Paulie had chosen to rather inconveniently die of a heart attack mid-beating rather than reveal that information. Shark's only clue was the red leather ledger with the rambling, scribbled out, crisscrossing columns of numbers, and the gold-stamped *Fred Abernathy* on the cover. There had been efforts to find the wayward accountant, but so far he was in the wind.

A vacuum cleaner started up on the far side of the room. Shark both ignored and enjoyed the sound. He didn't know if the layer of filth covering every surface was due to Rolling Thunder Lanes being a closed suburban bowling alley or because it was the base of operations for wise guys, but he was starting to feel like the OCD germophobe in his cell block who had eventually tried to scrub his cell mate's face off with a potato brush. Fortunately, Shark was now at the top of this particular pyramid. He might be dead in a week if he couldn't find Geier's money, but at least he'd go out in a damn clean bowling alley. He'd even had them open the blinds on the front windows. Bright October sunlight streamed in, illuminating all the grime and blinding him as it bounced off the white pages of the ledger.

He put on his sunglasses and flipped another page. He had no idea what he was staring at. He sensed a YouTube video on accounting in his future. Later, once he was alone, and no one would know.

Someone slid into the booth across from him and he looked up, expecting one of the low-level scumbags that floated through here. He wasn't sure why these suburban dipshits seemed to think he could be pushed around, but he was getting tired of correcting their misunderstanding. But sitting across from him in the booth was a girl—thick brown hair pulled into a loose braid on the right side, purple hoodie, hazel eyes, no make-up. She looked somewhere between fifteen and twenty. He had a hard time judging, since every sixteen-year-old girl he'd known since he was ten had looked over twenty-one. He had no idea what to say to her.

"We're closed," he tried. "No bowling."

"Do I look like I'm here to fucking bowl?" His mysterious apparition had a potty mouth. It was an incongruous as it was cute—like an aggressive Corgi.

He looked around the empty bowling alley. He had no idea what bowlers looked like; he'd never actually been bowling. His supposed bodyguards were lounging against the bar, unaware of the five foot four inch security breach sitting across from him. He flipped the ledger closed.

"How did you even get in here?"

"Through the kitchen. If you look like a kid and stay out of people's way, they assume you belong to somebody."

"OK," he nodded, trying to figure out how he was going to block that in the future. "How about, *why* are you here?"

"I'm here because you just took over from Big Paulie, so now you run the Fives and Blue Street," she said.

Took over, that was a polite way of putting it.

"And what is any of that to you?"

"Blue Street." She pulled his unused fork over to her side of the table, then paused to make a disgusted face when the fork proved to be sticky. He sympathized. "Blue Street is in an ongoing turf war with the 38th Street crew"—she pulled the spoon into an L shape with the fork, bowl to tines—"which is where Lincoln High School is." She put a sugar packet in the corner of the adjoining silverware.

Shark heaved a sigh. This had been going somewhere. She had been interesting. "And you want me to call them off your high school?"

"No, I want you to apply your foot to Blue Street's ass and

get them to do their fucking jobs."

Behind his sunglasses, Shark blinked.

"Look, I get it," the girl said. "You're new, and you're probably hearing a lot of chatter about how they can't push too hard because one dead kid in the schoolyard and the police will crack down, and then everyone gets rolled up like a window shade."

"The metaphors haven't been as good as that, but yes."

She flashed a smile. "They're not wrong. Dead kids equals bad. But everyone is stuck staring at the problem from here." She tapped the fork. "When you need to be looking at the problem from here." She laid the pepper shaker down parallel to the fork, but at the end of the spoon. There was a huffing sound as Zip and Marko jogged up. "Oh good," the girl said, showing zero fear. "Which one of them is the waiter?"

Shark looked at his bodyguards. Marko was Italianish, heavyset and forty-something, usually in jeans and a black leather jacket, and hadn't said one word about working for a younger man. Zip was a decade younger, equally well-padded, always dressed in a track suit, and had been pissy about the assignment, but so far he had followed Marko's lead on everything. "Either one," Shark said. "Seems like that's what they're good at."

"Great. I'll take a cherry Coke," she told Zip.

Zip looked at Shark.

"You heard her," said Shark.

Zip's expression said he wanted to argue. "I'll just…" He glanced at Marko for support, who gave him nothing. "I'll just go do that then." He headed for the bar, while Marko unfolded his Sports section and took a seat a few tables over. It was a location that said *I know you can handle a kid, but I feel like I should look like I'm doing something.*

The girl watched them leave. "What are the odds that Coke comes back spit-free?"

"Not good," said Shark. He slid his Jack and Coke across the table to her and she took a sip.

"Oh." She made a face. "How do you drink that stuff?"

"It's an acquired taste."

"But why acquire it?"

"Because at some point," Shark said, "you like feeling bad."

She didn't say anything, but looked like she was thinking it over. She tried another sip and slid the drink back. "Not today."

"So tell me about the pepper."

"The pepper is everything above Jackson."

"That belongs to the Ukrainians," he pointed out.

"Yes." She smiled, and this time there were teeth. "I know. And up until now the Ukrainians have been staying out of it."

"What do you mean *up until now?*"

"38th Street's been getting restless. They want a bigger slice of the pie. They've been intending to take it out of Blue Street, but would it be such a huge surprise if they hit the Ukrainians' stash house on Jackson?"

"Not a surprise. But what would they make them do it?" She had a firm grasp of the politics of the territory—probably better than he did. He hoped it didn't show.

"They don't really have to do it. You can do it. It just has to *look* like they did it."

Shark did a quick mental calculation about the amount of money they could expect to find in a Ukrainian stash house at the end of the month. It seemed like a possible solution to Geier's money problem. Although, the last time a girl had come to him with a plan he'd ended up in prison, so maybe he should be hearing alarm bells, not seeing dollar signs.

He wasn't sure what to make of her. Most girls, most women, if they wanted something from him, they hedged, they angled, they hinted. Things were suggested, but never actually stated. Also, there was generally a lot more cleavage. He stalled, trying to get a feel for her. "And what if the Ukrainians decide to just roll through 38th Street and onto Blue Street? Then you're right back to where you started."

"My focus is on 38th Street's current personnel; I need them gone. But for what it's worth, the Ukrainians are set to have a civil war."

"There haven't been any indications of that. My intel says they're stable."

"Your *intel* doesn't sit next to Andriy's younger sister in Pre-Calc. They don't know that she's been sleeping with his second-in-command and that she's pregnant. The right words to the right people at the right time and the Ukrainians could be pretty damn unstable."

"Cherry Coke," offered Zip.

"Cherry Coke," said Shark. "That sounds good. Why don't you give me that one, and go get another for the kid?"

There was silence. Shark didn't have to look up to know

Zip was sweating.

"You know," said Zip. "I didn't do the garnish right. I'll be right back."

Marko looked after him with a frown. "I'll help him," he said, folding his paper. Shark ignored them both, focusing on the girl.

Shark took off his sunglasses and set them on the table. Born with pale gray eyes, he knew most people found a hard stare from him creepy, an effect enhanced by the scar running through his right eyebrow. Leaning forward, he stared at the little shark who didn't like alcohol. She met his stare levelly. "Why come to me? Why not take this directly to the Blue Street crew?"

She shook her head. "Blue Street won't listen to me. Too many boobs, not enough dick. I did some recon and I think you're the first person on the food chain with more than two brain cells to rub together and enough power to make it happen."

"What's in it for you? Why do you care?"

"No one owns the school because all the crews have family there. That makes it an open territory for independent operators."

"Such as yourself?"

"Such as myself. But that arrangement doesn't mean we're unaffected by what goes on out here. And right now 38th Street is inconveniencing me. I need them, and specifically their leader Tall Jimmy, to go away. Preferably permanently, and without a lot of fuss or a long lead time."

"Two cherry Cokes," announced Marko, setting down the glasses with a flourish. This time there were cherries dangling from the rims.

Shark leaned back and put his sunglasses back on. "What are you bringing to the table?"

"Intel, a plan, and a few other items." She took a cherry off the glass and crunched it between her teeth, leaving the stem on the table.

"I'll think about it."

She slid a card across the table. "This is my number."

It was blank except for digits. How did she have better business cards than he did?

"I need to know by tomorrow."

"What happens tomorrow?"

She slid out of the booth. "I move on to plan B."

Shark watched her walk out the front door. She walked quickly, with firm feet. No hip wiggles, but no tripping or awkwardness either. She knew they were watching, but she didn't waver. Even some of the guys who had been around awhile couldn't walk from the table to the door without looking back. The girl had balls.

He tapped the card on the table. "Call Blue Street," he told Marko, when the door closed behind her. "Tell them I'm coming for a visit. Tell them to call in anyone in their crew who goes to the high school."

ABOUT THE AUTHOR

Bethany Maines, a native of Tacoma WA, is the author of action adventure and fantasy tales that focus on women who know when to apply lipstick and when to apply a foot to someone's hind end. When she's not traveling to exotic lands, or kicking some serious butt with her black belt in karate, she can be found chasing after her daughter, or glued to the computer working on her next novel.

OTHER WORKS BY BETHANY MAINES

BULLETPROOFMASCARA
A **CARRIE MAE** MYSTERY

COMPACT WITH THE **DEVIL**
A **CARRIE MAE** MYSTERY

SUPPORTING THE **GIRLS**
A **CARRIE MAE** MINI-MYSTERY

POWER OF **ATTORNEY**
A **CARRIE MAE** MINI-MYSTERY

HIGH-CALIBER CONCEALER
A **CARRIE MAE** MYSTERY

Shark's Instinct
Shark Santoyo Crime Series

Tales from the City of Destiny

An Unseen Current

Wild Waters

Find out more at:
BethanyMaines.com